The Picture House Girls

ROSIE ARCHER

The Picture House Girls

Quercus

First published in Great Britain in 2021 by

Quercus Editions Ltd
Carmelite House
50 Victoria Embankment
London EC4Y 0DZ

An Hachette UK company

A CIP catalogue record for this book is available
from the British Library

HB ISBN 978 1 52940 527 9

10 9 8 7 6 5 4 3 2 1

Typeset by CC Book Production
Printed and bound in Great Britain by Clays Ltd, Elcograf S.p.A.

Papers used by Quercus are from well-managed forests and other responsible sources.

For Constance Radford. Connie is such a lovely name.
Thank you for allowing me to borrow it.

Chapter One

May 1942

Connie lay perfectly still in the Anderson shelter, on the wooden bunk bed, listening and allowing her eyes to become used to the darkness. The sound of the engines grew louder as the bombers advanced. Below her, Aunt Gertie snored, the noise almost as deafening as the planes. Stale cigarette smoke hung in the air, diluting the hut's dankness. It occurred to Connie that, so far, she'd not heard one blast from exploding bombs. Why?

Sliding free of the scratchy blankets, she crawled across the quilt to the end of the bunk and, careful not to wake her aunt, climbed down to the packed-earth floor. For a moment she stared at the comatose Gertie Mullins, satisfied that nothing short of a direct hit on their sanctuary would wake her, then crept past the Primus stove on the upturned wooden crate to the shelter's entrance. She eased back the oiled bolt, pushed open the metal door a few inches and peered out.

Planes were emerging from behind dense cloud. They reminded Connie of a swarm of bees, although the buzzing was pitched much higher. She could hear in the distance the pop-pop of anti-aircraft guns, and see puffs of smoke, lit by far-off searchlights criss-crossing the sky.

There appeared no end to the German bombers, more than she'd ever seen before, while smaller aircraft danced attendance at their sides, clearly hoping to keep them safe. Now she could make out the shapes of RAF Spitfires and Hurricanes greeting the invaders with thunderous bullets and flaming fire.

Connie had been confused by the absence of exploding enemy bombs. Now she realized clouds had concealed Portsmouth's Royal Naval Dockyard, preventing Hitler's planes from shedding their loads and successfully hitting proposed targets.

As if in confirmation bombs began to drop.

The Hurricanes were retaliating against the marauding invaders. Gosport's anti-aircraft guns reverberated, cracking into the sky, as enemy bombs found targets. Shrapnel fell, like burning hailstones, and the sharp stink of cordite and scorched wood reached Connie. She pulled the door closed to keep it out of the shelter, reached for the bolt and slid it home.

Connie was sweating but her mind and body were under control. She felt a surge of energy that, unlike the last time she'd witnessed a raid, enabled her to accept that what had occurred then was unlikely to happen again. Connie Baxter would never, ever forget the previous raid that had changed her life completely, but neither would she be haunted by fear. She would and could cope with whatever Fate had in store for her.

A racking cough broke into her thoughts. When it subsided, a cracked voice said, 'As you're already up, love, light the Primus and make some tea. But first, pass me the matches. I'm gasping for a fag.'

At that, Connie's face creased into a smile.

Ace Gallagher, head in hands, sat on a wooden bench at Gosport's ferry facing the stretch of Solent Water that looked towards Portsmouth's dockyard.

The all-clear had sounded.

He didn't need to look back at his club, vestiges of which were still smouldering, despite the firemen's best efforts, to know his dream had been shattered.

Ace wanted to cry. He couldn't remember when he'd last shed a tear and he wasn't about to start now. Sitting there alone was all he was fit for until his head cleared and he could work out a plan of action. Eventually he'd find a solution, of course he would.

The waves below were gently slapping against the rocks and concrete pilings underpinning the ferry gardens. The sound soothed him. After a while he lifted his head and gazed across the narrow stretch of sea. Portsmouth's broken buildings stood out against the orange glow in the darkness. It looked as if one of the ships moored at HM Naval Base was on fire, mountainous clouds of flames billowing uncontrollably. The stench of smoke from burning homes surged across the water on the wind, mingling with the brick dust and soot from Gosport's demolished properties. It stung his nostrils. Bloody war! Bloody Hitler!

Ace's fingers massaged his temples. It was quieter now the planes had left and the emergency vehicles had gone. But he didn't think he'd ever block out the terrifying sounds of the explosions that had rocked and destroyed his club, the Four Aces, while he and Jerome had cowered in its cellars.

Another, more familiar, smell reached him. Food cooking? Ace decided it was probably his imagination. But it stirred his memory of Jerome protesting that he didn't want to leave the cellars for the Dive café, which had miraculously escaped the bombing.

That recollection caused Ace's mouth to curve into a smile. Jerome, as near to a father as Ace had ever known, had finally agreed to evacuate only if Tom, the café's owner, provided a saucer of milk and a titbit of fish for the black-and-white stray cat that never left his side.

His smile lingered as Ace remembered that safe, too, were the many boxes of black-market goods stored beneath his building. Those commodities represented money. And more might follow.

Money wasn't a problem to Ace – it never had been. Either he had it or he didn't. Losing his beloved club was a setback, though. Nevertheless, luck had still been with him: the club had been closed for the night so there were no deaths on his conscience.

He sighed. His flat above the Four Aces had been decimated so he needed somewhere to stay while he con-templated the club's reconstruction. After all, Gosport was his home now, his future: German bombs wouldn't drive him out. Cash passed to local councillors would ensure 'difficult to get' building materials appeared promptly. Ace knew money had the loudest voice.

A priority, too, was somewhere for Jerome to live. Another

smile lifted his lips. Jerome would do what Jerome wanted. He always had, he always would. But Ace would oversee his safety.

The smell of frying was stronger now. It was making him feel hungry and it definitely wasn't in his imagination. He stood up, turned, and forced himself to look at the smoking remains of his empire. The once-vibrant business was a sad shell. He shook himself and followed his nose towards the comforting aroma. In his mind's eye he saw Tom, in his white overalls, hard at work before the gas stove in the Dive. Fried bread? Bacon, maybe. Chips, and perhaps cod if he could get hold of it – at least fish wasn't rationed. And a cup of strong tea to wash it down. That was what Ace needed to help put his world to rights.

Chapter Two

Clark Gable's shoulder blades received a final dollop of paste before Connie put down the brush and tenderly fingered his torso, staring at him lovingly. 'You certainly deserve to be centre stage,' she said softly, placing the full-page picture of her favourite film star, cut from *Picturegoer*, face up in the middle of the scrapbook's empty page. Then she smoothed the paper gently but firmly to make sure the paste was evenly distributed. Sometimes the flour and water mixture was lumpy and didn't stick so well.

Clark Gable firmly tethered, Connie was satisfied with the result, although his left side appeared slightly distorted where he had been crushed against his co-star's glittery dress. She had snipped Joan Crawford out of the picture and discarded her: Connie liked to imagine she was the only girl in his life. She wondered what it was like for Clark Gable to be surrounded by so many beautiful women in magical Hollywood.

Ginger Rogers was the star Connie strove to imitate. She spent ages taming her fair hair into the blonde actress's pageboy style. Alas, the moment she set foot outside the house the wind remodelled it into its wayward tumbling waves.

Connie sighed. How that woman could move, her feet twinkling in shiny slippers! Connie had watched her dance excitingly, sinuously, on film with Fred Astaire. She was sadly aware that she herself had two left feet and little sense of rhythm.

The last dance she'd been persuaded to go to with some of the girls from her previous workplace had been a disaster, a nightmare. Miserable, she'd ended up a wallflower, sitting disconsolately on one of the chairs placed around the ballroom's edges.

A small cough disturbed her daydreams. She turned from the kitchen table where she was sitting, all her paraphernalia in front of her, to the tall, smiling man in the doorway. 'Why doesn't a gorgeous girl like you,' he suggested, 'forget about film stars' pictures in magazines and get involved with a real man, like me?'

Connie laughed.

Ace Gallagher had appeared soundlessly from nowhere to stand between the kitchen and the hallway with one hand on the door-frame as if he, alone, could save the wall if it suddenly tumbled down. His gold watch glittered on his wrist below his initialled cufflinks set in a pristine white shirt-cuff. 'I could take you into town,' he added, 'so you can see how my club's coming along. The rebuilding's going just fine. Or . . . you could come out for a drive to the sea shore. Watch the waves through the barbed wire protecting us from the land mines?'

Aunt Gertie's lodger was, as usual, teasing Connie, or trying to humour her, she could never make up her mind which it was. She shook her head. In another time and another place, she might have been tempted to go with the chirpy club owner but at present Connie had no intention of rushing into a relationship, however temporary, with any man.

To Ace's credit, his well-meaning banter shook her out of herself and momentarily raised her spirits. It also had the benefit of making her think of something tart she could snap at him in reply. She remembered Gertie's words spoken within hours of her moving into her terraced home.

'Don't take no notice of my lodger, Ace. He tries it on with all the girls. He's a heartbreaker, a right ladies' man, that one.' With a twinkle in her eye, Gertie had added, fiddling with the metal curlers that were hardly ever out of her hair, 'Mind you, if I was twenty years younger, I'd give him a run for his money . . .' She'd blown out a cloud of cigarette smoke without removing the fag from the side of her mouth.

Eighteen-year-old Connie was wise enough to know she'd be out of her depth with Ace. He was in his thirties and reminded her of Clark Gable as Rhett Butler in *Gone with the Wind*, without the moustache, of course.

She'd had boyfriends and she wasn't backwards in coming forwards, but carrying on with her childhood passion of collecting film stars' photographs was a soothing influence while she was grieving. She took a deep breath, put on a mocking voice and asked, 'What? Me and you?'

Connie thought about the shiny black MG VA Tourer parked outside her aunt's two-up-two-down house in Gosport's Alma Street, a car most men would sell their wives for. No doubt girls queued up for a ride in it. 'Been let down, have you?' she added.

He laughed, showing very white teeth with a slight cross-over in the front, an imperfection that only enhanced his good looks. 'Never,' he protested. 'There's plenty of girls lining up for me to take them for a drive.'

Somewhere from deep inside her a curl of anticipation began to unfurl as she wondered what the outcome might be if she went out with him. She crushed it. 'Well, I'd sooner be sick in the lavvy at the bottom of the garden!'

Ace's smile turned to a throaty laugh. 'You're attracted to me, really, aren't you?' he said. 'I can tell!'

She mimed sticking her fingers down her throat and choking. 'Whatever gave you that idea?'

He was staring at her with those hypnotic silver-grey eyes. For a long moment neither spoke. Then Ace said softly, 'You'll want me one day.' He winked at her as he stepped aside from the door-frame and smoothed his brandy-coloured hair, which he wore combed straight back. Connie tried not to stare as he pushed away an unruly lock. It fell straight back to his forehead. The scent of his cologne, a subtle lemony fragrance, wafted towards her.

'In your dreams,' Connie said. 'In your dreams.'

Ace smiled as he turned away. A moment later, the front door slammed behind him, causing the key, hanging on its string, to jangle against the wood.

Then she heard the letterbox being raised, the door opening again and heavy footsteps coming along the passage lino. Once more Ace stood before her. 'I forgot to say good luck.' He smiled. 'You're starting your new job today, aren't you?'

And then he was gone again.

Chapter Three

'Was that Ace I heard?' Gertie poked her head around the open doorway between the scullery and the kitchen. She gave Connie an enquiring look. Then, without waiting for an answer, she set the enamelled washing bowl on the small table. 'Thank God that's the last of it pegged out. All it's got to do is stay dry today and I'll be happy.'

'He's just left,' said Connie. 'I haven't heard his car start up, but if you want him, I could see if he's still in the street.' She rose from her chair.

'You sit still, love. It's just that he usually shouts goodbye to me.' Gertie stepped into the kitchen and went to the black-leaded range. She picked up a metal lever from its place on the hearth and used it to prise up the round hob-plate. With her other hand, she dropped in a log from the pile in the scuttle. Then she replaced the hob-plate. 'It's cold out there for May,' she added, standing up straight, stretching her back and wiping her hands down the front of her flowered wraparound pinafore.

'He wished me luck for work today,' said Connie, sitting down again. She began tidying the table, putting the discarded bits of *Picturegoer* to one side and the star cut-outs she was saving on the other. She couldn't go on filling her new scrapbook with Gertie hovering: in no time her aunt would be standing behind her, looking over her shoulder and saying, 'Oh, I like him. I remember him in . . .' Connie would then have to listen politely while Gertie lit a cigarette, then told her all the ins and outs of where and when she'd watched a particular film, with or without the right actor in it.

Connie's concentration would be shattered as Gertie would lose her train of thought and fall to gossiping about her Alma Street friends and neighbours.

No one knew how special her scrapbook was to Connie. How she needed to fill its pages while remembering all that had happened when she was younger. It helped her keep alive memories of the many other scrapbooks she'd filled with film stars' pictures, sitting at a table just like this one while her mother occupied the armchair nearby, reading or knitting.

Those scrapbooks had gone up in smoke the night she'd lost her mother when one of Hitler's bombs had destroyed their Portsmouth home.

'He's not a bad lad,' said Gertie, breaking into Connie's thoughts and feeling in her pocket for the packet of Woodbine cigarettes and the box of Swan Vesta matches she kept there. 'He's a good lodger. Always gives me the rent on the dot, he does. He's quiet and very clean – and I should know! I does his washing.' She laughed, a deep, throaty cackle, enhanced by years of smoking.

Connie watched as Gertie struck a match, then sucked hard at her cigarette. When a bright red tip appeared, she breathed out a plume of smoke. 'Aah, that's better,' she said. 'Now all we need is a nice cup of tea.' Connie was slowly getting used to the smell of cigarette smoke, which clung to Gertie like some exotic perfume.

'I'll help.' Connie moved quickly. Her chair scraped on the lino.

'Don't bother, love. The day I've no strength to make a pot of tea is the day they put me in my box.' Amazingly Gertie's words were clear even though the cigarette hadn't left her lips.

Gertie made her way past the faded green velvet arm-chair placed by the window that looked down the long thin backyard to the brick lavatory and the Anderson shelter. She winked at the framed picture, *Bubbles*, as she passed it. It faced *The Blue Boy* on the opposite wall. Both hung on twine suspended from the dado rail. The table was covered with an oilcloth, in the centre of which stood half a bottle of milk, a glass sugar bowl, with a crusted spoon standing to attention, and a saucer used as an ashtray that always seemed full of dog-ends.

Opposite the scullery doorway was a large wooden sideboard where Gertie kept everything that had no other home. Connie knew the ration books lay in one of the overflowing drawers, nestling among odds and ends, bits of brown paper carefully folded for later use and string, like tangled worms. If anything went missing in the house eventually it would turn up in that drawer. Not the other one: that was for cutlery, a wide selection of mismatched knives, forks and spoons.

Before Gertie disappeared into the scullery, she blew out another cloud of smoke, keeping the cigarette firmly attached to her thin lips. 'Nice of Ace to remember you was starting work today,' she said. Connie watched it move up and down as she spoke.

She listened to the swish of water in the kettle as her aunt shook it to see if there was enough to fill the teapot, then heard the flames pop on the gas stove. 'You're not worried, are you, love? First day an' all that?' called Gertie. Again, without waiting for Connie's answer, she added, 'You'll be all right. I've been a cleaner at the Criterion Picture House for years and they're a good bunch of girls as works there.'

Now Connie could hear the rattle of crockery. Gertie poked her head into the room. 'Mind you, the manager is the one you got to look out for. Don't let him take the key out of the lock if you ever gets summoned to his office. Stand with your back as close to the door as you can. Else he'll turn that key, slip it into his trouser pocket and tell you if you wants to leave the room you'll have to put your hand in his trousers to fetch it out!'

Connie, shocked, opened her mouth to say something, thought better of it and closed it.

Gertie removed the cigarette, which was now a quarter its original size, and laughed loudly. 'He's a randy old bugger, and would be even worse if his missus let him. Just you be firm with him and tell him you won't stand for any hanky-panky. Queenie, the ice-cream girl and head usherette, has got him weighed off to a T. She don't stand no nonsense. He really has got the hots for her. If ever you need to go into his office, take Queenie with you.' Gertie replaced her cigarette in her mouth and her head disappeared back into the scullery.

Connie stood up. Her heart was pounding as she swept up the discarded paper cuttings and scrunched them into a ball. Whatever was she getting into? It sounded as if she was entering a den of iniquity instead of a dream job as an usherette at the local picture house! At the range she picked up the metal lever, lifted off the hob-plate and threw the rubbish into the hole where it flamed immediately.

Was Mr Arthur Mangle really as awful as Gertie made out? He'd seemed polite when Gertie had accompanied her to her interview for the job. But she hadn't been alone with him, had she? Gertie, of course, had done all of the talking. Mr Mangle had been standing next to the kiosk, and the commissionaire in his gold-braided suit was about to allow in the queue of people waiting to purchase their tickets for the main film.

'How old are you, dear?' Mr Mangle's eyes behind his gold-rimmed glasses looked her up and down.

'She's eighteen,' Gertie said.

'Why do you want to work in a picture house?' Mr Mangle asked, pushing his face nearer to Connie's so she could see the hairs growing out of his nose. 'I . . .' She was trying to ignore the queue's muttering at being kept waiting but she'd got no further for Gertie had interrupted again.

To his credit Mr Mangle had listened politely. 'Start

Saturday at four, dear. You'll get a uniform. It's your respon-sibility to keep it clean.'

Later, Gertie had told her, 'I been working there so long I'm part of the furniture, and most vacancies gets taken by a relative or a friend of a friend. You being my niece and a pretty little thing, it was a foregone conclusion he'd give you the job.'

Now Connie looked at the wooden clock on the mantel-piece. It was nine o'clock and her stomach was feeling like it was full of the wriggling maggots from a fisherman's bait tin. Today she was starting work as an usherette.

A cloud of smoke preceded Gertie, who came bustling in carrying a tray with the brown teapot, steam curling from its spout, and two mismatched mugs. She set it down on the oilcloth with a clatter. 'I'll cook you a nice bit of breakfast in a minute, love. Got some lovely streaky bacon. How does egg, bacon and fried bread sound? Bit of bread with proper butter that Ace brought home? He's a treasure, he is. I don't ask no questions when I finds bags of sugar, packets of bacon, butter, and tins left on this here table after Ace has been down at his club. He's a proper gent, he is, not a spiv . . .'

Connie allowed Gertie's voice to fade out as she glanced at the wireless sitting on a doily on the sideboard and settled herself at the table. Glenn Miller was playing 'In The Mood', one of her favourite recordings. She watched as Gertie took off the knitted tea cosy and began pouring the strong black tea.

Without Gertie, Connie wouldn't have a clean bed to sleep in. There'd be no food in her belly or a job to start this afternoon in a picture house where she'd be able to gaze at her beloved screen stars. But, oh, how nice it would be to listen to the wireless without Gertie's voice competing . . .

Then Connie was angry with herself. Without Gertie she'd have no home.

'Yes, I'd love some breakfast,' she broke in. 'But I can make it. Why don't I cook for both of us?'

'Don't you worry yourself, love. It's nice to have you to fuss over.' Gertie frowned. 'In different circumstances it would be even better. Poor Jean,' she said. 'I heard you crying last night. I miss her too, you know.'

Chapter Four

Connie swept the chrome-backed brush through her shoulder-length fair hair. Every time she used it, she was surprised by its unfamiliar bristly touch. She missed the plain wooden-backed one she had used since she was a child but, like practically everything she had owned, it had been burned in the fire at her home.

She studied her reflection in the oval swing mirror on the top of the chest of drawers in her bedroom, which was actually the front room of Gertie's terraced house. Her large green eyes stared back at her. Connie was aware she was lucky to have a hairbrush, any hairbrush, and, like practically everything else she now owned, including the faded candlewick dressing-gown she wore, it had come courtesy of her mother's sister.

Her eyes swept over her pale oval face. She wasn't beautiful, not by any means, but she wasn't dissatisfied with her looks. Behind her, reflected in the mirror, hanging from the door of the near-empty wardrobe was a straight black skirt, and her white cotton blouse, the sleeves turned up to the elbows just the way she liked them. Newly washed and ironed, they were ready for her to put on when her aunt accompanied her to begin her new job.

Those were the clothes she'd been wearing while she worked behind the bar at the Sailor's Return in Portsmouth's Queen Street on the night of the raid she would remember all of her life.

There had been other air-raids since then, of course, Gertie and she scrabbling into the Anderson together as soon as Moaning Minnie screamed.

In the Sailor's Return, Sadie and Fred, Connie's ex-employers, had never seen the need to turn their customers out into the street when the siren announced an attack was imminent. Sadie said they could just as easily get blown up running to a shelter as they could while they were enjoying a pint. As long as the Sailor's Return had a supply of ale, the customers stayed.

The pub's pleasant ambience was enhanced by the blazing fire, the beer and a few candles in saucers dotted about. The blackout curtains were so dense that nothing could penetrate them.

Connie had liked working a few nights a week behind the bar of that busy pub on the Hard near the dockyard gates. Her mother, Jean, had had a day shift cleaning there. In the evenings there was always plenty going on, especially as Fred fancied himself a vocalist and usually started the patrons singing.

During the day Connie had worked at the corset factory in Lake Road. The women were loud and good-natured and the hours went by swiftly. Then, due to the war effort, supplies of rubber and corset-steel had been diverted from making underwear to helping to produce tanks and planes. The women coped well with the change-over, and went on being just as loud and good-natured as ever. Connie missed the camaraderie.

'Are you decent?' Gertie called.

Connie's memories faded. 'I am,' she said.

Gertie entered and put down the cup and saucer she was carrying on the chair next to the iron-framed bed. 'We got a while before we needs to leave so I thought you'd like a cuppa.'

'Bless you.' Connie smiled at her. Gertie lit a cigarette.

There were traces of Jean's prettiness in Gertie's arched brows and finely shaped nose but there the resemblance ended. Gertie was rounded: her body and her bright blue eyes were practically circular, her arms fleshy and her ankles heavy. Jean had been slim, almost waiflike, and Connie was virtually her mirror image.

Around her snug house Gertie had scattered framed family photographs. On the mantelpiece in the kitchen a young girl stared sternly into the camera. Marlene, Gertie's daughter, looked as if she'd been spirited away from her real mother and placed in Gertie's care, so alike were Connie, Jean and she. The two girls could easily have been mistaken for sisters, except for Marlene's hard expression, which the lens had picked up.

Jean had rarely spoken of the rest of her family. There'd been no photographs on display in Connie's Portsmouth home and certainly no family albums. Jean and Gertie, separated by the stretch of water between Gosport and Portsmouth, visited each other regularly, and when they did the occasions were happy, but they tended not to live in each other's pockets. Connie was always filled with apprehension when a visit was imminent, for Marlene, six months older, was in the habit of pinching her or giving her Chinese burns for no other reason than that she could. Not liking to make a fuss, Connie tried never to be alone with her. Perhaps, she thought, Marlene had mellowed with age. She hadn't seen her for ages.

There weren't any photographs of Connie's father. She must have had one, of course, because all children had fathers, didn't they?

Marlene's father was gone. Gertie didn't talk about him. She never said where or why he had 'gone'.

On the odd occasion when Connie had asked about the father she'd never known, Jean's eyes had clouded with tears and she'd said, with a half-smile, 'I loved him. That's all you need to know.' Or, 'We'll talk about it one day.'

Now Connie knew that that day would never come,

Gertie sat down on the faded patchwork quilt, the bed creaking under her weight. 'Nearly ready, love?' She squinted at Connie and a couple of lines creased her forehead. 'Are you worried?'

'Yes, and yes,' answered Connie, making faces at herself in the mirror while she applied her lipstick. 'I'm never going to be able to thank you enough for getting me this job . . . and taking me in. But I'm worried the other usherettes won't accept me.' Gertie had told her that most of them had been at the Criterion since before the war and they all mucked in together.

Tom Doyle, the commissionaire, had been employed at the picture house when it had first opened back in 1912. He'd been a young man then and now he was middle-aged, grey-haired, with grandchildren. He was a highly respected *gentleman* – Gertie had stressed the word. Her aunt had told her there wasn't much that went on in the Criterion without Tom Doyle finding out about it.

She tutted and shook her head. 'Where else was you going to go to live?' She sniffed. 'There wasn't any room at the Sailor's Return, though it was good of them to put you up that first terrible night. Anyway, what with my Marlene being evacuated out at Shedfield, to help look after some of the local kids from Alverstoke's children's home and her bed here going spare . . .' she patted her apron, smiling when her fingers made contact with her cigarettes '. . . where else was you to go?' Out of her pocket came the green packet, which Gertie pushed open to slide one out, and the matchbox. 'My Jean would come back and haunt me if I hadn't taken you in.'

There was a sudden silence. Connie's eyes had filled with tears at her aunt's words.

'Oh, my dear!' Gertie exclaimed. 'I let my stupid mouth run away with me. I'm sorry, so sorry!' She placed the cigarette and matches on the chair next to Connie's tea, then foraged in her cardigan pocket and handed Connie a folded and ironed handkerchief. 'I really am sorry, my love. It's not easy remembering my only sister's gone. I'm such a thoughtless cow!'

Connie could feel her aunt staring at her as she shook out the cotton hanky and wiped her eyes, then dabbed at her nose. She doubted she'd ever get over leaving the pub after her shift, turning the corner into the street where she lived and discovering a huge crater where her home had been.

She'd stood among the rubble, the smoke stinging her eyes, uncomprehending until she saw the blue wool, unravelled from the knitting needles, trodden into the wet brick dust that the firemen had damped down. When she'd left for work her mother had been sitting by the fire and had said, 'I'm nearly up to the armholes now. Might get this back piece finished before you comes home tonight.' Now she knew her mother wouldn't finish another cardigan ever. Of the special bag with the bone handles that her mother had kept her knitting in, there was no trace but Jean had never gone far without her knitting.

Connie had begun screaming. She'd felt as if she was in some terrible dream when the middle-aged Women's Voluntary Services lady had led her away, sat her down on an upturned box and pressed a mug of strong tea into her hands.

ARP men were still digging and scrabbling among piles of smoking, broken furniture. The air stank of cordite, and while Connie's befuddled brain was trying to think that maybe, just maybe, her mother was safe after all, a neighbour, Mrs Willis, had shouted, 'Here's Connie! Thank God she isn't in that lot!'

The men had stopped searching in the rubble.

They'd already found her mother, what was left of her.

After that, everything was a blur, but Connie remembered Sadie coming from the Sailor's Return – someone must have run and fetched her. How she got back to the pub Connie had no idea. She had a recollection of brandy, which she wasn't used to and didn't much like, burning her throat. She woke on a lumpy sofa with Sadie standing over her holding a mug of tea. On the floor next to the sofa was Connie's black handbag.

'That nearly got left behind,' Sadie said. 'Hope you didn't mind but I looked inside to check you had your identity papers and ration book.'

After making Connie drink the tea, she said, 'You can stay here as long as you want. You've always got a roof over your head and a job here, love.'

But Connie didn't want that. Everywhere she looked in the pub she thought she saw her mum, sweeping the floor, dusting a picture frame. Sometimes she seemed so real that Connie wanted to touch her, speak to her, but she knew it was all in her head.

She'd taken the ferry-boat across to Gosport to give Gertie the bad news.

'You can't stay in a place without a proper bed,' Gertie had pressed, blowing out a cloud of cigarette smoke. 'Neither is it good for your nerves knowing your mum died just around the corner from where you're working. You're staying here, with me.'

Connie and her handbag had moved in.

Now she shook away those thoughts. 'I promise I'll try to save enough money after I've given you my keep so that when Marlene's ready to come home from the country I can move on,' she said.

'Don't you worry your pretty little head about that,' Gertie said. Connie watched grey ash drop from the end of Gertie's cigarette onto the bedspread. Gertie removed the small damp dog-end from her mouth, squeezed the remains between her fingers to extinguish it and laid it in Connie's saucer.

'I only took in Ace to help me out moneywise, and because I needed a bit of company,' she said, rubbing the ash into the bedspread until it faded away. 'With the extra he gives me I'm well fixed, but as soon as the bomb damage is repaired on his club, he'll be away from here and living back in his own premises. But you don't need to worry about

Marlene coming home unexpectedly and needing a bed. My girl's in Shedfield for the duration. She loves it there.'

Shedfield was a tiny place without even a village shop. Something or someone must be keeping the normally gregarious Marlene happy there, Connie decided.

Gertie's round eyes were searching Connie's face. Connie could never tell her aunt how frightened as a child she'd been of Marlene. She picked up one of Gertie's rough hands. 'You've done so much for me,' she said. 'Without you I'd have nothing. I certainly wouldn't be looking forward to starting a dream job—'

Gertie broke in, 'You and Jean loved the films. I remember how she'd cart you off to the pictures every time they changed. She knew all the stars' names, she did, just like you do. What better place for you to get a job? You got nothing to fear from the Criterion girls. I told you, they're a good bunch.' She paused. 'Some got a few problems but then . . .' Her eyes took on a glazed look but within seconds it had passed. She smiled and brought out her packet of Woodbines again. 'This is wartime,' she said, 'an' we've all got problems, haven't we?'

Chapter Five

'When d'you reckon you'll reopen?'

Ace Gallagher looked up from his accounts book. Irritably, he stared at the blond young man standing in front of him. On the bar his coffee had gone cold. Ace frowned. It wouldn't smell or taste of anything now, except the ever-present odour of sawn wood and fresh paint, which was giving him a headache. The sooner the builders finished the better, he thought, trying to ignore the sawing and hammering that accompanied the renovations.

'Bloody coffee's cold,' he muttered. 'Can't you exist without the old dears' gifts, Tommo?' He pushed the mug along the polished wood and caught the eye of Jerome, a tea-towel as usual in his hand.

'Leave it to me,' mouthed the elderly man with horn-rimmed spectacles. He put down the cloth he'd been using to polish glasses and removed the offending mug. Careful not to spill any of the liquid, he limped out to the kitchen, which had recently been refurbished. Ace saw Tommo's eyes follow Jerome and widen dramatically as the double swing doors opened to reveal brand-new electrical goods and boxes piled on the parquet flooring from which copious packets of tea, sugar and tins of fruit could be seen.

'Just asking,' said the pretty boy. He laughed nervously.

Aware, no doubt, Ace thought, that he had been caught staring at what didn't concern him.

'I've got my regulars but new blood's always exciting,' said Tommo.

'So long as you don't ask too many awkward questions, like how I can have this club up and running soon with brand-new fittings when there's sod-all in the shops.' Ace set down his newly sharpened pencil in the middle of the page and closed the book with a slap. 'Ask no questions, you'll get fed no lies.' Ace touched his nose with his index finger, meaning for Tommo to mind his own business. From a wireless at the back of the bar, Vera Lynn was singing that, one sunny day, everyone would be meeting again.

Tommo smiled nervously. 'I meant no harm, boss,' he said.

'You're a taxi-dancer, Tommo. A ghost dancer. A pretty

little Fred Astaire. Women who think they've still got what it takes when they haven't buy tickets at sixpence a dance to have you put your arms around them. There's no harm in that. What you get up to when my club's closed is no skin off my nose, as long as it doesn't implicate me.' Ace stared intently at the younger man, then laughed. 'You bring the old girls in to dance and gamble, and I make money because they get hooked at the tables. You take 'em home, fleece 'em of whatever else is on offer. I'm happy, you're happy, right?' Ace slid off the bar stool, put out a hand and let it rest on Tommo's shoulder. 'You're not special, Tommo. You're just one of my boys. I'll let you know when we're back in business.'

Ace saw the blush rise over the young man's face. Tommo, embarrassed, looked down at his perforated two-tone shoes. He wasn't wearing a hat but his dark blue suit was well pressed, his white shirt collar clean.

Ace knew Tommo realized he'd been dismissed.

'See you later, then, boss,' he muttered, slouching away.

Ace could smell the fresh coffee before it reached him. None of that war-issue chicory rubbish: good coffee, strong coffee.

'He's a good kid, that one,' said Jerome, setting a tea plate on the counter with the steaming mug, fresh and fragrant.

On the plate there were several Bourbon biscuits: Ace's favourite. He smiled at Jerome, noting that his skin was more papery-looking than ever. He knew the old man cared about him as if he was his son. Ace appreciated that.

'I know you don't rate the lad but give him a chance,' Jerome said.

'I'd give him the benefit of the bloody doubt more if he didn't copy the way I dress,' Ace said, biting into a biscuit and glancing at his own two-tone shoes. 'Anyway, shouldn't the little bastard be in the army?'

'Copying isn't a crime, Ace, and you know what they say. "Imitation is the sincerest form of flattery." That youngster couldn't get in the forces. He had rheumatic fever as a kid. His heart don't beat properly, so the doctors said. It broke his heart he couldn't enlist.'

'He doesn't act like his heart's dodgy.' Ace crunched the last of the biscuit. 'He should be in the pictures the way he dances. All those fancy steps. All that pent-up energy wasted on them old dears.' Ace grew thoughtful. 'I'm more inclined to think he'd like to step into my shoes and wear my double-breasted suits.' He picked up the mug.

'Why?' asked Jerome. 'Because that's what you did with Billy Hill?'

'I did a proper apprenticeship under a gangster with a

solid reputation. He killed a bloke with a knife when he was fourteen. That's a back-story to set any man up for life – it tells people he's not to be messed with.' Ace set the empty mug down with a clatter on the polished wood. He licked his lips. 'Good coffee that,' he said. Then, 'I served my time under Billy Hill. I was a ten-year-old bookie's runner for him . . .'

'I know, I know. Billy's my mate and always will be. He still dishes out extreme violence and coins it with his protection rackets, but don't forget it was because of me he lent you the money to buy one-armed bandits from that geezer up north – Yorkshire, wasn't it? And look at you now . . .'

'You've always been there for me, Jerome.' Ace laughed. Then his voice became serious. 'I'd be in the services myself if you and Billy hadn't paid that doctor to sign me off as unfit—'

'The first war buggered my knee,' Jerome interrupted. 'We was only trying to keep you safe and out of the second lot of fighting, you silly young whipper-snapper. You want to keep on the right side of Billy . . .' The older man reached for the empty coffee mug.

As he moved Ace saw a spasm of pain cross his face. He leaned across the bar and put his hand on Jerome's arm. 'Why don't you go and have a lie-down? The trouble with you, you daft beggar, is you think you're still sixteen.'

A smile rose to Jerome's eyes. 'I wish I was sixteen again. That sounds like a good idea, a lie-down. I wouldn't mind a rest. You sure you'll be all right?'

'All right? What d'you think's going to happen?' Ace pulled a comical face. 'You think the painters are going to whitewash me? The chippies nail me to the floor? Get off upstairs now and I'll bring you a cuppa before I lock up.' Ace watched him hobble away. As the kitchen doors swung closed, Ace made himself as comfortable as he could on the stool and opened his accounts book again.

He looked across the bar at the early-summer sun disappearing on the horizon. Outside on the high street a lone car passed. There was hardly any traffic about now. Petrol rationing had taken care of that. Fuel for private use had been withdrawn. He smiled to himself. He had a deal with a farmer at Rowner. In exchange for black-market goods Ace took delivery of dyed pink agricultural fuel that had been strained through bread to get rid of its colour. That petrol was the lifeblood of his beloved MG Tourer.

A sudden memory of Connie putting her fingers down her throat to feign sickness when he'd offered her a ride caused him to chuckle. She was a strange one, he thought. Collecting film stars' pictures and pasting them in books was a comfort, reminding her of the life she'd had as a child.

Losing her mum like that had broken her. She'd certainly had a rough time lately. He knew Gertie would do all she could to mend her. He'd help too. He'd never met a girl who intrigued him as much as Connie did. She could be a feisty little bitch, not at all his usual type, but he'd wear her down, eventually.

Chapter Six

'We're off now, Mr Gallagher.'

Ace was surprised to see one of the carpenters standing in front of him with curls of wood shavings clinging to the front of his hair and on his work-shirt.

'The day's gone so fast, Harry,' said Ace. He pushed aside a pile of receipts and invoices, closed the accounts book and grinned up at the middle-aged man.

'We should be finished here soon.' The man scratched his ear without removing his flat cap. 'Sorry to disturb you, like.'

'Not a problem. Just cooking the books.' Ace looked down at the ledger. He could smell the man's sweat after his day's labour. 'The taxman doesn't need to know everything, does he? When d'you want your money? Cash in hand, all right?'

Harry was grinning back at him. 'The weekend is fine,

Mr Gallagher.' He fingered his cap as though touching a forelock. 'See you tomorrow.'

Ace nodded, and as the man walked away to join the rest of his workers idling at the front door, he rose from the stool and stretched. He hadn't realized he'd been sitting so long. Outside the sky was darkening. He should draw the blackout blinds and put some lights on. He glanced at his watch. Time to check on Jerome. He could do with a cuppa. Or something stronger.

He walked about his club examining the work done that day. Yes, it was coming together again nicely. He'd be happy when the Four Aces reopened and he could recoup some of the money it had cost to get the club in shape after Hitler had razed it to the ground.

'Why don't you renovate an empty building in the town? One that won't cost the earth to rebuild,' Jerome had asked him. 'Leave this pile of stones to rot?'

'You don't understand, old man,' Ace had retorted. 'This place is special. It overlooks the ferry and the waterway between Gosport and Portsmouth. When the American sailors and our other allies pull in at the Dockyard, the Four Aces is the first place in Gosport they see. It's here they spend their pay. Here is where the girls are, the gaming tables. They can buy American beer and whatever else makes them happy.'

Jerome had turned away but with a smile on his face.

Ace knew deep down Jerome understood him. Understood why his first club should be the Four Aces. It would be one of four clubs Ace would eventually own on the south coast. He was making a good living from black-market ducking and diving. Smuggling helped, as did his stream of one-armed bandits sitting in pubs and cafés up and down the country.

He ambled into the kitchen and put on a kettle. He thought about making a sandwich for Jerome but guessed he wouldn't eat it. Ace had often arrived at the club in the mornings to find whatever delicacy he'd conjured up for Jerome the night before hadn't been eaten. He'd crumble it up and throw it into the yard at the back of the club where screaming seagulls pounced on it. That's if Gosport's mangy stray cats didn't scare the birds away. Jerome was very fond of cats.

Ace sometimes wondered what kept Jerome going. Deep down he knew that hard living and extremely hard drinking had taken its toll on Jerome's kidneys, and the shrapnel in his leg didn't do him much good, either.

It was Jerome who'd cuffed his ear one late night outside the Running Bear pub in Hackney. Ace had tempted the drunks into putting down money to play Take Your Pick, a confidence game with straws, similar to Find the Lady with cards. He had no cards but was always going to win the straws game by sleight of hand. This time his audience had got nasty, until Jerome had come from nowhere, slapped him about the head and pulled him to the back of the bar by the scruff of his neck. Jerome had winkled out his age – ten – and discovered it had been twenty-four hours since Ace had last eaten. He hadn't sent him back to the uncle who was a drunk and knocked him about, but suggested to Billy that he was sharp enough to be a bookie's runner.

It wasn't long, remembered Ace, before he was better dressed, better fed, and had discovered he could make a bit more pocket money by not bothering to submit the bets on races he thought the chosen horses had no chance of winning. That had worked out fine until an outsider, Police Patrol, came in first and Ace had no idea where he was going to find sixty-six pounds to pay a bare-knuckle fighter who couldn't read or write but could pulverize a man with one punch.

Ace had finally confessed to Jerome, who'd handed him money out of his own pocket to pay the fighter and save his skinny arse. It was then Ace knew he'd found the father figure he'd never had.

That had all happened a long time ago.

Now, Ace made a pot of tea and when it was set he

poured Jerome a mug, then carried it up the wide stairs at the other end of the kitchen to the small flat he'd had furnished especially for Jerome, even before his own apartment had been finished.

Jerome was sitting on the side of his bed. He sent Ace a grateful wink. 'Just what I could do with, a cuppa,' he said. Ace saw that he was freshly shaved and dressed. The black-and-white cat curled on the bed opened one eye, blinked, closed it again and ignored him.

'There's no need for you to start prowling about down-stairs,' Ace said. 'I've closed the blackout curtains. The men have gone for the night and it's all locked up. Why don't you take it easy, go to bed?'

'When you're not here after dark it doesn't do for Gosport's villains to think the place is empty.' He sipped his tea and swallowed. 'That's good, just the way I like it.' He looked at Ace. 'Them petty thieves would think Christmas had come early if they knew what was stored in this place.'

'I'd still rather you came to stay at Gertie's, with me.'

'You're falling over each other in that little place,' Jerome said. 'Anyway, I like me own company, you know I do.' His shaking hand firmed as he stroked the cat's sleek coat. 'Well, me own company and a mate that don't answer back!'

'You won't be on your own much longer,' said Ace. 'I've

got furniture arriving soon for my quarters.' He waved an arm around Jerome's bedroom, with its en-suite bathroom, and the door that led into a good-sized sitting-room. 'And I'm going to make this place into a palace for you,' he said.

'I don't need a palace, lad,' the older man said, 'but I wouldn't mind you leaving another cuppa on the top down-stairs before you get off for the night.'

Ace nodded. 'Should I cook something for you?'

Jerome shook his head. 'Anything I need I can get for meself,' he said. 'Or I can pop over to the Dive for some-thing.' Ace turned to leave when Jerome started speaking again. 'I left a brown carrier bag with some bacon, butter and a few tins of peaches on the table-top in the kitchen. Thought Gertie might appreciate them. There's coffin nails in it as well.'

Ace knew he meant cigarettes. 'What would I do without you? You think of everything, don't you, old man?'

Jerome laughed.

As he was driving back to Alma Street Ace didn't really want to remember how Jerome's final laugh had turned into a violent fit of coughing. 'Bloody old fool!' he muttered to himself. But he said the words lovingly. Jerome was all the friends he needed in the world, wrapped in one. That damned moggy he'd adopted didn't help his sinuses much though, shedding hairs everywhere, he thought. Jerome should never have started feeding the stray in the first place. Now it thought it lived in the club with them.

He glanced at the string-handled brown bag on the seat next to him, wriggled around in his seat a bit and extracted from his pocket two lipsticks in gilt push-up cases. Gertie would like the cigarettes but Connie might appreciate the Scarlet Dream American lipstick. Just the other day he'd noticed she was using her nails to scrape colour from hers. So that Gertie wouldn't think he was taking liberties with Connie, he'd appropriated a lipstick for her as well. He slipped them in with the rest of the gifts.

Gertie always appreciated the little extras he took home to her, but he was the lucky one, he thought. Clean sheets, his washing done for him and a meal left under a saucepan lid on the gas stove made him appreciate home. Home? It wasn't really his home, was it?

He'd answered her postcard advertisement pinned in the paper-shop window near the ferry for a male lodger. Her daughter had decided to escape the bombing and had removed herself to a place of safety near Wickham in Hampshire, leaving a bedroom empty. Gertie would have taken him and Jerome but the old fool refused to leave the club. He'd said he wouldn't fit in with family life, and instead would become a sort of night-watchman. At first Jerome had slept in the cellar. Ace knew better than to try to dissuade him. Jerome would please himself anyway.

Ace had never met Gertie's daughter. The photos dotted about the house showed her to be a pretty young woman rather like Connie, except there was a knowing look in her eye that said she had a streak of wildness.

Gertie was easy to win over. He could see she had a soft spot for him. He teased her mercilessly. And he soon discovered that the more outrageous he was, the more she revelled in it.

There was little traffic about, which was just as well: the amount of light his lamps were allowed to show in the blackout was bloody dangerous. He parked outside Gertie's house, went up to the letterbox, pulled out the key and let himself into near silence. Connie and Gertie were no doubt fast asleep. He wondered how Connie had fared on her first night as an usherette. The thought of her tucked up in bed just the other side of that door in the passage warmed his heart.

Chapter Seven

Connie couldn't sleep. The events of the past evening were tumbling around in her brain and wouldn't allow her to settle.

Of course, the blackout curtains had leached all the colours from her room but in her mind's eye the costume was vibrant. Wearing it had made her feel special.

She thought back to when she and Gertie had first arrived at the Criterion earlier that evening.

'Thanks for reminding me to bring my gas mask,' Connie had said. 'Nobody likes carrying them around all the time even though the government warns us never to leave the house without them.'

'Well, you won't be carting it about in the picture house,' Gertie said. 'But at least the management will see you can obey government orders by always having it with you.' Her footsteps paused as she joined Connie, who had stopped to look at the film stills in the glass-fronted cases advertising the forthcoming attraction: *Suspicion*, starring Cary Grant and Joan Fontaine. 'You can leave the gas mask in the staffroom,' said Gertie. 'That's what the other girls do.'

Connie was now avidly staring at photographs of the main feature film, *High Sierra*, with Humphrey Bogart and Ida Lupino, whom she admired greatly. Photographs of a western, *Virginia City*, starring Errol Flynn, Randolph Scott and Humphrey Bogart again, accompanied them.

'Just imagine,' said Gertie, 'you'll be able to watch them without paying. I never get to see the films, meself.' Gertie, as a cleaner, worked in the early mornings and left before the afternoon showings began.

'Thanks as well for coming with me. I must admit I was a bit scared of walking in . . .'

'It's called moral support,' said Gertie. 'Go on push the doors and get inside.'

Connie's heart was beating wildly. Panic set in. She could no more open the swing doors to enter, than fly to the moon. On the opposite side of the picture house a small queue of people had formed, chatting while waiting to buy tickets.

'Just look at all those shiny green tiles,' said Connie, standing back on the pavement and looking upwards at the handsome façade, which was topped with a high, crenellated roof. The picture house stood in the centre of three roads, forming a sort of island. To its left and right were shops. Outside the sweetshop she could see the bus stop for Fareham. Across Forton Road, she could wait for a bus to Gosport ferry.

'You two coming in or not?'

Connie gulped and swallowed. It was time to conquer her nerves.

The tall commissionaire had pulled open one of the heavy glass doors. 'Mr Mangle said you'd be in tonight to do a shift to find out if the job suits you and if you suit us,' he said. His voice was gruff but he had spoken kindly. He kept the door open so Connie and Gertie could enter. He was resplendent in a maroon suit splashed with gold braid. His coat was three-quarter length and his black shoes so shiny that Connie thought, if she looked, she'd be able to see her face reflected in them. His peaked cap showed just a little of his grey hair.

The glass door softly closed behind them.

'Wasn't expecting two of you,' he said, with a smile.

'I popped along to introduce Connie to a few of the others, Tom,' said Gertie. Already she'd opened her handbag and taken out her Woodbines, offering him one.

'I shouldn't really, Gertie,' he said. 'You know I'm on duty so, if it's all right with you I'll smoke it on my break.'

Gertie nodded approval as he slipped the cigarette into his top pocket, and lit her own. 'He'll pop in the lavatory later and smoke that,' she muttered to Connie, then waved towards a door with 'Gents' on it, next to another labelled 'Ladies'.

'Oy! Don't I get one?'

A peroxide-blonde head topped by a red pillbox hat popped up from below the counter of the kiosk. Connie stared at the pretty young woman holding a roll of shilling tickets in one hand.

'Just cos I'm out of sight don't mean I'm out of mind. I'm refilling the ticket machine for the stalls,' she said. She saw Connie looking at the roll. 'It's one and six upstairs in the circle.'

Gertie gave a laugh that nearly dislodged her Woodbine from her lip. 'This is Queenie,' she announced, delving into her handbag again for the green packet, taking out a cigarette and slipping it below the glass cover onto the metal tray where the patrons placed their entrance money.

'Welcome to the house of fun.' The young woman spoke in a low, husky voice. Her curled hair was almost white. Connie was reminded of the platinum-blonde star Jean

Harlow. Queenie gave Connie a huge smile as she reached for the cigarette. Despite the wall of glass between them Connie could smell the heavy scent of Californian Poppy.

'Thanks, Gert,' Queenie said.

'You're welcome,' came Gertie's reply. 'Is his lordship about?'

Queenie was lifting small plates of metal to insert the ticket roll. She shook her head.

'Nah!' said Tom. 'He's been summoned to the town hall to collect his missus from one of her many charities, and you know he daren't defy her wishes.'

'He's right under her thumb,' added Gertie.

Gertie took the dog-end from her mouth and threw it on the floor.

'You shouldn't do that,' whispered Connie, even though she couldn't see an ashtray. There wasn't even a bucket of sand that did double duty as a receptacle for dousing cigarettes and a safety measure in case of fire.

'God love you, Connie, it's me what's got to clean the place up tomorrow morning, ain't it?' Gertie remonstrated. 'This is a picture house, not Buckingham Palace!' She looked at Tom, laughing, and winked at him as though there was a secret between them. Connie, embarrassed, stared at her shoes.

'Take no notice of Gertie, my duck,' said Tom. 'She likes dog-ends!'

He raised an eyebrow at Queenie, who said, 'I'll tell you later, Connie, why Gertie likes dog-ends, if she doesn't!'

'How long's Mr Mangle gone for?' asked Gertie.

'Said he might be back by the last showing,' answered Queenie. 'He'd like to know how his new girl,' she jerked her head towards Connie, 'gets on with the job. Told me to keep an eye on her.'

Connie looked at her in surprise. Seeing Queenie behind the machines in the ticket kiosk, she'd automatically thought that that was her allotted work. Now it seemed she did other jobs as well.

Her eyes fell on a coloured poster from *Gone with the Wind* that showed Clark Gable holding Vivien Leigh in his arms. It was set above carpeted steps that led, she surmised, into the stalls.

Connie had already noticed painted signs proclaiming 'The Circle', one each side of the foyer pointing up wide winding stairs. Huge framed pictures of film posters featuring the stars adorned the walls, no doubt encouraging patrons to pay the extra money for a seat upstairs.

Opposite the ticket kiosk another booth sold sweets and crisps. It wasn't particularly well stocked and the electric light inside it was switched off. Obviously, thought Connie, whoever worked in there hadn't yet turned up.

Just then a dark-haired young woman came hurrying down the stairs. 'About bloody time, Edna,' said Queenie. 'I thought I was going to have to do your job as well as mine tonight.' Queenie came out of the ticket kiosk and Edna, out of breath, squeezed her way in. She was already dressed in her uniform.

'I've been upstairs looking for the watch that bloke said he lost this afternoon,' she said. She turned to Gertie. 'If you finds it, Gert, when you cleans up in the morning, let me know. He seemed a nice young fellow, army lad.'

Gertie nodded. 'Edna, this is my Connie. She's starting here tonight.'

'Hello, love,' said Edna, with a welcoming smile, as she settled into the booth.

Gertie whispered to Connie, 'We got a special cupboard for lost and found stuff.' She winked at Queenie. 'Sometimes we finds some unusual lost things.'

The women laughed.

Now Queenie was standing next to her, Connie discovered she wasn't as tall as she'd thought. In fact, Queenie was a couple of inches shorter than herself.

'I need to take Connie down to the staffroom,' Queenie

said, 'so she can change into her uniform. The B picture's going to end in about twenty minutes, then it'll be the intermission and time for me to serve the ice-creams. I'll be back here before the main feature and the queue's allowed in, Tom, so I'll keep a look-out while you go to the Gents for your smoke.'

Tom gave her a grateful look.

'I can take her to change and meet some of the others,' broke in Gertie.

'No! Ol' Mangle told me to do it.' Queenie was firm. Now she wasn't behind glass the smell of Californian Poppy was much stronger. Connie had read somewhere that a woman should buy her perfume to suit her personality and decided that the heavy, sexy scent was ideally suited to Queenie. She resolved that as soon as she had some money to spare, after she'd begun paying Gertie for her keep, of course, she'd buy a fragrance that people would automatically associate with her and wear it all the time. A sort of signature scent. She gave a small sigh. Here she was, thinking about buying perfume when there was practically nothing in the shops. Connie breathed in more of the Californian Poppy. She'd been so interested in what was going on in the foyer she'd hardly spoken a word.

'People are queuing up outside,' she said now.

'That's because a lot of folk don't like sitting down in the middle of a film, Connie. Some don't mind. They go in, and when the film comes round to where they started, they soon put it all together in their heads.' Queenie looked at Gertie, who had about an inch of ash on the end of another cigarette. 'If you want to come along to settle her in as well, Gert, that's fine by me.'

'No, I know when I'm not wanted,' she replied.

Connie breathed a sigh of relief. Her aunt had uttered those words with a smile. Obviously, she wasn't put out by Queenie's suggestion that she was surplus to requirements. The ash fell off Gertie's cigarette and sank to the carpet.

Now she was closer to Queenie, Connie realized she wasn't that much older than herself, certainly no more than three or four years. A torch was tucked into her skirt top, causing her jacket to ruffle up a little at the side, but her uniform couldn't conceal her ripe figure. Heavy red lipstick and eyebrows like Marlene Dietrich's above long lashes coated with mascara gave her the look of a film star. Connie had already decided she liked her enormously.

Gertie was pulling open the heavy glass door. 'I'm away home to start making a Woolton Pie for Ace when he gets in,' she said, to no one in particular. 'Ace likes my cooking. An' you'll need something warm in your belly, our Connie.

Bloody 'ell, it's started raining,' she said. 'Tom, shall I tell that little crowd outside to come in and wait?'

He nodded. 'Good idea. Don't want the poor beggars getting wet through before they sit down.'

'Might as well,' called Queenie. 'And don't worry about Connie getting home in the dark, Gert. Remember, I go that way as well. See you tomorrow. Come on, Connie.'

Dutifully, Connie followed Queenie up the first set of stairs, admiring her seamed nylons and high-heeled black shoes. Queenie certainly knew how to make the best of herself. And how kind of her to offer to walk with Connie on their way home.

Her stomach was tied in knots. She hoped she wouldn't make any mistakes, and if she did, she prayed the other usherettes would be kind to her.

It was exciting following Queenie to start learning the ropes of her dream job. She thought of the many times she had walked past the Criterion. This was the first time she'd been inside since she'd come to live in Gosport, even though she loved watching films. Going to the pictures reminded her of her mother: she and Jean had spent many happy hours at the Regal in Portsmouth's Queen Street.

Why did the picture houses always have such glamorous names? Eldorado, Forum, Embassy? Their names enticed people to discover magic doorways to places only ever before seen in books.

Queenie pulled open a large door at the top of the steps, then slid back a dense curtain on silent runners. She stopped and put a finger to her lips. When she and Connie were in the darkness of the auditorium, she pulled the curtain back into place and switched on her torch.

Chapter Eight

The smell of cigarette smoke, sweat and stale perfume engulfed Connie as soon as the curtain in the doorway swished closed behind them.

'Stand still a moment and let your eyes adjust to the dark,' Queenie whispered, putting out her free hand to stop Connie moving in the vast blackness. 'I don't want you falling arse over head on your first night!' Although Queenie had switched on her torch, she kept it shining low, on the carpet. 'When I give you your torch it's not for waving all over the place!'

She could hear a few paper bags rustling but Connie's eyes were drawn to the screen, where Randolph Scott's larger-than-life image was remonstrating with a sheriff. His voice was as clear as a bell, she thought.

From the room above the circle's seats, the projectionist

was working his magic and Connie was mesmerized by the shaft of gleaming light showing the images. Smoke from cigarettes wafted through the flickering beam in changing colours from white to grey and black.

'Ol' Randy's just about to catch the bad men,' confided Queenie, glancing at the screen.

The smoke in here was worse than it had been in the Portsmouth bar where she'd been working. It stung her eyes and already she felt like sneezing. She'd get used to it, Connie thought. She'd never really noticed before how many people smoked. Her mother hadn't taken to cigarettes. Neither she nor Connie could afford to. She remembered Jean saying, 'If God had meant us to smoke, he'd have put chimneys in our heads!' And at school, when the girls in her class had disappeared into the toilets to light up, Connie hadn't gone with them. She'd always had a library book in her satchel and preferred to read somewhere quiet.

She knew there were ashtrays between the cinema seats. Hadn't she been embarrassed once or twice when, in the dark, someone sitting next to her, extinguishing a fag, had accidentally brushed against her knees?

'Is that the new girl?' The loud whisper came from one of the two usherettes sitting in the back row watching the film.

'Sssh!' said Queenie, but she nodded. Two faces stared

at Connie. One broke into a welcoming smile but the other glared at her. Nevertheless, Connie smiled at both. Automatically her mouth formed the word 'Hello' but she didn't speak. Randolph Scott was now hiding behind the corner of a wooden saloon ready to fire a gun at the bad men. And there was almost complete silence in the picture house, except for the dramatic music from a non-existent Wild West orchestra.

'C'mon.' Queenie grasped Connie's hand and pulled her down the aisle towards signs that said 'WC' and 'Exit', and a door marked 'Private'. She pushed against it, and thrust Connie inside.

Queenie switched on the electric light. The bare bulb showed the small room furnished with a table, some mismatched chairs and a couple of metal filing cabinets. A row of pegs contained coats and jackets. Another open door showed a room only a little larger than a cupboard, containing a sink, a gas ring on the draining-board and a table on which the makings for tea were set out. Another door opened to reveal a lavatory. A cistern on the wall had a chain pull to flush. Connie could smell disinfectant. Queenie went to a large built-in cupboard and took out a uniform from among other clothes hanging inside. She handed it to Connie. 'You're about the same size as the last girl so it should fit. Go through to the kitchen to change. The outfit's been washed, but if it needs altering you'll have to do that yourself. As, no doubt, you've already been told, you're responsible for it now, and when you leave it has to be returned spotless.'

'Thank you,' Connie said. She pursed her lips. She suddenly felt eaten up with shyness. Then she noticed how quiet it was. The film's dialogue could not be heard in this room.

Queenie had taken a box of matches from her pocket and was lighting her cigarette. She sat on one of the uncomfortable chairs, sighed, then breathed out a stream of smoke. 'I needed that,' she said, 'though I can take it or leave it.' Then as if she was reading Connie's mind, 'This room's soundproofed, like the projection room upstairs. The staff use it to chat, make tea.' She pointed to the kitchen's open door through which Connie was about to go, the uniform over her arm. 'Mangle doesn't come in here. It's our special place.' She took another deep drag on her cigarette. 'Some of the girls arrive at work in their uniforms. It's up to you.' Queenie lifted her head and contentedly blew a lungful of smoke into the air. 'Pull the kitchen door closed if you're a bit shy.'

Connie, eager to start work, was in the kitchen changing her clothes. She was a bit ashamed of Marlene's cast-off underwear. Her own was in the wash and Marlene's was grey with laundering, but Connie was glad to wear it until she could buy new. After all, she'd arrived at Gertie's with only the clothes she stood up in, hadn't she? Queenie had raised her voice so Connie could hear her.

'You can put stuff in here. It will be reasonably safe, but don't leave money or anything precious. Sometimes a picturegoer might come in, by mistake, but from the seats we're allowed to sit in when we've nothing else to do, it's easy to keep an eye on this room.' She paused. 'I'll have to leave you soon. I'm the ice-cream girl as well, you see!'

Connie came out of the little kitchen in her dark red uniform with her day clothes over her arm. The cheeky pillbox hat felt funny clamped over her hair. She hoped it wouldn't fall around her neck and strangle her. She put her folded clothes on the table. Now her eagerness had turned to fear. Queenie must have noticed her stricken face: 'You'll be all right. Shirley and Lucie will look after you. You just follow them around, helping where you can. I'll come back for you later.' Softly, she added, 'They won't bite!' She smiled, showing strong white teeth. 'That outfit could have been made for you. You look lovely in it. But most of us wear the elastic round the back of our heads.' She pointed to Connie's hat. 'Let me do it.'

Feeling better after her hat had been adjusted, Connie admired herself in the foxed mirror hanging on the wall. She twisted and twirled, and Queenie stood smiling at her. 'You're only going to show people where they can sit, not take part in a beauty parade!' She pointed to a torch that had appeared on the table. 'Stick that in your belt.' Connie laughed.

'By all means you can tell the patrons to stop rattling crisps bags and sweetie wrappers, if they're lucky enough to have some. Just remember, coming to the pictures is a treat for them and we're here to serve. Keep your eyes open for dirty old men . . .'

Connie's eyes widened.

'We get all sorts in here, like most cinemas. This place has over seven hundred seats, so keep your eyes peeled. Our job's not just walking people to their seats in the dark, you know. Watch out for courting couple who go too far. I like to stick them in a back row where they can't upset other folks. It's good to advise women in big hats to remove them before they sit down. After all, the poor bugger behind has paid for a ticket to see the film as well.' She took another drag on her cigarette. 'Watch out for men who purposely sit next to young girls or boys . . .' she added, grimacing. 'Keep your eyes open, Connie. I can't repeat that enough.

Sometimes people act funny in the dark and Mr Mangle don't want trouble.' A smile came over her pretty face. 'Don't ever,' she said seriously, 'call the Criterion the Bug-hutch or the Flea-pit. He'll get really cross if you do.'

After blowing out more smoke, Queenie said, 'When I was little my mum sent me to the pictures with a hatpin to stick in any bloke's hand if it started wandering to my knees.'

Connie hoped she'd remember all that. She was still admiring herself in the mirror while she listened to Queenie's words of wisdom. Now she had the elastic at the back of her head to keep her hat in place, it felt much better.

Amazingly she still had colour on her lips and, while no one would notice it in the dark, Connie felt properly dressed as an usherette. Soon she'd not be able to hook any more lipstick from her tube. Bloody war, she thought, making it hard for people to buy the things they wanted.

Queenie looked bandbox fresh and so glamorous – Connie envied her.

'Stop admiring yourself.' Queenie stubbed out her cigarette in the overflowing ashtray on the table and picked up Connie's clothes. 'Put them in that cupboard over there and hurry up.' She looked at the clock on the wall. 'It'll be intermission soon, that queue will be needing seats after the other patrons have left, and I've got to get the ice-creams out.

Come and meet Shirley and Lucie. Of course,' she added, 'there are more usherettes working tonight, upstairs and on the other side of the auditorium, but I won't bombard you with names tonight. You'll meet everyone tomorrow.'

Connie must have looked confused because Queenie continued to talk.

'Before the first performance each day, every usherette usually congregates in the foyer, Mr Doyle as well,' she added, 'and Arthur Mangle has us stand to attention while he checks us over. He likes us to be smart and clean with not a hair out of place.' She paused. 'I don't know how much Gertie's told you but he does have wandering hands . . . If he starts to fiddle with your collar or buttons, just move away sharply. He's not daft – he'll know you're not going to play his game. It's just the way he is. I've told him I'll kick him in the bollocks if he tries anything with me. But as you're new here, just glare at him and move away. He'll get the hint.'

Connie had heard Gertie say he was like an octopus but now she didn't know what to think. 'What about his wife? Does she know?'

Queenie shrugged. A cloud of Californian Poppy rose from her and Connie breathed it in deeply. 'Some men are like that, aren't they?' Queenie said. 'Anyway, most days he's too lazy even to get here on time so don't worry too much.'

Connie wasn't a child. In the pub, she'd often been touched by the men, and she could cope quite well with a smack on the bottom, or an occasional cuddle or hug from a beery bloke. She knew they meant nothing. Men usually got a bit flirty as the evening wore on and the drinks kept coming. Sadie and Fred kept an eye on what was going on in the bar and had a sharp word with any customer who got out of hand.

'Queenie,' said Connie. She broke the sudden silence between them. 'I just want to say thank you.' She knew she was blushing but she was grateful for the kindness shown her.

Queenie coloured. 'Don't be daft, Connie. We're all put on this earth to help one another, aren't we?' She smiled, and Connie felt warm and happy until Queenie added, 'Hurry up – I don't want Tom moaning at me. He'll be wanting his fag break if he hasn't already taken it.' She smiled again as she opened the door into the auditorium and the soundtrack burst forth from the actors onscreen.

'The programme tonight is a newsreel, a cartoon, trailers, the big picture and the B, and if this job's not to your liking, that's the end of it. I've a feeling, though, you're like me, here to stay. I'll catch up with you later, all right?'

Queenie led the way back to where Shirley and Lucie

were still sitting in the back row. She pulled down a spare seat and nudged Connie into it. 'She's Connie and ready to start now, so look after her.' Both women nodded, and the one next to Connie whispered, 'You'll be all right, ducks.' Then her eyes slid back to the screen.

Connie watched as Randolph Scott went into a clinch with his leading lady. Her head was in a whirl but her own adventure had just begun.

Chapter Nine

Gertie had already lined the pie plate with shortcrust pastry and was now filling it with the Bakewell mixture, containing strawberry jam, dried egg, margarine, sugar and almond essence. She was lucky to have such luxuries, with most food rationed or on coupons and little in the shops. Thank God for Ace and the bits and pieces he brought home, she thought. She hummed along to the wireless with Vera Lynn singing 'Yours' and wondered how Connie was getting on at the Criterion. She'd left her in good hands with Queenie.

Ace liked her cooking. 'Gertie,' he'd said, 'you're a damn fine cook. If I ever get my kitchen in the club up and running again, I'll make you my chef.'

She knew he probably didn't mean it. Anyway, she didn't think she'd like to spend her days and nights cooking for a lot of people she didn't know, but it was nice to hear Ace say that. And he liked a bit of Bakewell Tart.

The table was filled with her bowls, spoons, rolling pin, ingredients and a fine dusting of flour. The smell of the Woolton Pie in the oven wafted in from the scullery to the kitchen making her feel happy and contented. Gertie drew a breath of nicotine from the Woodbine that hadn't left her lips since she'd first lit it.

Later, she'd dish up dinner for Ace, cover it with a plate and leave it over a saucepan of water so he could heat it up when he got home. She'd know then that he'd had a decent meal today. She often did that for him when he wasn't around at normal mealtimes. He was such a considerate lodger. She might have to start doing it for Connie as well. Of course, that depended on what hours Mangle wanted her to work. It looked like she'd be on the six until eleven shift, the same as Queenie, though Queenie seemed to work all hours at the picture house. Mangle took over when Queenie didn't work, but often as not he was absent so the girls mucked in. Gertie worked every morning from eight until midday. The women's rotas were supposed to be set so that the different shifts covered all the hours the films were shown.

Gertie looked at the clock on the mantelpiece. She was

tired. She wanted her bed. To oversleep was a sin. One thing she prided herself on was good time-keeping. Being late had once caused a bit of bother for her – actually, it had erupted into a bloody great row. She felt mean about it now, but at the time she hadn't known what the real problem was, had she?

'Bloody Sara Cantrell!' The other cleaner's name came out of her mouth in a hiss.

It was well known that Gertie had an arrangement with Mason's the tobacconist. She would collect the cigarette ends off the floor and out of the ashtrays and bag them up ready to take home with her. She'd open them and save the unsmoked tobacco shreds, which would go into another bag. It had to be clean, mind, Fred Mason wouldn't pay for ash – no, not at all. She would then deliver it to the tobacconist, who would mix it with his shag for rolling tobacco to sell on to customers who preferred to make their own cigarettes in Rizla papers. The cash she got for it was money for old rope – or money for smoked fags . . .

Gertie still felt shame remembering.

Coming in late one morning she had caught Sara Cantrell picking up the bigger butts and putting them in her overall pocket. From the bulge she was trying to hide, she'd quite a few fat ones.

'You don't pick up any dog-ends until I've seen 'em first!' Gertie had shouted. 'Don't think you can muscle in on my game! You do it again and I'll stuff one down your bloody throat!'

Meek Sara had run out of the auditorium crying, but not until after Gertie had scooped the dog-ends from her pocket. Gertie had then got on with her job and was really surprised when Ol' Mangle had waltzed up to her and demanded she apologize to Sara.

'It's her should apologize to me,' she'd ranted. 'Bloody thief!'

Of course Sara, standing at his side with a cigarette in her hand, cried all the more.

'Apologize or get the sack!' There was steam practically coming out of Mangle's ears.

'I won't!'

'You will!' Mangle looked like a demon from Hell. He didn't like being challenged.

Suddenly Gertie feared for her job. She mumbled, 'Sorry,' and the morning's work went on.

It was only later she found out from Queenie that Sara had been desperate for a cigarette and didn't have any money to buy some. The previous evening her husband had walked out on her, leaving her with three kiddies, the rent and the grocer's bill unpaid.

The grocer had caught hold of her and she'd had to pay off the slate money and didn't know which way to turn because he wouldn't give her any more credit. Coming to work she'd looked in the gutters for big dog-ends she could pick up. In the auditorium she'd pocketed some. Gertie had seen her and laid into her before she'd had a chance to explain.

Gertie felt awful. She was in the wrong.

The next morning Gertie slipped ten Woodbines into Sara's hands, ignoring the terrified look on the woman's face. 'Sorry, Sara,' she'd said. 'We've all been there. But next time, for God's sake, say something.' Gertie hadn't been late for work since. She usually arrived fifteen minutes early so she could listen to all the gossip.

Now she looked at the Bakewell Tart. It was finished and ready for the oven.

'Bugger!' She couldn't help but swear because the long end of ash had fallen from her cigarette and landed on the pastry close to the almond-flavoured topping. Quickly she flicked it off with her thumb and smoothed the floury surface.

'What the eye don't see the heart don't grieve over,' she whispered to herself.

Satisfied the tart was as perfect as she could make it,

Gertie carried it out to the scullery, bent down and opened the oven's door. A wave of heat nearly took the skin off her face. The Woolton Pie was coming on nicely. She slipped the tart onto the lower shelf and closed the door, careful not to burn her fingers.

Gertie, cigarette in mouth, hummed along to Jimmy Dorsey and His Orchestra as she began clearing the mess from the kitchen table. She thought about her dead sister: when Jean was a little girl Gertie had had to take her with her wherever she went. 'Look after Jean, our Gertrude,' their mother would say, as she helped Gertie slide the big old pram over the step in the mornings. She was always 'Gertrude' when her mother wanted her to do something. Pretty little Jeannie, thought Gertie, not with jealousy but with fondness. After all, it wasn't her sister's fault she was pretty as a picture.

People always stopped to admire Jeannie's pale curls. Of course, when they looked at Gertie they didn't say, 'Don't you have lovely curls too,' because Gertie wasn't pretty and didn't have blonde curls. She was referred to as 'my good girl' or 'Gertie, my little helper'.

She didn't really mind having Jeannie with her. Their mum had to work. Gertie didn't remember her dad very well. When she thought about him, she remembered a moustache, the smell of tobacco and peppermints.

He wasn't home a lot because he was in the navy, and then he never came home at all. Her mother cleaned other people's houses. They had a terraced house opposite the Hard at Portsmouth, which shared a WC with five other households, and they took water from a standpipe in the street. Cleaning's in my blood, Gertie thought, for it was all she'd ever done.

There was never any question of not taking Connie in. She'd looked after Jeannie, so it was only natural she'd do the same for Jeannie's daughter, wasn't it?

When the table was cleared and the unused ingredients packed away in the kitchen cupboard, Gertie made herself a pot of tea. Another peek in the oven told her the pie and the tart were ready to come out. The tart went on the wooden draining-board to cool and the pie she left on the gas stove. Pleased with her efforts, she went back into the kitchen to have a sit-down.

She looked at the clock on the mantelpiece. She was longing for Connie to come home and tell her all about her first night at work. Connie was a lovely girl. She'd been in her house for five minutes, and Gertie could tell she'd not be the handful her Marlene was. They were alike as two peas to look at but there the similarity ended. Marlene was Gertie's daughter but she had a mind of her own, did that one.

Marlene had always been in trouble at school, and Gertie was forever receiving notes asking her to report to the head-mistress of St John's School. 'Marlene has been standing out of sight behind the main lavatory door with a scarf tightly rolled as a long weapon. Whenever the door opens, she whacks the person coming out.'

Marlene's big blue eyes would open wide as she apol-ogized. 'It was only a game,' she'd say. The staff's hearts would melt and all would be forgiven. Then there was the pilfering and lying. Gertie stopped sending her daughter to the shops: Marlene conveniently 'lost' the money before she got there. Later Gertie would find empty sweet wrappers under Marlene's bed.

Keeping Marlene in her bedroom to teach her a lesson did no good: the girl found she could climb out of her window onto the shed roof and escape down the alley.

Gertie wondered how on earth she'd ever kept her out of a policeman's clutches.

Marlene was high-spirited and highly strung, and if Marlene wanted something, Marlene made sure she got it.

Jeannie never had any such bother with Connie, especially as Connie seemed accident prone when out playing with Marlene. Marlene said Connie was a fraidy-cat and she did seem to fall over and hurt herself a lot.

When Marlene began working at Priddy's armaments' yard, Gertie thought she was settled for as long as the war was to last. There she met Alex, a handsome young man who tried to get kids off the streets after they'd left the children's home in Alverstoke to go to foster parents. He took them to a church hall in the town where they could play billiards and table-tennis, listen to music and drink orange squash. Marlene revelled in the responsibility of leadership and volunteered to go to Shedfield, a country village, as a helper when the kids were evacuated.

Without Marlene to look after, Gertie was lonely. However, when Ace knocked on her door saying he'd seen her card in a shop window, she'd taken one look at his posh car and decided he'd definitely be an asset to Alma Street. She didn't know him from Adam until he'd said, 'I own the club near the ferry that was flattened in the big air raid. I need somewhere to stay that's homely and clean until I can get the place rebuilt.'

She'd done a double-take at his good looks and fancy suit, invited him in, shown him the upstairs bedroom and given him a cup of tea. He'd fallen for her bread pudding, which she'd left steaming on the stove.

'Is all your cooking as good as this?' he'd asked. She'd tried not to blush and was glad she'd bothered to take out her curlers.

He'd looked at the photograph of her Marlene on the mantelpiece. 'Is she your sister?' She'd decided then and there that he'd do very nicely as a lodger. They'd agreed on how much he should pay, very generous it seemed to her, and he'd moved in.

Now Gertie heard the key being pulled through the letterbox. Excited, she got up and went down the hall to welcome either Ace or Connie.

Chapter Ten

'I really enjoyed myself tonight.' Connie stumbled in, already divesting herself of her coat. She threw down a brown carrier bag containing the clothes she'd worn earlier to the Criterion, slung her coat over a peg in the hall and fell into Gertie's arms. 'Oh, it was lovely,' she said.

'Don't knock me off me feet, you daft 'aporth! You're not supposed to like working! It's not natural!' But Gertie couldn't help feeling Connie's happiness had infected her as well.

'Oh, Auntie! Thank you for putting in a good word for me. What wouldn't I like about the job?'

Connie was waltzing Gertie down the passage and into the kitchen, where she let go of her to collapse onto a chair. Gertie, breathless, blew out her cheeks, took in a big gulp of air and held onto the back of another chair to keep her balance after her unexpected and hectic dance.

'C'mon, then, tell me everything!' Gertie wheezed, pulling out the chair and plonking herself opposite Connie. 'I need a fag to calm me down after that lot,' she said, one hand in her apron pocket for her Woodbines and matches.

'I'll tell you if you let me know what that gorgeous smell is – I'm as hungry as a horse!' Connie was smiling but a huge yawn overtook her. 'Oh dear,' she said, putting her hand over her mouth. 'Not only am I hungry but tired as well.'

Gertie preened. She liked her cooking to be praised. 'That's Woolton Pie and Bakewell Tart, and I'll dish you some up when you've told me how your first shift went.' She took a deep pull on her cigarette and sighed happily.

Connie's eyes were shining like diamonds. 'My normal shift will be six until eleven at night. I'll be taking tickets in the foyer, tearing them in half and giving the stub back to the customers – we have to call them patrons. Then I'll show them to their seats either inside in the stalls or upstairs in the circle, depending on whether I'm up or down. Everywhere in the Criterion is carpeted, except for the lavatories—'

'I know that! Have you forgotten I work there as well? I do clean the place!'

Connie started laughing. 'Whoops!' she said. 'I'm only telling you the things I've learned tonight.' She paused. 'I now know there are three separate showings of films a day.

On our last shift we have to raise all the seats ready for the cleaners to work their magic early the next morning.'

'Did you see Arthur Mangle?' Gertie asked.

'No, the manager didn't come back from wherever he'd gone with his wife.'

'So, you don't know if he's pleased with your first evening at work?' Gertie looked at her thoughtfully.

'Queenie said I was doing fine,' said Connie. 'You didn't tell me she's head usherette! I'm hoping she'll tell him I learned a lot this evening.'

Gertie smiled at her. It was like the happiness was bursting out of the girl, she thought. Her own heart lifted. Gertie so wanted to do what was best for her sister's girl.

Connie broke into her thoughts. 'I know you've been cooking but what else have you been up to while I've been gone?'

'I had the wireless on earlier,' Gertie said. 'The announcer said our planes had decimated Cologne. Over two hundred German factories destroyed. I hate it when they talk about bombing. That was when I turned the wireless off, but not before they said that lots more American servicemen have landed in Ireland. We'll soon be overrun with them . . .'

'Queenie's boyfriend is American.'

'Didn't take you long to start winkling things out of her, did it? That's something I didn't know.'

'Well, she walked me home, didn't she? We chatted about all sorts of things,' said Connie. She yawned again. 'I like Queenie. She's a straight talker and there's no airs and graces with her . . . And I really like sitting out of the way at the back and watching the films in between doing my job.'

'You'll soon get fed up with watching the main film, the B picture, the news, the adverts and the cartoon over and over.' Gertie laughed.

'Never,' said Connie. 'It's my dream job.'

'And did you make friends with some of the other usherettes?'

Connie sighed. 'I tried to be as nice as I could to everyone. It'll take me a while to put names to faces, though. There was only one woman I found it hard to speak to. I had to make all the conversation, if you know what I mean. I felt like I was talking at her instead of to her.' Gertie nodded. 'Gwen, her name is. She seemed a bit off with me. Perhaps she's one of those people who don't make new friends easily but she seemed to dislike me instantly. I could feel her disapproval. We used to get women like that in the corset factory. Everyone would be falling over backwards to include the new ones in what the firm had to offer, but if a girl's face didn't fit, there wasn't much anyone could do about it. I think—'

'Gwen Cadogan!' The name came out in a burst from Gertie. Connie nodded. 'Yes, that's her . . .'

'Don't take any notice of her, Connie. She wanted her friend to get the usherette's job but Queenie thought you'd be better suited.' Gertie saw Connie yawn again. It wasn't food or a cup of tea this girl needed, she decided, it was her bed. Even though, no doubt, the minute she laid her head on the pillow she'd be wide awake with everything whirling in her brain.

'What d'you think of my uniform, then?' Connie leaped up from her chair but staggered against the table. 'Oops,' she said.

Gertie would have commented on it sooner but she was finding it hard to get a word in edgeways, with Connie animated one minute, yawning the next.

'It fits you like a glove and you look really professional . . . There's hot water in the kettle if you want a wash in the scullery. Hang your outfit up behind your bedroom door. Get into bed. I'll bring you in a cuppa and something to eat.'

Gertie was surprised when the girl leaned across and kissed her cheek. 'Thank you,' Connie said. Gertie sniffed to hide the wave of emotion that suddenly coursed through her.

A while later when the tea was made and a slice of tart sat on a plate, Gertie nudged open Connie's bedroom door. Her niece was fast asleep.

Chapter Eleven

'Thank you,' said the young man, his gaze holding Connie's eyes as he made his way through the row of patrons, forced either to stand or make themselves small so he could reach his seat in the middle of the row.

Connie kept her torchlight low on the carpet so it wouldn't disturb anyone. Though it was amazing, she thought, how quickly your eyes became accustomed to the darkness. The man pulled down the seat and nodded gratefully at her before his gaze was drawn towards the screen and he removed his trilby.

'Hurry up and get comfortable, mate! We don't want to miss anything,' said the man in the seat behind.

Connie waited until he was settled, then walked back up the aisle and sat down on one of the designated staff seats.

'He was lucky to get in,' Queenie whispered. 'Everyone

wants to see *Citizen Kane* – it's been running to packed houses everywhere.'

Now the newness of the job was receding, Connie was beginning to recognize a few of the regulars. It wasn't the first time she had seated the tall, slim, immaculately dressed young man. It was, however, the first time she had become fully aware of him. In the foyer she had torn his ticket in two, eager to return to her staff seat to find out what Orson Welles as Charles Foster Kane was buying next for his mansion, Xanadu.

But on handing him back the ticket stub, their fingers had touched and something, she wasn't sure what, had forced her to look into his eyes. She knew then that, whatever the future held, the moment they had just shared would remain with her for ever. His eyes were a deep, deep, penetrating blue.

Embarrassed, she'd stuttered, 'Will – will you come this way, sir?' She felt at a disadvantage that her stock sentence was all she could say to him, despite the magical thing that had just happened to her. Switching on her torch, Connie had shown him to the last unoccupied seat.

'He's been in before, hasn't he?' she whispered, now she was back sitting with Queenie.

'Are you sleepwalking when you show people to their seats?' Queenie asked.

'What do you mean?' Connie stared at her friend.

'Ssh!' came a woman's voice from across the aisle.

Queenie nudged Connie's arm. 'C'mon, I don't think anyone's likely to move from their seats for a while, and if they do, Shirley and Pat can cope.' She nodded across to the other side of the picture house where the other usherettes were engrossed in the film. 'Come on,' she repeated, getting up from her seat. Connie followed her down the aisle, the smell of Queenie's Californian Poppy accompanying her.

'I need a cup of tea,' Queenie said. As she entered the staffroom and switched on the light, she added, 'We can tell Ol' Mangle I didn't feel too good and you came to look after me.' She sighed. 'He's probably not in the building. Anyway, I haven't seen him. I don't mind him leaving everything to me, but sometimes . . . He knows I can cope, and Tom Doyle's still on duty. Anyway, it's not a lie. I do feel a bit queasy.' She pulled out a chair and sat down heavily. 'You make the tea, will you?'

Now they were in the light Connie could see Queenie's face was devoid of natural colour. Her heavy makeup gave her the appearance of a painted doll. Queenie put her folded arms on the table and leaned her blonde head on them.

'You really are poorly, aren't you?' said Connie, frowning, 'Do you want to go home?'

'No, it'll pass. It usually does,' Queenie said, without raising her head. 'Go on, put the kettle on. I could also do with one of those cream crackers you'll find in a tin on the top shelf.' She said it in such a way that Connie felt it was more an order than a request. She gave her a last worried look, then went into the kitchen. A few minutes later, bearing a tray with a metal teapot, two mugs and spoons, a bottle of milk. Connie set the tray on the table. A few crackers lay on a saucer. 'Tea's up!'

Queenie grinned at her.

While she'd been preparing the tea, Connie had been worrying about Queenie. She'd said she'd felt like this before. What if she was really ill? Should she go and see Tom Doyle if she couldn't find Mangle?

Her fears were unfounded: Queenie was sitting back on the chair with a cigarette in her hand. She gave Connie a bright smile. 'I could really do with that tea, thanks, love.'

Her colour was back in her cheeks, real colour, noted Connie, not artificial. She breathed a sigh of relief. Queenie knew her own body better than anyone else did, but Connie couldn't help asking, 'You feeling better now?'

Queenie took a long drag on her cigarette. 'I told you, it comes and goes. Let's leave it at that.'

Fair enough, thought Connie. After the tea had been

partly drunk, Queenie seemed eager to talk again about the enigmatic young bloke. 'Whenever he comes in here, which is at least a couple of times a week, he spends more time looking for you than he does at the screen.'

'Are you sure?' Connie was amazed that Queenie should be aware of something that had obviously slipped her notice. Not that it was surprising, Connie thought. She missed her mum and often caught herself feeling so sad it was difficult think about what was going on in the present. 'Do you know who he is?'

Queenie blew out a stream of smoke. 'I was at school with him. He's a Gosport bloke, Tommo Smith, a bit of a chancer. He got a black eye for rescuing me from a lout who'd been following me home and suddenly made a grab for me. I'd have been in a right state if he hadn't intervened. He wouldn't come home with me so my mum, she was still alive, could attend to his eye. He's smartened himself up since then. I remember his shoes had holes in and were stuffed with cardboard.'

Connie remembered his smart two-tone shoes. His fortunes must have changed for the better since then, she thought.

'Usually he comes to the early screenings,' continued Queenie. 'He must have a pretty good job now to dress so smartly.'

'Perhaps he comes to the early showings because he doesn't like going to bed late!' Connie was happier now that Queenie seemed more like her old self. She watched her friend drink more of her tea.

'I never pointed it out to you because I know you're still in a fragile state and grieving for your mum,' Queenie said. 'If you knew some bloke was eyeing you up, and that wasn't what you wanted, I thought you might pack the job in.'

Connie opened her mouth to answer, but Queenie, who seemed in a talkative mood, went on: 'The usherettes often get blokes after them. Most just shrug it off, but that was how I met my Chuck. He bought an ice-cream when the spotlight was shining on me and gave me that corny line, "You looked like an angel beneath that spotlight."'

Her eyes went all dreamy and she looked like she was in a world of her own. 'And to think when I felt that spotlight on me for the very first time, I wanted the floor to open and swallow me. I felt so exposed. But it produced a lovely American soldier boy for me.' She smiled at Connie. 'It doesn't bother me now, the spotlight. And, let's face it, I wouldn't be able to give out the correct change without it, would I?'

They sat in companionable silence until Queenie took the lid off the teapot, looked inside and said, 'All gone. Tea break's over, Connie.' She replaced the lid, lifted the tray and said, 'I'll take this into the kitchen. We'll wash up later. First, I need the lav. I'm going every five minutes, these days.'

Connie watched her leave the room, then went over to the mirror and patted her hair while waiting for Queenie rejoin her.

A few minutes later they were walking back to their designated seats when someone shouted, 'Sit down!' The man's tone carried across the stalls.

'I'll go,' said Connie. She didn't want Queenie upset after her funny turn. She switched on her torch and went to investigate. She found a man remonstrating in a seat behind three young lads, who were messing around and obviously disturbing other patrons. A cigarette packet was being thrown about. *Citizen Kane* was classified as U, which meant there was no age restriction and anyone could watch the film.

Connie walked swiftly up the aisle and shone her torch on the youths. 'If you three don't pack it in, you'll be thrown out! You might not want to watch this film but others do!' She fixed her eyes on the one who appeared to be the oldest. He was staring back at her.

Connie's heart was thudding in her chest. This scene could play out in one of two ways. Either the boys, who looked no more than twelve, would recognize her authority or they would take no notice and cause even more bother. Connie watched indecision cross each face and glared at the one she considered the ringleader. 'And I'll make sure you never come inside this picture house again.'

To her utter amazement the eldest hung his head and mumbled, 'Sorry, Miss.' Then he turned to his cohorts and said, 'Pack it in, you two!' Connie thought her eyes were playing tricks on her when the two boys sat back in their seats, closely followed by the third, and focused on the screen.

Connie switched off her torch and stood watching for a few seconds. Then, seeing the boys had actually become immersed in the film, she turned to walk to her own seat, but not before the man shouted, 'Thanks, love!'

'Little monkeys, they get bored easily,' whispered the woman on the end of the row. Connie smiled at her and went to sit with Queenie, who put a hand on Connie's knee. 'Well done, mate!' Connie preened. 'Little sods,' Queenie added, settling back to watch the film.

Allowing herself to look around the full house, Connie could just see the back of the young man's head in the centre of a row. He seemed lost in the film. She wondered why this stranger should be claiming her thoughts. She also wondered why he wasn't in the services. Most men his age would be. And why was she thinking about him at all?

On the screen Charles Foster Kane was professing his love for a young singer, who was clearly tone deaf. Love made people do funny things, thought Connie. Momentarily she was glad she had no feelings for any man. So far in her life she had witnessed the disappointment and unhappiness love brought. Her mother had been proof of that, hadn't she? Although Jean had refused to talk about Connie's father, it was clear to Connie that she had loved him. Oh, how she wished her mother had confided in her. And now it was too late.

Connie tried to push thoughts of her mother from her mind. Forwards: she must look to the future, not back to the terrible past. Hard to do, she thought, when the war was all around her. Surely it wouldn't last for ever, would it?

There was a sudden sharp dig from an elbow in her ribs and Connie turned to Queenie. 'Sorry, I forgot to tell you. It went clean out of my head. Arthur Mangle told me he wants to see you. He said to go to the projection room.' Then she added, 'Fancy you going there. I've never set foot in the place. Mind you, the projectionist is a bit of all right!'

Panic rose within Connie. No wonder Ol 'Mangle had been out of sight if he was up in the projection room. This would be the first time she'd ever been summoned to meet him. So far, she'd managed to keep a low profile. Why did he want to see her now? Had she done anything wrong? Surely not.

'The one good thing about the old devil is that as long as things run smoothly, he's not on our tails all the time,' Queenie had once confided to her.

'Will you come with me, Queenie?' There was a begging note in her voice.

'I can't disappear upstairs with you, Connie, and leave the rest of the workers down here. Anyway, you won't be on your own. Len'll be there.'

Connie must have looked mystified.

'Len Gregory, the head projectionist, and he'll have his lad with him.'

'I've not met him, or his lad, have I?'

'Not many people have. He hides away with his films and sound system and hardly anybody knows he's there, but we wouldn't have anything to watch if it wasn't for him.'

Part of Connie was thankful she wouldn't have to be alone with Mr Mangle in his office. The manager's reputation for trying to feel women up had filled her with disgust. But she daren't ignore his request.

As she looked at the screen, the credits rolled up. The film had ended and the audience had discovered what 'Rosebud' meant and with it the key to the behaviour of Charles Kane. Patrons began to move about. Cigarette smoke made patterns in the light coming from the projection room. Connie couldn't put it off any longer.

'I don't want to go,' she said to Queenie.

'You want to lose your job?' Queenie was getting to her feet – she had duties to attend to.

'No!' Connie's voice was indignant.

Patrons were leaving their seats: the lights had come up.

'Well, go and find out what he wants,' Queenie said.

'How do I get to the projection room?' Connie asked pathetically.

Queenie grinned. 'Up the main stairs, into the circle and the door is marked.'

Chapter Twelve

Tommo looked at her sagging flesh with displeasure. He could have been an actor, the way he managed to fake his feelings, he thought. Then his eyes moved to the table at the side of the bed where the pound notes lay that she'd placed there before he commenced her massage. It was Friday night and this was Mrs Keating, wealthy widow of Samuel Keating, who had left his beloved wife five greengrocery shops in Gosport, which provided her with an excellent income, and a large house in Western Way. There had been no children from their union. What her husband hadn't left her was affection. Angela Keating paid Tommo for that.

'I'm getting old, Tommo,' she whispered coyly, into the feather pillow.

'You have the skin of a twenty-year-old,' he soothed, as

his hands manipulated her flesh. The lie caused her to sigh in contentment. The scent of Joy perfume filled the air.

He glanced at his suit and shirt hanging over the back of the cane chair in her opulent bedroom. She liked to feel as much of his bare skin touching her as was possible. He resented getting highly scented greasy oils over his clothes. He bent down and allowed his lips to caress the back of her scrawny neck. Then he moved from the bed. 'I need the lav.'

As he crossed the thick carpet, he heard her sigh. 'Don't be long, Tommo.'

When he reached the downstairs lavatory in the hall, he kicked the door open. He could spin out the time longer in here than if he had used her bathroom. He was angry with himself and the situation that, over time, he'd got himself into.

Once safely inside, he stared at his reflection in the mirror. He'd been told he looked like Alan Ladd. Tommo knew he was much taller than the film star. He wouldn't need to stand on a box to kiss his leading ladies. That made him think of Veronica Lake, who was often teamed with the blond male star. Veronica Lake, who looked remarkably like Connie Baxter: she had been working at the Criterion Picture House for some time now and had stolen his heart. If only he had the guts to ask her out. But what would a nice girl like her want with him?

He remembered when their fingers had touched. It had been like an electric current welding them together. She'd felt it, too, he knew she had. It wasn't a surprise to him: he spent so much of his free time in the picture house on the off-chance that he might catch a glimpse of her.

But how could he ask her to go on a date with him? He didn't even have a proper job, did he? He had money, but he didn't earn it like most men worked for theirs. Standing in the Four Aces bar, now the club was up and running again, and waiting for some old dear to press a ticket into his hand so he could dance with her certainly wasn't a proper job.

And when the elderly woman whispered in his ear, 'Are you free later?' he'd say he was, and accompany her home to be her fawning sycophant.

It definitely wasn't a proper job, or one to be proud of. Connie Baxter would be horrified if she knew about it.

But what was he to do? Dancing was the only skill he had. His mother had paid for his lessons from an early age in the hope he could do something glamorous with his life. She didn't want him to work manually. She had visions of him becoming a music-hall star.

To pay for those costly lessons she'd taken any job offered to her. Economizing on clothes and outings, and with barely enough food for them both, she was planning for his future.

He'd protested about going to school in ragged clothes. The bullying he'd been subjected to had made him aggressive, and he'd fought for other children who had become objects of derision.

When he danced, he could forget everything that troubled him. He was transported to a different world, a magical place where nothing else mattered and he could be anything, anyone, he wanted to be. New dances were effortless to learn.

Unfortunately Rosa, his mother, had had dreams above her station. When he was a child, he, too, believed in those dreams. But as he grew older the harsh realities of life had crushed his hopes.

When Rosa had become ill with consumption, the wasting disease, he was forced to take a job. He'd liked working for the newsagent, the first job he'd had on leaving school. His wage barely kept the two of them. And then a customer had bragged about a club in Portsmouth that hired male dancers to take a turn around the floor with lone women who went there to dance and play at the gaming tables. All they had to do was buy a ticket and take their pick of the young men on offer.

At his interview for his previous job, the club owner had told him, 'I like your looks. You dance like Fred Astaire. You need decent clothes.'

Tommo's heart and face had fallen. He had no money for new shoes or a suit, but the manager had simply opened a drawer and thrust pound notes from it into his hand. 'You can pay me back, with interest.'

Tommo had been a hit straight away with the elderly women. To curry favour with him, they'd tuck pound notes into his top pocket. Soon he was able to buy his own clothes and, best of all, pay for a woman to live in and look after his mother when he wasn't around. Most importantly, he could pay doctors' bills. He went home with the women and offered massages because he didn't want to get into bed with them: that was prostitution and there he drew the line. He was paid to accompany women to concerts, dinners, anywhere a lone woman was frowned upon. He didn't mind being called a gigolo.

He knew his mother would never recover but he aimed to make her remaining time as free of worry as he could. He'd told her only that he was dancing for a living. It enabled her to feel her sacrifices hadn't been in vain.

When Ace Gallagher had opened his club in Gosport and advertised for male dancers, it seemed as though a prayer had been answered. Tommo could spend more time with his mother because he didn't have to take the ferry to Portsmouth to work. His biggest regret was that he hadn't been able to join the forces: naval pay would have been secure. 'Irregular heartbeat,' the doctor had told him.

'Rubbish!' he'd pleaded. Everyone knew how strenuous dancing was. He was as fit as a fiddle! He had no symptoms so his life carried on as normal. Then he'd met Connie Baxter and wished he'd embarked on any other career than the one he had now. He was caught in a trap of his own making. He loved his mother dearly; he would go on looking after her. She coughed up blood relentlessly now, and his own peace of mind was as nothing when he wanted to do the very best he could for the woman who'd given him life.

'Are you all right, Tommo?' Angela Keating's voice shook him from his reverie. He was about to shout back to her when his ears picked up the sound of plane engines. His first thought was that it had been a while since a night raid.

Tommo walked swiftly into the sitting room and pulled back a tiny corner of the blackout curtain. There'd been no air-raid warning. However, in the moonlight planes were emerging from behind clouds. Groups of German bombers, more than he could count, surrounded by smaller fighter planes, protecting them.

'Angela!' His voice was loud, harsh. 'Get down here this instant.'

Tucked away in the corner of the sitting room, a Morrison

shelter was covered with a large chenille cloth. The top was of heavy steel and the sides made of mesh. He pulled back the covering and breathed a sigh of relief that inside there was a feather mattress, blankets and pillows. Angela was well prepared for air raids.

Now he could hear whistles: ARP men giving warning of an impending attack.

Angela came bustling downstairs, swamped in a heavy dressing-gown and wearing fur slippers. In her arms she carried his clothes.

'You'll be needing these,' she said, throwing them onto an armchair. Then, 'I'll make a flask of tea.' She eyed the shelter. 'We'll be safe in there.'

The bombers had drawn closer. Anti-aircraft guns opened fire with an almost deafening noise. Now he could see the searchlights and puffs of black smoke from shells bursting around the planes. He heard explosions. The noise seemed to be coming from Portsmouth – no doubt the invaders were aiming for the docks. He let the curtain fall back.

He could hear Angela clattering crockery in the kitchen. She was a good cook, was Angela, and a nice woman. Tommo wondered if she would bring to the Morrison some of the excellent bread pudding he'd tasted earlier.

While he was slipping into his shirt and trousers, he said

a little prayer in his head for God to keep his mum safe – and Connie. He didn't want to leave her out. In his trouser pocket his fingers found the notes from the bedside table that Angela must have put there. He smiled to himself. Luck was with him after all.

Chapter Thirteen

Connie clung to the brass rail so she wouldn't be swept back to the foyer in the tide of people coming down the wide stairs from the circle. Their bodies gave off the stink of cigarettes and warm sweat. From fragments of conversations she discovered they'd enjoyed the film.

It might have been easier to find the projection room if she'd waited until the crowd had finally dispersed, but as she had no idea why Mr Mangle wanted to see her or exactly when he had asked for her, she thought it unwise to keep him waiting longer than necessary. At the back of the circle she spotted the door marked 'Projection Room' and in smaller letters beneath, 'Keep Out'. She went over to it and knocked respectfully. On the screen the Pathé News was just starting. An elderly usherette said, 'Go in and up the stairs.'

At the top of the short flight another door was marked

'Keep Out'. She knocked. It was opened almost immediately by Mr Mangle himself. Queenie's description of the manager had been accurate. 'I was wondering where you'd got to,' he said. 'Connie, this is the projectionist Len Gregory. Len, this is our newest recruit, Connie Baxter.'

Connie put a smile on her face. 'Hello.'

Mr Mangle moved aside slightly, beckoning her to enter. He left barely enough room for her to pass. As she squeezed past his rotund stomach, she could smell the Brylcreem on his thinning hair, which had been combed across his scalp to hide his baldness. She couldn't help but stare at its strange arrangement. The long hair at the back of his head had been combed forward and arranged in a circle to sit on top.

He was only as tall as he was round yet his bulbous eyes seemed to strip her naked. Connie shivered, glad to be inside the room, away from him as he closed the door behind her. Exceptionally tidy and clean, the dull-lit workroom showed two more doors, one partly open. She could make out the corner of a table with a Primus stove standing on it. The other door, closed, said 'WC'. She thought how self-contained it was up there, high above the picture-goers watching the films.

She was aware of the noise. A soft click-clacking, a fast and even-sounding clatter that didn't falter. It brought to mind the rustle that the pages of a book made when she flicked through them, and she found it intensely soothing.

The sound was coming from two machines rather like enormous cameras, with spools at the back and very long lenses. They stood side by side, pointing down towards the cinema screen through an aperture in the wooden wall. Only one machine seemed to be working. A reel of film was unwinding, slowly rotating on a spool to be reclaimed and automatically rewound to a second spool. She stepped closer to look through the aperture. Mr Mangle had already moved up beside her.

A shaft of light emitting from the camera's lens reflected scenes of war news onto the screen below. Connie was thrilled. She could hear the correspondent's voice as clearly as if he was standing next to her.

'Welcome!' Her trance was broken by another voice, softly spoken. The tall man to her right put a finger to his lips, suggesting she speak quietly. 'This is where the magic begins,' he said. 'This room is supposed to be soundproofed but it doesn't always absorb all the noise—'

'Good to meet you properly at last, Miss Baxter. I'm Arthur Mangle,' the manager interrupted. At her left, Mangle put his plump hand on the sleeve of her uniform. He moved his arm forward and she realized she was supposed to shake his hand. His fingers, slightly damp, held on to hers just a little too long for her liking. However, when he released her Connie smiled at him. He was, after all, her boss. Mr Mangle was talking: 'Normally I'd have welcomed you in my office, my dear, at the very start of your employment, but I've been exceptionally busy of late.' He'd now moved close enough for her to catch his sour breath. 'However, today I've been in conference with Leonard Gregory here,' he gave a small nod towards the other man, who had bent down to pick up a large canister from a tall pile of round tins. 'Len, as you know, is our projectionist. Gary over there is his second in command.' She turned in the direction of his waving hand. A thin, tow-headed lad sat on the floor reading the *Dandy*. He looked up and grinned. He could have been any age from twelve to nineteen, she thought.

Leonard was now settling what she supposed was a large flat roll of film into a circular tin, handling it with great care. When he pressed on its lid, she saw that two fingers were missing from his right hand. He glanced up, clearly aware of the lull in the conversation between her and Mangle, whose arm was crushed against the side of her body, pressing so hard that she could feel her breasts being pushed together. She stepped away from him. Mangle stepped after her. She didn't turn her head to look at him for she was well aware he knew what he was doing. She felt intimidated.

Leonard had straightened. His eyes were long-lashed, dark with a mischievous glint, and he was watching Mangle closely. His hair, in the dull light, was almost black and very curly. He looked from Mangle to Connie, then gestured towards the lad. 'You wouldn't think to look at Gary that he's an asset, would you?' He grinned, showing strong white teeth. 'I don't know what I'd do without him.' Connie could see the boy was embarrassed. 'I was fourteen when I started in here and rarely leave the place. If it wasn't for him, I probably never would.'

Len moved towards the huge projectors, watching the cinema screen, then plucked a cloth from his back pocket and reverently dusted the side of the machine. He wore a yellow waistcoat over a white shirt, with its sleeves rolled beyond his elbows. 'I can trust Gary. He stands in for me if I need time off,' Len continued. He ran his fingers through his hair but it promptly fell back across his forehead. 'You're extremely honoured, Miss Baxter. There aren't many usherettes who've been inside my little empire. Anything you'd like to know about the screening process?'

Connie decided she liked Len Gregory. 'I'm sure there's much you could teach me about film, Mr Gregory,' she said formally, 'but it's Mr Mangle I've come to see.' She hesitated. 'Actually, he sent for me. Oh!' Arthur Mangle had silently moved so close to her that she could feel his breath on her cheek and the heat from his paunch against the side of her body.

Panic filled her. Here she was in a small room, alone, with three males, one of whom was rumoured to be a lecher and seemed intent on gluing himself to her.

Her stomach roiled. She felt trapped. Supposing . . .

Len, still polishing, suddenly flicked his cleaning cloth right in Arthur Mangle's face. 'Damn dust!' he said. 'Can't have it destroying the film.' He gave another flick. Connie jumped backwards out of the way of the flying duster just as tiny particles of dust caused the manager to sneeze several times in succession.

Mangle moved, knocking over the pile of canisters that rattled as they rolled on the floor. He looked down at them with alarm and sneezed again into a handkerchief he had whipped from his trouser pocket.

'Steady the Buffs!' called Gary.

Connie recognized the local catchphrase. It meant 'Keep calm.'

'You all right, old chap?' Len asked solicitously. 'I must ask you to be careful not to damage the cans of film, unless you don't mind the house takings being cut severely.' He smiled at Connie and winked. She knew then that Len had intended to help her when he'd seen the anxiety on her face. He, too, knew what a crude man Mangle was and had cleverly upset his plans while pretending nothing out of the ordinary was happening. Had he openly challenged the manager, it could have cost them both their jobs.

'Mr Mangle! Mr Mangle! Your wife's in your office waiting for you.' The woman's voice was accompanied by insistent knocking on the projection room's door.

'I'd best go,' said Mangle, immediately perturbed at the news and replacing his handkerchief. 'Coming,' he called. He stared at Connie and Len. 'Can't keep my good woman waiting.'

As if pulled on strings he turned quickly towards the door, then glanced back as if he might have forgotten something. 'As I say, I'm very pleased to meet you properly, my dear. I've heard only good things about your work. Especially as I witnessed, from up here during the big picture, how you kept your head and told off those lads causing mayhem. Well done. Keep it up.'

Connie let out a sigh of relief as the door closed behind him.

'Greasy git!' said Gary, his comic now on the floor because he was carefully re-stacking the canisters. 'Clumsy, too. These films are due to be collected tomorrow and changed for new ones.'

Connie took a deep breath. 'Thank you, Len,' she said. 'I really thought the old devil was going to grab hold of me.'

'I don't know whether he'd have been foolish enough to go any further while I was here but I'm not deaf to the stories told about him. I could see you were distressed. I had to do something without jeopardizing both our jobs. You are all right, aren't you?'

Connie nodded. Then she gave a big sigh. 'Yes, thank you. At least he said he was pleased with my work. I expected a telling-off for something I couldn't remember doing!' She tried a smile.

'He was looking out over the audience and saw you remonstrate with those lads,' Gary put in. 'He said, "That new girl's got some guts. She's a real asset to the Criterion."'

'He really is pleased with the way you're shaping up,' Len said, 'but if he oversteps the mark in future just tell him you'll have a word with his wife. Or give him a good sharp dig in the ribs, like Queenie does.' He paused. 'I'm sure it's the chase old Mangle likes . . .'

Gary chipped in, 'He wouldn't know what to do if a girl gave in to him!'

Connie began to feel better. But at the mention of Queenie's name she said, 'Oh dear, if I don't get back downstairs, Queenie'll wonder where I've got to.'

'She won't worry about you,' he said. 'Not when she sees Mangle. And he won't be hanging about downstairs for long if his wife wants him.' He peered at the clock on the wall. 'Anyway, Queenie'll be checking the ice-cream tubs and choc ices for the next film just about to start. She's a good girl, is our Queenie.'

Connie thought she heard a hint of admiration in his voice when he uttered Queenie's name. She smiled at him. 'Thank you for looking after me. There wasn't any dust anywhere near that projector, was there?'

He shook his head. 'Our secret?' he said.

He moved to the second projector and began threading film onto the spool from a can Gary handed to him. 'Second feature,' he said. He must have seen her watching his deft movements despite the missing fingers.

'Kids in the playground,' he said. 'It was my seventh birthday and I was given the bumps by my pals.'

Connie remembered being hustled into a blanket that was held by classmates shaken as high in the air as they could manage.

'Unfortunately when I fell my hand was sliced by glass.' He stilled her horrified look with a laugh. 'There's nothing I can't do with the remaining fingers, including pick my nose!'

He was a man who didn't take himself too seriously, thought Connie, laughing because she knew it was expected of her.

'I wanted to join the air force.' There was regret in his voice. 'I pleaded but they wouldn't take me.'

'But it's obvious you love your work here.'

He nodded and, having finished threading film, placed the empty can on a different pile. Connie allowed herself to look around the room. There was another aperture, smaller than the ones used for the projectors. A torch-like object on a tripod pointed not at the screen but to a part of the aisle down in the stalls backing onto a wall.

'That's the spotlight,' Gary said. Connie noted its position would light up the area where Queenie usually stood with the tray of ices for sale.

Len added, 'I can train the light practically anywhere in the stalls and circle.'

Connie remembered Queenie saying her American had said she looked like an angel in the spotlight. 'Queenie says it took her a while to get used to being under such a bright light,' she said.

A smile lifted the corners of Len's lips. 'She looks angelic beneath it,' he said.

Connie smiled to herself. Queenie was admired by many

people. It gave her a good feeling that she and Queenie were friends. 'That's what her boyfriend said.'

Connie noticed his smile had dimmed.

It came back again in full force as he said, 'Queenie *is* an angel.'

She nodded. 'It's nice in here.' She felt perfectly at ease with the pair of them, especially now Mangle had gone. She resolved never to be caught alone with the manager, ever again.

'Well, this is the heart of the picture house,' Len said. 'I'm proud to do this job and happy with the fine equipment installed here.' His eyes glittered. 'This picture house opened thirty years ago—'

He got no further because Gary chimed in: 'We've got a Western Electric Sound System and the best American audio amplifiers for film that money can buy and seating for seven hundred people . . .' The lad glanced at the reel of film that was practically rewound on the second spool and moved speedily forward to attend to it. It was obvious he, too, loved his job, thought Connie.

'I hope we haven't bored you talking about the equipment we look after,' said Len. He went to a small table and picked up some papers. 'Queenie told me you keep a scrapbook.' He handed her some stills of film stars.

Connie flicked through the glossy photographs and remembered seeing some of them in the glass cases outside the cinema. She was overwhelmed that he'd thought of her. 'Are you allowed to give these away?'

'Normally undamaged stills are sent back with the canisters of film but damaged ones aren't. We can pretend these aren't perfect.'

'Thank you,' she said, smiling at him. 'I've enjoyed seeing what goes on behind the scenes. And, again, thanks for sorting out Ol' Mangle.'

Moments later, running down the empty stairs, she thought, Apart from Mangle, I *do* like working here.

Chapter Fourteen

The July sky was filled with stars as Connie and Queenie walked arm in arm along the near deserted streets, careful to watch for the white lines on the pavements that showed where the kerbs dipped dangerously.

Connie was chattering nineteen to the dozen, the stills from the films in her uniform pocket. 'Len Gregory's a nice bloke, isn't he? He gave me some stars' photographs.'

'Yes, but he's a bit mysterious . . .'

'Do you mean because of his fingers? He told me how that happened.'

'No. It's just that he doesn't mix much with the rest of us.'

'Probably because he's a bit older.'

Connie felt Queenie shrug her shoulders. 'He's an intelligent bloke. You don't get many of them to the pound in

Gosport.' She laughed. 'An' he lives alone in that big house on the corner of Old Road and Mayfield Road.'

'Nothing wrong in living by yourself. You do!' said Connie, smartly.

A bicycle rattled by. 'That's right! Hurry along home quickly, girls!' sang out an ARP man. Connie watched his overripe bottom wobbling on the saddle as he pedalled.

'Get stuffed!' called Queenie, then to Connie, 'I live by myself only because my dad died last year.'

'Oh, I'm sorry. I didn't know.'

'Why should you be sorry? I'm not!'

Connie stopped walking and stared at Queenie, who pulled her gas-mask case onto her shoulder and said, 'Look, come back to my house and I'll make us a cuppa. I could do with talking to a friend just now. Or will Gertie be waiting up for you?'

Connie shook her head. She wondered at Queenie's remark about not being upset by her father's death: it seemed out of character for her warm-hearted friend.

'She leaves me something under a plate for supper but she's often asleep when I get in. She puts something out for Ace as well.'

'Is he that gorgeous chap with the car?'

'If you mean he knows he's good-looking, then yes.' Connie laughed.

'Has he asked you out?'

'He's always trying to get me into his car!'

'An' I suppose you'd rather be sticking pictures in that blessed scrapbook of yours?'

Connie was taken aback. Queenie's words had stung even though there had been no real malice in them.

They now stood on the corner where they usually parted to go their separate ways. But Connie didn't want to leave Queenie without knowing what she'd meant by her cryptic remarks. 'I'll come back to your place. I need to know what's going on in your head, Queenie.'

They walked on in silence past the closed chip shop where the smell of oil and fish lingered, and greasy newspaper not yet blown away in the breeze littered the pavement. Queenie pointed to a piece of ground covered with rubble and broken furniture. Either side of the space, the damaged walls of the shops were propped upright by wooden struts. The stink of burning hung on the air. 'That was the cobbler's shop and his home, a nice old bloke. He'd been there for ever until last Sunday when a German bomb landed. Oh, Connie,' she said, 'I'm so fed up with this war.'

'Everyone is,' said Connie. The despair in Queenie's voice worried her.

At the bottom of Inverness Street Queenie paused. 'Don't be expecting a palace, will you?'

Connie followed her along the uneven pavement. The back-to-back house was similar to Gertie's two-up-two-down. She waited while Queenie inserted the key in the lock and stepped inside after her. Queenie shut the door behind her before she turned on the light, mindful of the blackout.

'Sit down while I make us some tea,' said Queenie, taking off her usherette's jacket and hanging it over the back of a chair, then disappearing inside the scullery.

Connie saw the room was about the same size as Gertie's kitchen but there the resemblance ended. It smelt of lavender polish, not cigarettes. The furniture was old-fashioned. Some pieces had obviously been mended, not very professionally, but they sparkled brightly with coats of white paint. Colourful bedspreads had been thrown over the two armchairs and a sagging sofa. The range dominated the room, black-leaded to within an inch of its life, and on the floor in front of it was a handmade multi-coloured rag rug. The drawn curtains shut out the evening's blackness and these, Connie saw, were made of small diamond-shaped patchwork pieces. Matching cushions sat on the chairs and sofa. The overall effect was welcoming and bright. Connie couldn't help saying, 'Why, it's so clean and colourful in here!'

Queenie put her head around the scullery door and frowned, 'Did you expect me to be scruffy and dirty, then?' Before Connie could answer she'd returned to making tea and Connie heard the rattle of cups and crockery.

Taking off her jacket and putting it on the arm of the sofa, Connie walked towards the scullery. 'Do you need a hand?' she asked, not replying to Queenie's previous barb. Boiling water was being poured into a shining silver-plated teapot and already a tray had been set with cups and saucers. A quick glance around showed the whitewashed scullery to be spick and span. Queenie put the lid onto the teapot and picked up the tray, carried it into the kitchen and put it onto a small table. As if reading Connie's mind, she said, 'The place didn't look like this when my father was alive. I never brought anyone home. If he wasn't ranting and raving and breaking stuff he was passed out on the floor.'

She spoke with ease as if that was an everyday happening. Connie thought maybe it was, for her.

'I was at work when he drank himself to death, choking on his own vomit, or so I was told. I felt nothing but relief.' She smiled. 'Sit down, then. You're making the place look untidy!'

Connie did as she was told.

Queenie began arranging the cups on the saucers. 'You could never understand how wonderful it felt being on my own. It was my wages kept a roof over our heads, you see, and that made him feel even more inferior. I was treading on eggshells every time I came home from my shift at the Criterion.'

'Why didn't you leave if you were earning enough to support yourself?'

'Connie, my love, he was my dad. And he was a different bloke down the pub. The other customers bought him drinks – he could chew the hind leg off a donkey telling tales – but then he came home and took it out on me or the house. Said I killed my mum . . . She died giving birth to me, you see.'

Queenie was carefully pouring tea into the cups, using a silver-plated tea-strainer.

'The drink had made him forget how different it had been when I was a kiddie and he'd loved me, bringing me up the best way he knew.' She paused. 'Those were the good times,' she said. 'Drink does that, changes a person's way of thinking. Milk?' she asked.

Connie nodded and watched while Queenie poured milk into the cup from a small china jug. She handed the tea to Connie. 'Sorry I haven't any sugar. It got used up.' She sighed. 'Bloody rationing!

'Anyway, after my dad had passed away, I sorted this place out and my job kept me from going around the bend. After a while I began to go out when I wasn't working. I love dancing!' She grinned at Connie. 'We should go dancing, you and me.'

'I'm not very good,' Connie said. 'Actually, I can't dance at all.'

'You just let yourself move to the rhythm,' Queenie said, then, thoughtfully, 'That's what I meant about you packing away your scrapbook and beginning to live again.'

Connie was horrified. 'But—'

'But nothing! Your mum would rather her little girl was out enjoying herself than staying at home filling empty pages with film stars' pictures, wouldn't she?

Connie opened her mouth to protest but instead said quietly, 'And how long was it before you took a dose of your own medicine, after your dad . . .?'

She didn't finish for Queenie said, 'Too long! Look, I was glad to see the back of my dad. That doesn't mean I didn't love him. It's just I think sometimes we expect too much of our parents.'

She picked up her cup and drank deeply. Connie was

thinking over everything Queenie had so far said. She came to the conclusion her friend knew what she was talking about. Queenie nodded towards the teapot and Connie said, 'Please.'

While Queenie poured, Connie studied a photograph propped against the wooden clock on the mantelpiece above the range. 'Is that your boyfriend?'

Queenie nodded. 'He's a bit of all right, isn't he?' The very blond, short-haired young man with a mouthful of sparkling teeth smiled down on them. He was every inch the typical American serviceman. Queenie's eyes filled with tears. 'Looks are only skin deep, Connie. The bastard's left me,' she said, 'and I'm pregnant with his kiddie.'

Chapter Fifteen

Tommo stood against the bar, his fingers clutching the glass of lemonade. He wasn't a big drinker, never had been. In any case it wouldn't be the done thing to be seen whirling an elderly lady around the dance floor half cut, would it? Ace Gallagher would soon give him the push, and where would he be without a job?

He looked down at the highly polished refitted dancing area, at the small tables of white-painted metal with matching chairs all set against the background of Ace's refurbished club.

The women bought tickets to dance with him but it didn't end with a foxtrot or a waltz. His job was to get them to the gambling tables upstairs. While he whispered endearments, their greed took over from there.

They'd win a few times and, encouraged by those small

sums, would go for higher stakes. Maybe they'd win larger amounts, depending on the croupier's handling of the wheel or cards. If their money ran out, Ace gave credit. Why wouldn't he? He charged high interest rates, of course he did. But women past their first flush of youth, and eager for undivided attention from Tommo and the other ghost dancers, were happy to appear generous. Sitting at the gambling tables distracted them while they waited for Tommo's attention. The more money the women laid out, the higher Tommo's wages. And he needed every penny: his mum had taken a turn for the worse. The doctor was now calling daily, and his visits and the medicines had to be paid for.

Tommo was spending more time at home during the day, his picture house visits severely curtailed. The last time he'd seen Connie had been at the insistence of his mother's friend, Nellie, that he get out of the house. 'You're no good to anyone if you don't have a break,' she'd said.

In the past he'd envisaged asking Connie out on a date. He'd had to put that idea on the back burner. His priority was his mother. How could he possibly concentrate on a nice girl like Connie or expect her to have anything to do with him when his life was such a mess? How could he tell her what he did for a living when she asked? And of course she would ask. To lie would be unthinkable. She wouldn't want to know him when she found out the truth about him. And he cared too much about her to run the risk of that happening. He was caught between a rock and a hard place.

He raised the glass to his lips and took a sip. Cigarette smoke swirled about him, mixing with the perfumes and the smell of fresh paint. He thought about the last time he'd spoken to Connie. As she'd taken his ticket and torn it in two the look in her eyes had betrayed her. His heart had lifted as if it had wings and might at any moment fly from his body. He'd laughed at people who'd said they'd fallen in love at first sight. That was a load of old guff from films and magazines, wasn't it? Until it had happened to him.

'Hello, Tommo. Got a brand-new film today,' Connie had said. He smiled because she'd used his name. He hadn't told her what he was called so she must have been asking about him. He hoped his name was all the information she'd gathered.

She had shown him to a seat in the rear of the stalls. The film was *Gaslight*, with Anton Walbrook, who was trying to make the actress Diana Wynyard believe his lies. Almost a parallel of his own life. After all, Tommo lied to elderly women, didn't he? He told them untruths of exciting wins at the gaming tables, told them they were beautiful . . . Told them, told them, told them until, just like in *Gaslight*, they believed his lies.

He'd watched Connie's trim uniformed figure walk away. There was so much that was unspoken between them. He could tell she was interested in him. All he had to do was ask her to meet him away from the picture house.

And he couldn't do that because he wasn't worthy of her.

During the picture it had come to him that he would have to put Connie from his mind.

Certainly, he must stop coming to the Criterion. He could offer her nothing but unhappiness and she was worth so much more.

'Wake up, sleepyhead!'

A ticket was being waved beneath Tommo's nose. He gave an automatic smile at the same time as putting his glass down on the bar. The sweet smell of Joy filled his nostrils. 'Hello, Angela, darling,' Tommo said, as he bent to kiss her cheek.

'You look like you've lost a quid and found sixpence.' Jerome slid a glass of lemonade across the bar towards Tommo. He'd been keeping an eye on the young fellow because it seemed he'd lost his sparkle. Tommo was dancing mechanically with the old dears who had bought his company, but Jerome could see tonight his heart wasn't in it, not at all. Jerome was genuinely worried about Tommo's lack of interest. If the lad wasn't careful, he thought, his number-one position among the ghost dancers' pretty boys would slide.

'Take that back and give us a whisky,' Tommo said. Jerome raised his eyes. Over the sounds of laughter and voices Tommy Dorsey was playing 'Stardust'.

'Not like you to have a drink so early,' said Jerome. He pulled back the lemonade and replaced it with a decent measure of golden liquid from a bottle hidden beneath the bar.

'I hope that's the good stuff and not the rubbish you serve the punters,' Tommo said.

'Of course,' Jerome replied. 'In fact, it's so good I'll have a drink with you.' He poured a second glass.

Tommo gave him a rare smile. Usually his smiles were reserved for the women.

'Wanna talk about it?' Jerome asked. 'Is it your mum?' There were few secrets among Ace's employees.

Tommo shook his head, took a sip and licked his lips. 'I've accepted she won't be around for ever. I do what I can.' He stared at the glass. 'Nice that,' he said, swirling the whisky around. His eyes met Jerome's. 'You ever been in love?'

'Only when I was young and silly,' Jerome said. The moment those words were out of his mouth he wished he could pull them back. It was obvious Tommo needed to unburden himself. Making a joke about love wasn't the right way to go about helping him do that. He added, 'I remember it hurt as much as scraping my skin with a pen nib. But being in love with the right person and having them love you right back is the best thing in the whole world.'

Tommo was still staring at him. The corners of the young man's mouth lifted and he smiled. 'You do know what I mean, then?'

Jerome nodded to the other bartender to go on serving. 'Is it one of your harem of ladies?'

'God, no!' Tommo took another sip. 'If it was, that would be the easy way out.'

Jerome waited. He knew he'd set the ball rolling and that Tommo needed to talk. He also knew Tommo would do better if he did it in his own time.

'I've met a girl and I can't get her out of my head.' His eyes narrowed. 'Know what I mean?'

Jerome knew all right. He nodded. 'Does she feel the same way?'

Tommo took his time draining his glass. 'I know she does.'

Jerome reached for the bottle and poured again into Tommo's glass. The poor bloke needed to talk, he thought, and if the whisky loosened his tongue then it wouldn't be a bad thing, would it? He looked at his watch. It was gone midnight and wouldn't be long before Angela Keating came downstairs to claim Tommo, hopefully for the night. There'd be no problem with him having a few drinks. Ace wouldn't worry – it wasn't as though Tommo made a habit of it.

'What's the problem, then?'

'She doesn't know what I do to pay bills . . .'

'This is Gosport, lad. It's wartime.' He was trying to console Tommo. The lad was young: he didn't yet know that women in love could forgive practically anything. 'I don't know of anyone who doesn't bend the rules a bit to get by . . .'

'She's just lost her mother, living with an aunt . . .' Tommo was eager now to talk.

'She working?'

'An usherette at the Criterion. Connie's only been there a little while.'

It was then something clicked in Jerome's mind. He drew in a breath and pushed Tommo's glass towards him. 'Drink up, lad,' he said. His heart was beating wildly. General chit-chat might be normal in a workplace such as this but Ace kept his own cards very close to his chest. That the girl who lodged with Ace's landlady wouldn't go out with him would make him a laughing stock. That Connie was interested in Tommo didn't bear thinking about.

He looked towards the wide stairs and saw Angela stepping daintily down. 'Listen to me, Tommo,' he said. 'Seems like you've got to a crossroads in your life.' He paused. Angela had spotted Tommo and was pushing through the last of the punters to reach him. 'You just take the road well travelled. The road you're used to. That'll be better for all concerned.'

Chapter Sixteen

Loyalty was all very well, thought Jerome, but where did it lie with him?

He'd been awake most of the night thinking about the dilemma. He swallowed some tea, put down the tin mug on the table in the kitchen at the Four Aces and felt the cat rubbing its head against his ankle. 'I haven't forgotten to feed you,' he said. 'Just got a lot on my mind.'

The cat gazed up at him with amber eyes that held all the secrets of the universe. Jerome picked up the sardines, disconnected the metal key, inserted it into the flap of metal on the tin and began to turn. He could hear the cat's loud purr.

'If you could talk, you'd tell me the right thing to do,' he said. The cat's purr strengthened as the fishy smell escaped from the tin. Jerome bent back the lid and, with a fork, pulled the oily fish onto a saucer. 'Half the tin now, and you'll get the other half later,' he said. He tried to ignore the pain that ran from his knee to the small of his back as he bent down and set the saucer on the floor in front of the cat next to a small container of milk. Outside, the rain hit the windows as though it wanted to break in.

The sound of footsteps on parquet flooring told him Ace had arrived so he took another mug off the shelf and began pouring thick brown tea. As he added milk, he wondered how people would manage now the government had cut the milk ration to two and a half pints a week. Mentally he thanked his lucky stars that Ace had ways and means via the black-market.

'I reckon this is the wettest September on record,' said Ace. He shook his auburn hair and droplets flew in all directions.

'If you lived in your apartment upstairs instead of traipsing backwards and forwards to Gertie's place you wouldn't need to get wet,' said Jerome. He was aware that the only reason Ace trotted back and forth to Alma Street was Connie. He also knew Ace would ignore his comment.

Ace was looking at the mug. 'Is that for me? Good!' He took off his jacket and hung it on the back of the door. 'Those German bastards bombed Canterbury last night,' he said. 'Made a right mess of it.'

'I heard,' said Jerome. 'The wireless didn't give too much away in case Ol' Hitler starts thinking he's got one up on us. But I guessed it was in retaliation for us bombing Cologne.'

'Quite so,' Ace said. He ran his fingers through his hair. 'You need anything?' His eyes dropped to the cat licking the saucer.

'No, I don't need a thing,' said Jerome.

'That's the best-fed cat in Gosport,' Ace said, turning back to the door. 'I'll be in my office if you need me.' He left taking his mug with him. Jerome heard him whistling 'You Are My Sunshine' as he walked away.

Half an hour later Jerome stood over Ace watching him write cheques while he sat in his leather chair. He thought his head was going to split in two if he didn't say something.

The early-morning cleaner had already done her job and the room smelt of polish.

The lipstick in its gold case, which Connie had rejected when Ace had offered it to her a while ago, lay on the shiny oak desk.

'Connie never did take that lipstick off you, did she?' He lifted it and twisted the outer case, revealing the bright colour.

Ace laughed. 'No. She told me she didn't take gifts from men. Gertie, though, was a different kettle of fish. Practically snatched hers out of my hand.'

Jerome knew it was now or never to speak. He liked young Tommo but he loved Ace like he was his own son. He didn't want to see Ace made a fool of. Certainly not by a young girl.

'Connie's in love,' he said, blurting it out like it was something nasty he'd tasted.

'I bloody hope so.' Ace chuckled. 'I've been pursuing her long enough.'

A silence followed. Jerome stood the lipstick back on the desk. Then he searched and held Ace's eyes. As the penny dropped, he watched Ace's face change from contentment to undisguised concern. They stared at each other.

'You mean . . . you mean someone else has been sniffing around her? Someone I know nothing about?'

'You know now because I'm telling you.' Jerome was trying to pacify Ace before Ace's feelings got the better of him.

'Jesus Christ! How is this possible? Surely Gertie would have said something if Connie was out meeting some toe-rag—'

'That's just it,' interrupted Jerome. 'She hasn't been out meeting him. It's one of those good old-fashioned real-life love-at-first-sight jobs.'

Ace banged the flat of his hand down on the desk top.

The noise was loud. Papers and pencils flew upwards, rolled, then settled. The lipstick sprang into the air, then arced to the carpet. Ace's eyes were dark as he looked at Jerome, who said gently, 'He's only ever met her in the picture house.'

He was expecting Ace to erupt with fury. Instead, after what seemed an interminable pause, Ace said, 'An' I've been taking my time with her . . .'

'He's not touched her.'

'How do you know that?' The question came sharply.

'He told me. I believe him. The kid actually loves her so much he's barely spoken to her and is terrified she'll have nothing to do with him when she finds out how he makes a living— '

'What is he? A hired killer or something?' Ace swung his body from the chair and moved towards the window where he stood looking out at the rain falling in sheets across the Ferry Gardens. Jerome, following his gaze, saw it had practically eclipsed the ferry-boat waiting to depart on its journey to Portsmouth.

He knew better than to interrupt Ace when he was in this sort of mood. He waited.

After a while, when the only noise was the rain lashing the window-panes, Ace turned slowly. His eyes held Jerome's.

'If this bloke has talked at length to you, you must know him pretty well . . .'

'That's the trouble. So do you.'

Ace continued staring, frown lines creased across his forehead.

'It's young Tommo.' Jerome's words were spoken softly. He watched as Ace assimilated his words. What would happen next was unimaginable.

Ace started laughing. 'You've got to be kidding. He's got next to nothing to offer any woman.' He shook his head as though the whole thing was unbelievable. More laughter followed.

'That's why he's not made a move on her.'

Ace's laughter stopped. He was digesting Jerome's words. After a while he said, 'To think about her needs instead of his own, he must really care about her, then?'

Jerome waited in the long silence after Ace's question because Ace already knew the answer. And he'd want revenge. Ace didn't like to be bested by anyone, certainly not a copy-cat kid who worked for him. Jerome took off his spectacles, polished them on the end of his tie, then put them back on, using a finger to push them up on his nose.

'Tell Tommo to come up to the office when he arrives tonight.' Ace's words were clipped.

Jerome shook his head. 'I don't think that's a good idea. You've got to think about this. You give him the sack or beat him up and it'll push that young girl straight into his arms. She'll hate you for ever more.' He stared at Ace as he added, 'Trust me.' He gave Ace a little smile. 'I've got a much better idea.'

Chapter Seventeen

'Sorry we're so late, Gertie,' called Connie, slipping the key back through the letter-box, then ushering Queenie inside the house. 'Ol' Mangle got caught out touching up that new young usherette.' Connie could smell warm pastry.

Gertie, in her dressing-gown with metal curlers in her hair and a cigarette in her fingers, stood in the passage at the bottom of the stairs. 'Gawd! I thought that happened yesterday,' she said.

When Connie reached her, she saw the lipstick she'd applied earlier had disappeared from her thin lips and settled into the lines around Gertie's mouth. 'You're right, it did happen yesterday but it was tonight the girl's father came in and punched Ol' Mangle on the nose!' Connie saw Gertie's mouth had dropped open. The cigarette clung to her lip.

Queenie jumped in: 'It happened just as the queue was

being let in to see *Old Mother Riley's Ghosts*. The blood was pouring from Ol' Mangle's nose and dripping everywhere! I had to take the manager down to our staffroom and put a wet compress on it. Tom Doyle saw the kid and her dad off the premises. That little girl won't be coming back to work.'

'He's had it coming to him for a long time,' said Gertie, fully in control of her cigarette once more.

'I dunno how he's going to explain the size of his nose to his missus,' said Queenie, shrugging off her coat and putting it over the back of a kitchen chair. She had on her uniform. Then she sat down and eased off her high-heeled black court shoes, relief showing on her face. 'You got that kettle on?'

'Wish I'd been there,' said Gertie, going into the scullery.

'You'll hear all about it in the morning,' said Connie. She, too, had removed her coat, now hanging on a nail on the back of the kitchen door.

Connie could hear the sounds of cups rattling and the pop of gas being lit beneath the kettle in the scullery. The dark shadows beneath Queenie's eyes made her look older. Connie put out her fingers and covered her friend's hand. 'Don't worry. It'll be all right. Trust Gertie,' she soothed.

Queenie gave her a weak smile. 'Can you smell something meaty and nice?'

Connie said, 'Maybe Gertie made something tasty for us. She likes to feed Ace when he gets in.' She looked around the kitchen. It was obvious Ace wasn't home yet as there was nothing of him left lying about: no keys, no empty mug, no clothes slung about the place. She was glad he was still down at the club. They'd all find it difficult to talk if he was there.

Momentarily she wondered what his club looked like now he had it up and running again. It wasn't for want of his offering to take her to the Four Aces but she knew if she went anywhere with him in his car he would act as though she was his personal property. She wasn't ready for that. But she was allowing herself to think that there was more to life than work and cutting out film stars' pictures to stick them into a scrapbook.

She'd thought a lot about the young man she'd met in the Criterion who had sent her senses reeling. Unfortunately, she'd exhausted Queenie's knowledge of him, and now Queenie had problems of her own to worry about. It didn't seem right to contemplate her future when her friend was worried about the present.

Gertie came in with a tray, set it on the table and began to pour the tea. She stopped in mid pour and stared at Queenie, 'I could see it in your eyes long before you told me about the kiddie. Are you sure you want to get rid of it?'

'If I could keep the baby, I would,' Queenie snapped.

Connie had never seen Queenie shed a tear but now one rolled down her cheek. She took her hand from Connie's and wiped it away, then sniffed. 'I need my job to pay my way. Even if I can go on working, how will I manage afterwards? Ol' Mangle won't keep me on at the Criterion when I begin to show, and you know how people treat unmarried mothers . . .'

'Does Chuck know about the baby?'

Connie saw Queenie swallow as a second tear followed the first.

Gertie pushed a mug of tea towards her. 'Get that down you. You'll feel better.'

Obediently, Queenie lifted the mug to her lips and sipped. 'So, do you know of anyone . . .?'

'I asked if you'd told that American of yours.'

Now Connie saw that Gertie had tipped Queenie over the edge. Queenie pushed the mug away and stood up with such force that Connie's untouched tea slopped over the rim of the mug and pooled on the table.

Her voice was a shout: 'Course I bloody told the bugger! That's when all the nonsense he'd been talking about us living with his parents in San Diego while we found a place of our own and got married melted away, just like he did when my front door closed on him.'

Queenie took a deep breath. Connie could see her hands shaking. After a while, she said, 'I'm sorry. I know you're trying to help me.' She sat down again and stared at the table.

Connie rose, went into the scullery and picked up the dishcloth from where Gertie had left it draped over the tap. Back in the kitchen she made short work of wiping up the spilled tea. 'So, do you know of someone?' Connie didn't wait for an answer but took the grubby dishcloth back to the scullery and left it on the draining-board.

Back in the kitchen she watched as Gertie picked up her packet of Woodbines from the table and lit up. Her aunt took a long drag. 'Did you try to find the bugger?'

'What's the use?' Queenie said. 'I'm not making a fool of myself running after some bloody Yank who don't want me or his kid. I'm not the first and I certainly won't be the last to fall for a bloke's lies.'

'I went to see Etta Hines earlier this evening,' Gertie said. 'She obliges from her house in Old Road. She asked how far gone you were and I told her three months. She don't like to do anyone much later on that that. Not knowing how far gone you are I took a chance. Was I right?'

Queenie gave a huge sigh of relief, then tried to smile. 'That's about right.' She looked longingly at the fags. 'Do you mind?'

'Of course, love. Sorry I didn't offer.' Gertie leaned across the table pushing the packet in front of Queenie. She used the lighted tip of Gertie's to suck life into her own cigarette. She breathed deeply after that first long drag.

'When? It's got to be done as quick as possible. There's already been a few comments about me looking peaky.' She ran a hand across her stomach. 'My skirt's tightening up, as well.'

'Is tomorrow morning soon enough?' Gertie opened her eyes wide, questioningly.

Queenie did smile this time. 'How much? And will you be with me?'

Gertie said, 'If you haven't got it, don't worry. I got money put by.' She was interrupted by the wail of Moaning Minnie, but managed, 'Course I'll be with you. I should be in work but I'll tell Mangle I've got a dentist's appointment. I'll get up early to go and pick up my dog-ends, no sense in wasting money.'

Connie looked surprised. 'Doesn't he know you've got false teeth?'

Gertie laughed, 'He doesn't look at old girls like me! He wouldn't know if my teeth were sky-blue-pink.'

The alarm was piercing. 'For God's sake,' said Queenie, stubbing out her cigarette on a saucer. 'Just what we need, an air raid.' She was poking about beneath the chair with her feet, trying to find her shoes. 'I'd better make a run for home.'

'You're going nowhere except into my Anderson,' said Gertie, squeezing the end of her own cigarette and popping it back in the packet. She smiled at Queenie, who was staring at her. 'I'm not so wasteful as you young 'uns,' she said. 'Besides, I gets paid for decent second-hand tobacco, don't I?'

'I can't stay here.' Queenie was struggling into her jacket. 'I can't spend the night sleeping in my usherette outfit. It'll be like rags in the morning.'

Gertie was already taking off her dressing-gown to reveal a winceyette long-sleeved nightdress underneath. 'Take this,' she said. 'Go and change in Connie's room. Borrow a nightie off her. She won't mind, will you, love?'

Connie shook her head. Of course she didn't mind lending Queenie a nightdress.

'What about you? Have you got another dressing-gown?' Queenie asked.

'No, but I got an old warm coat that'll do instead.'

Connie, on her way to her bedroom, heard the scream of a bomb falling and stood rooted to the spot with fear. She felt the house shake from the blast as the shell landed somewhere nearby.

'Just take what you need, Queenie,' she shouted, tugging open a drawer.

'I need another cup of tea,' Queenie answered. Connie was glad that, despite everything and at a time like this, Queenie could be light-hearted.

'There's the makings down in the shelter,' Connie said, grabbing her own nightwear and a couple of wooden coat hangers to use for their uniforms. The sudden loud noise of explosives ripping through the night air made her shout, 'We've got to get under proper cover. Follow me!'

And then she was out of the house and running down the backyard, Queenie by her side. The stink of cordite and fine flecks of what appeared to be burning paper filled the air. Above the privet hedges the sky was glowing red. Using her elbow to shove open the shelter's door, Connie stood back and allowed her friend to stumble inside. 'I'll light the paraffin lamp in a minute,' she said.

'There's only two beds.'

'You better bags one quick, then,' said Connie. 'But there's a camp bed under the bunks and plenty of bedding.'

It was then she realized Gertie wasn't with them. She heard the slam of the back door and was relieved she didn't have to run to the house to search for her.

'C'mon, Gertie,' she said. 'What's keeping you?' A figure

was approaching along the dirt path holding a tray in front of her, reminding Connie of a picture-house ice-cream girl without the spotlight on her.

Puffing away on a cigarette attached to her lip, Gertie gasped, 'I had to go back and turn off the gas and electric. Then I remembered I'd made us some bacon turnovers. I couldn't be bothered to put them onto a plate so I've brought the bloody oven shelf an' all.'

Chapter Eighteen

Ace lifted the blind to get a look at what was causing the noise outside. Two anti-aircraft guns in Broad Street had opened fire. Caught in the searchlights, he saw black dots falling from large enemy aircraft while small glittery planes, like silver fish, hovered close by them.

'There's loads of 'em,' he said to Jerome. 'Thank Christ I shut up shop earlier than usual tonight. You get on down to the cellar. I'll be with you soon as I've cashed up.' He let the blind drop and turned back to the pile of banknotes and bills scattered on a small table.

'Not going to Gertie's tonight, then?' Jerome was standing in the doorway looking at him quizzically, with that flea-ridden cat in his arms. Thick, stale cigarette smoke hung in the air.

'You wouldn't send that animal out in this lot, would you?' Ace didn't wait for an answer. Instead he supplied one himself. 'No, you wouldn't. So why are you trying to get rid of me?'

'Don't think I haven't noticed you're not so eager now to get in the car and round to Alma Street . . .'

'You have no idea how much it kills me to go back there and make out I know nothing about Connie fancying that bloody sharp-dresser I have to pay to work in this club. You know nothing,' he repeated to Jerome.

Jerome bent down with a grimace of pain as he allowed the cat to run into the kitchen. 'When I said there was nothing physical going on between them, I was telling you the truth. Don't you believe me?'

'Yes, but to know she's thinking about him is tearing me apart.'

'Well, you're not going to win her if you blow your cover and she finds out your plans, are you? You've got to make her believe you know nothing and whatever happens is as big a surprise to you as it is to her.' Ace knew Jerome was right. His eyes followed the old man as he limped into the kitchen. Presently he heard the glass top of the milk bottle tinkle against the cat's saucer.

A deafening bang shook the building. Shrapnel began raining down on the road outside and distemper fluttered from the newly dried ceiling, like falling snow.

'Get down in the cellars, you daft old sod, and take that nit-bag with you before it starts chasing its own tail with fright!' Ace gave a sigh of relief as he heard the cellar door open.

Before it closed, Jerome was back again. 'I don't know why you feel so bad about keeping a secret like that from the girl. After all, there's plenty you don't need her to know, isn't there?' Jerome had a smile on his face and the cat in his arms.

Ace picked up a fountain pen from the table-top, and threw it at him. He sighed, rose and went over to pick up the pen: Jerome was making his getaway at the back of the kitchen through the cellar door accompanied by the cat, and didn't look back.

The air-raid warning had put a dampener on late-night business: many of the punters had left in search of the nearest shelters. A few had stayed until the bombing became serious, then they, too, had left. Never did Ace offer the security of the cellars beneath his club to customers. That domain, filled with drink and non-perishable provisions, was private and belonged to him, Jerome and Jerome's blessed cat, which didn't even have a name. In the beginning when Jerome had taken a fancy to it, he'd said, 'What's it called?'

Jerome had looked at him scathingly. 'It's a cat. It don't

need a name!' And he'd said it in such a way that Ace had felt stupid for asking.

Maybe, too, he was being stupid in feeling as he did about Connie. After all, she'd never once given him the slightest encouragement in all the time she'd been living at Gertie's. Oh, she'd thawed towards him. He felt she even enjoyed coming back at him with little insults. There was a warmth about her now that wasn't there when she'd first moved in. She didn't spend so much time with her scrapbooks, probably because she was one of the first to volunteer for extra shifts at the Criterion.

That made him wonder if she volunteered hoping to see more of Tommo. Immediately he castigated himself for that thought. Tommo was at the club every night, and when he wasn't there, he was at his mum's bedside, wasn't he? Jealousy was a powerful emotion. It twisted his thinking into knots that were impossible to untie. Thank God Jerome was clear-headed. Now he'd had time to think about his suggestion, Ace could see it was foolproof. All he had to do was wait. Of course, while he was waiting he could put into action the beginning of Jerome's plan. He'd have a chat with Tommo. Sooner rather than later was best, he decided.

All the staff in the Four Aces club knew how disappointed Tommo was that the forces wouldn't take him. The doctors had told him he wasn't fit enough. A smile hovered on Ace's lips.

Hadn't he been told he couldn't fight for his country because he too, failed the physical test? That was a load of codswallop! Ace Gallagher was as fit as a flea, but Jerome had fixed things with Billy Hill, and Ace had been only too happy to let other stupid buggers go and get killed. All it had needed was some medically unfit bloke to take his place. Billy and Jerome were only too happy to keep him safe. They could all benefit from this war then, couldn't they?

With his mum in the ground, Tommo would be only too happy to get away from Gosport, far from the claws of his dance partners, wouldn't he? He'd give anything for a fresh start. Ace, with Jerome's help, was going to give him one.

He was brought out of his thoughts by another huge explosion. Not so close as the last one but loud enough to make him duck his head when he knew it had landed outside and not on his club. He put the banknotes into a cloth bag ready to take down into the cellar with him and crossed the room to look out of the window. He lifted the blind.

The searchlights were zigzagging across the night sky. There were puffs of smoke from the anti-aircraft guns and brightness from flames burning across the water – Southsea, probably, he thought. Down in the street rubble steamed and dust floated like mist. Outside Woolworths, the stacked sandbags were untouched but a taped window was shattered, its broken glass glittering like diamonds on the cobbles of the high street. Further up he could see a gap, like a tooth missing from an old man's mouth, at the side of the India Arms public house. He remembered the closeness of the last explosion and hoped no one had been inside but guessed the chances of that were minimal.

Ace allowed the blind to drop. Gertie would be down in the shelter with Connie. Safe, he hoped. He picked up the bag of money, doused the lamp and thought of Jerome's snide remark about him not wanting Connie to know his past. Jerome knew how to keep Ace's feet grounded. Ace would lash out at anyone else who took liberties with him but he'd accept it from Jerome.

Belle was safe in Kent with Leon. He'd provided her with a nice house where the bombs didn't fall. He sent money regularly, enough for her to see he cared for his boy, and for her to spend on whatever she could find in the shops, and she knew she could do what she wanted as long as Leon was brought up properly. The only thing he wouldn't give her was his name. Marriage wasn't for him, and he'd told her so fifteen years ago when she'd fallen pregnant. Ace hadn't been much more than a kid himself then, but he had to admit she'd been a beautiful woman who'd taught him a thing or two, in bed and elsewhere.

Thank God Jerome had sorted everything out.

Ace was a private person. Jerome knew this and even he didn't talk about the boy. But that evening he'd flung a few words at Ace to let him know he had secrets he didn't need Connie to know. It was Jerome's way of telling him to rein back on the outrage he felt at her sentimental feelings towards Tommo.

'You've been given a lesson early in life,' Billy Hill had told him, all those years ago. 'Don't be an arse and repeat it.'

Sex was on tap when Ace wanted it but he'd never allowed his feelings to get in the way. Until Connie had come along.

'You only want her because she doesn't want you,' said Jerome. Was that true? Maybe it wasn't. Trouble was, he'd never find out how deep his feelings went until he had her, would he?

Chapter Nineteen

He turned his key in the lock and stepped inside his mother's house. Immediately Tommo could sense a difference, not just in the atmosphere, for the smell of disinfectant, stale urine and sickness hadn't altered, but there was a feeling, an awareness, that something was about to change.

Footsteps clicked down the thin-carpeted stairs, and before he reached the kitchen door Mrs Haynes was on the bottom step. 'She's going.'

Two words that in themselves held little meaning, but as soon as Margery Benn stepped into the hallway Tommo pushed past her, taking the steps two at a time. He heard his mother before he saw her.

She was little more than a small mound beneath the white counterpane. Tommo pulled up the chair that was already at the side of the bed and sat down. He made himself look at his mother's face, frightened of what he might discover there. Already wax-like, her eyes were closed, her lashes and eyebrows almost invisible. Her hair was white, where once it had been as blonde as his. It had escaped from its bun and lay in long lank strands across the pillow. He felt he should tuck it back behind her head, his mother hated untidiness, but he didn't want to disturb her.

Yet if he did move her, he thought it might break the regularity of the terrible strangled breaths that were coming from her throat: great waves of tortured sound drawn in and exhaled with tormenting persistence. His first thought was that she could not go on making sounds like that without her throat becoming raw. He hated his helplessness.

He felt for her hand beneath the counterpane. There was no automatic movement in her thin fingers. He thought then that it was impossible for those emaciated hands to have done all the things they had to keep him alive as a child. He wanted to cry but he'd be crying for himself, his selfishness, because she was leaving him.

'Come down and have a cup of tea.'

Tea, the panacea for everything.

He hadn't heard Mrs Benn enter the room but he felt her hand on his shoulder. 'You haven't even taken your jacket off,' she said, as though it was a necessary requisite.

Nevertheless, he carefully placed his mother's hand back on the counterpane and rose from the chair.

'How long has she been like this?' he asked, when they were down in the kitchen.

'Since I called the doctor earlier this evening,' the woman said. 'He said there was no need to fetch you too soon as she could go on like this for ages.'

Tommo, now coatless, nodded. Margery Benn was well-practised in caring for the sick and dying. She was more than just a neighbour to his mother and himself but she welcomed and needed the money he paid her to keep an eye on his mother while he worked.

For a while now he'd been refusing approaches from women to accompany them home after he left the Four Aces. Angela Keating wasn't pleased about that. He'd have given up dancing if he could have afforded it but the doctor's morphia didn't come cheap. He also worried about the time Margery spent away from her own family but it was what she did, she said.

'I'm going back to my lot for a while but you know where I am if you need me.' She smiled at him. 'There's dirty sheets and her nightdress in a bucket in the scullery. They're from when she had a bad coughing fit and made a mess. They'll be all the better for a good soak. That was when I sent for the doctor. He's coming back first thing in the morning, if he's not sent for sooner. I've stoked the range with logs, made sure the blackout curtains are drawn, and there's some corned beef and cabbage, freshly made, ready to warm up.' She searched his eyes. 'I don't suppose you've eaten?'

He shook his head but was too full of emotion to answer her. He'd hate it if he cried because of her kindness. He heard her footsteps go down the passage. His soft 'Thank you,' was obliterated by the noisy closure of the front door.

Her very last words had been 'Come for me if you need me.'

Tommo wanted to put the wireless on. Anything to block out the noise of those never-ending gasps that rang through the house, but transmission had ended for the night. He knew he couldn't force down a morsel of the food that had been thoughtfully left for him but he saw the steam rising from the spout of the brown earthenware teapot and upturned a cup onto a saucer. He was parched. In quick succession he drank two cups of tea while standing at the table. Then, when he felt sufficiently refreshed, he kicked off his shoes and went back upstairs to sit with his mother.

It didn't seem right for her to be lying in the darkness. He lit a bedside lamp. He was amazed at how the light leached even more colour from her skin. He knew it was only a matter of time before she was lying in eternal darkness but he felt she would sense his presence and feel less lonely if he sat with her, in the light, holding her hand, until the end.

The bedroom had no fire lit in it but was never cold when the range was burning in the kitchen. His mother's great ragged gasps seemed to fill the small house. Her jaw had fallen open. He knew his mother, usually so fastidious in her cleanliness and appearance, would not like to be seen as she was now, but he didn't know how to make things better for her.

Tommo hoped there would be no raid. But if there was, he would pick up his mother, bedclothes and all, and take her down into the shelter in the garden. He would rather she died in his arms than be blown to bits by one of Hitler's bombs.

He looked at her. She was his mother and yet she wasn't. His warm hand cradled her cool one. He leaned over, put his other arm across her frailty, his head on the counterpane, and cried.

Chapter Twenty

Nineteen-year-old Marlene Mullins was fed up. She'd told him the hall was hot, that the stench of cigarettes and body odour was choking her and that she needed a drink. Through the crowd of dancing couples, she could see Alex Huggins standing with the two cups of lemonade he'd offered to get and, of course, he was now looking around gormlessly to see where she'd got to. She stepped further into the shadows near the doors to the gardens and watched the American soldier she had danced with earlier shift his fingers lower down a girl's back until they were holding her bottom. Marlene smiled when the girl slapped his hand away. Harrison James the Third and she had had quite a conversation on the dance floor before the fast music made talking impossible. He'd also made her laugh when he'd said, 'Feel that!'

Instead of what she'd expected, it was packets of nylons in his inside pockets.

Another look at Alex Huggins showed he was now wandering towards the open door and out onto the lawn, still holding the cups. He hadn't been able to protest earlier when the American had wandered over and asked Marlene to dance – so politely that meek Alex couldn't demand she stay with him. After all, the dance had been held in honour of the Americans arriving in the area. She sighed.

The man she'd once thought was so wonderful now looked a complete and utter twit staring around as though he was a spare part at a wedding. With a bit of luck she could be on the floor, dancing with the American again, before Alex spotted her. Later, of course, she could ask Alex where on earth he'd got to, tell him she'd got fed up waiting for him to come back with the drinks, and felt compelled, when asked, to accept an offer of another dance. After all, Alex knew how much she loved the jive and the jitterbug. He couldn't possibly be rude to one of their cousins from across the sea when the Wickham village hall had opened its doors specially to welcome them to the south of England, could he?

The American Army base at Great Ashfield was practically fully staffed now, and the men with their suntanned faces, close-cropped hair and olive-coloured jackets, which for some reason they called 'drab', worn with light-coloured trousers and shiny brown shoes, set her heart racing.

Even their names were glamorous. Harrison James the Third, he'd said he was called, from Wyoming. Just imagine, Marlene thought, and he'd been so polite to her and smiled with those beautiful teeth, so straight and white she'd thought at first they were false, just like the ones her mum, Gertie, wore.

Marlene lowered her eyes but left the smile on her mouth as Harrison looked her way. She knew she was prettier than either of the two girls he and his friend were talking to, and she certainly had more exciting curves than the bag of bones he was trying to feel up. Marlene raised her long fake lashes and stared at the American invitingly. He had full lips like John Garfield, the film star – in fact, he was almost the dead spit of him. She wondered what it might be like to feel those lips on her own . . .

Marlene began to mentally count, one, two, three, four . . .

'Can't have a pretty little miss like you standing on her own, can I? Want to chance it on the floor again with me?'

'Well . . . I . . .' She mustn't appear too eager. Best to let him think it was his idea to ask her to dance again. But, oh, that heavenly American voice, just like John Garfield's.

'Was I so bad to dance with before, Marlene?' Demurely she shook her head and smiled again as she fell into his arms. No, he'd been great jitterbugging with her to 'In the Mood'.

Glancing back at the thin girl left standing with her friend, Marlene gave her a gloating smile. Why, Harrison James the Third had even remembered her name! 'Of course not,' she whispered, close to his ear.

'I'd have asked you for another dance before, but that man . . .'

'Oh, you mean my brother?' The lie came easily. God, but this man smelt so nice, she thought. Like lemons growing on a tree in the heat of the sun. Not that Marlene had ever smelt lemons on a tree, but she could imagine, couldn't she?

The dance was a quickstep, and as Harrison whirled her around the floor, she thought again how light he was on his feet, so different from the heavy plodding steps of Alex, who danced like a coalman delivering heavy hessian sacks.

Not that she disliked going dancing with Alex. At least it broke the monotony of looking after those kids. Marlene knew Alex cared about her. He'd paid for the dress she wore tonight and it was so pretty. Red with white spots, puff sleeves, a darling white belt to match the white collar, and large patch pockets, one on each side of the dress. It had cost her eleven of the yearly allowance of sixty-six coupons but it was so sweet, and not having to pay for it was a bonus.

Sometimes she wished she'd not volunteered to come to Shedfield to help him look after the Gosport brats but the pay was reasonable. She'd thought at the time that twenty-three-year-old Alex Huggins, with his dark curls and teaching degree, was a likely candidate for marriage. After all, being married had to be a step up from working at Priddy's armaments factory.

She was helping to care for twelve Gosport horrors, youngsters evacuated to the large country rectory where the clergyman, along with his housekeeper, Mrs Dummer, had kindly offered salvation so the children might escape the bombing.

Marlene hated the cold, draughty rectory, with its many rooms and wild gardens. Mrs Dummer lit a fire each evening in Marlene's room but it barely took the chill off the spacious, old-fashioned bedroom. She often thought longingly of her mother's small, warm terraced house even though she didn't like the constant smell of Gertie's Woodbines.

'You okay, honey?' Harrison looked down at her.

Her heart thrilled at his words. 'Of course. I'm with you, aren't I?'

A smile lit his face. She'd said the right thing.

'Great little band,' he murmured.

She glanced across at the bass player, the pianist, the drummer and saxophonist, all elderly and looking as though they might not last the night. 'I suppose so. The woman has a good voice.'

Every so often the band had played slower songs and a woman in a long dress had already sung 'Swinging On A Star' and 'I'll Never Smile Again' and, of course, as she lived locally and worked in the post office, everyone clapped exceptionally loudly.

Marlene, sadly, was not as enamoured of Alex as she had been in the beginning. Then she'd loved the knowledge he had amassed as a teacher. Now she thought of him as a know-all. He also had irritating habits that, at first, she'd not been aware of. Every so often he would cough, not a full clearing of the throat but a tiny, lacklustre sound. She'd got to the point where she was waiting for him to make the noise, and when he did, she cringed, then found herself waiting for the next. He also said, 'Er!' before every sentence. Now she didn't like to ask him too many questions for she'd be counting those, too.

Marlene knew she wasn't being fair to Alex. But when the magic had gone from a relationship and there was nothing left to keep the flame alive, wasn't it better to look around for something or someone else?

Her mum would tell her she had to put some effort into a romance. Well, that hadn't done Gertie any good, had it? Marlene's dad had still knocked his wife about, then left the house for ever. No man would leave Marlene Mullins. She was determined that she would be the one to say when the romance was over.

Just then she saw Alex, across the floor, near the band, still holding the two cups. He was scanning the dancers on the floor, looking for her.

'Let's get a bit of fresh air,' she said, almost pulling a surprised Harrison out through the doors she'd stood near earlier. She led him towards a tree near the fence and leaned against it, pulling his head down to meet her lips. Marlene guessed they were out of sight from anyone else taking a breather in the gardens, and hopefully Alex, already having decided she wasn't waiting for him in the gardens, wouldn't bother to come out and look again.

English girls were supposed to be 'easy'. Marlene knew all the Americans thought this and bragged about it to their countrymen. Well, she'd show him she was hot stuff.

Already Harrison James the Third was returning her kiss with ardour and his hands were all over her breasts outside her dress. For a moment she was sorry she'd not bought the one that had had buttons all down the front. She kissed him back, pushing her tongue into his mouth, which tasted sweet, with just a hint of chewing gum and the cigar she'd seen him put out in the ashtray on the table where he and the girls had been standing.

Marlene could feel him hard and full against her softness. His hand had rucked up her dress and begun feeling along the top of her lisle stockings, passing the suspenders to the elastic of her knicker leg. A very few fumbles, and he was spreading her open with his fingers. 'You're a bit hot, aren't you?' She managed to pull away. But slowly, teasingly.

'You know you want it,' he said, in that delicious Hollywood accent. 'You want me, I want you.' The look he gave her was half knowing, half enticing. 'Say, you're not wearing nylons, are you?'

'We can't get them here because of the war,' she said. She snuggled closer, giving him easier access to probe and push with his fingers. Another look at his face as he said, 'Relax, honey, I just love to do this. I can make it so-o-o good for you.' Marlene began to moan.

She went back into the hall, leaving Harrison James the Third buttoning and tidying himself. Her sharp eyes spotted Alex standing at the side of the hall near the table where the refreshments were sold. An elderly lady with grey hair was in charge of the tea urn. She was chatting to Alex, who was drinking from one of the cups he had been carrying around, the other now on the stained tablecloth.

Marlene walked around the edge of the floor so as not to disturb the dancers. When she reached Alex, she said crossly, 'Where the hell have you been? I've been wandering about for ages while people have been staring at me like I'm a lost sheep!' She put a hand to her forehead, pretending to stop tears falling. In a softer voice, she mumbled, 'I'm so glad I've found you.'

Alex put down his cup and gathered her into his arms. 'Er! Oh, my love, I've been looking for you as well.' He pressed her tightly against his jacket, which smelt of moth balls.

'I want to go home.' She sniffed. 'I feel such a fool.'

'Er! Then back to the rectory we shall go,' he said. She gave another sniff. 'Don't cry, love. This place is too crowded, it's not for us . . .' And he gave a little cough.

As his arm went around her shoulders and he led her away from the dancers to collect her coat, she heard the soft rustle of the cellophane-covered packets of nylons in her dress pockets, and smiled.

Chapter Twenty-one

'Do you want to borrow a pair of Marlene's slacks and a jumper? They're old but clean and serviceable.'

Connie, in the kitchen in Alma Street, watched Gertie hovering around Queenie, like a mother hen with her chick.

'Those beds in the Anderson are comfy.' Queenie continued her conversation with Connie. 'I didn't think I'd sleep a wink after the all-clear. Especially with worrying about what was going to happen today.' She stopped doing up the buttons on her white uniform blouse and stared at Gertie. 'Why would I want Marlene's cast-offs?'

Gertie frowned, then took a drag on her cigarette without it leaving her lips, which Connie thought a remarkable thing to do. 'Surely you're not wearing your usherette's uniform this morning. We're going round to get you seen to.'

That was Gertie all over, thought Connie. She was never one to mince words.

Gertie had arranged for Queenie to go to Old Road to Etta Hines's house just after nine. Etta obliged women in trouble. Connie saw Queenie's face was suddenly stricken. 'Gertie, tell Queenie the woman knows what she's doing!'

Gertie frowned at her. 'She knows I didn't mean it like that. Etta does it all the time.' Gertie looked tired.

Down in the shelter Connie had been wakened by Gertie getting dressed. It was still dark, but her aunt had borrowed a spare key to a back exit and was going into the picture house extra early to pick up the dog-ends. Mangle didn't mind when the cleaning was done as long as it was fully completed by the time the patrons were queuing outside. Gertie was hoping to curry favour with him by getting there early. Her excuse for being absent later was indeed a visit to the dentist.

'Surely it's not going to take all morning. I can't come back here just to get changed again.' Queenie frowned, 'I need to get to work, can't afford to take time off, Gertie. I'm only about three months gone, there can't be much there. Connie's given me a nice thick sanitary towel.' Gertie looked at Connie, who rolled her eyes heavenwards and shrugged. Obviously Queenie thought it would all be over and done with in five minutes. And why wouldn't she? thought Connie. Even she didn't know what was going to happen.

Queenie had grown up without a mother so must have learned about women's body changes and how babies were made from girls chattering in the playground. Sometimes, though, mothers were too shy to talk to their children about love and such matters.

Queenie was now standing in front of the range putting on her lipstick in the mirror. Despite her outward self-assurance, she was actually quite naïve, Connie thought. She liked her all the more for that.

Queenie turned to her. 'You're coming along as well, aren't you?'

'I will if you want me to,' said Connie. If Queenie needed support from her, she'd help in any way she could. Connie was due at the Criterion at lunch-time for the first house. If by any chance the woman at Old Road was running late, she could always go on ahead to the picture house, leaving Queenie in Gertie's good hands.

'Of course. You're my best pal, aren't you?'

'I'd like to think so.' Connie grinned at her.

Connie didn't like the area known as Old Road, in a poorer part of the town alongside Alver Creek. Gasometers, some empty, resembling leggy spiders, overlooked the run-down houses where police often visited the tenants.

It had been a half-hour walk to Etta Hines's house. Connie decided if she'd had to find this place on her own it would have taken her ages and she'd have got lost. Gertie, having been there yesterday, knew where to come.

Grubby, skinny kiddies played out in the street congregating around a burned-out car in front of a bombed house. 'Should be at school,' muttered Gertie.

'Most of the schools are shut,' said Connie.

'Should be evacuated, then,' answered Gertie, clearly eager to have the last word.

On the corner of Old Road, straddling Mayfield Road, there was a large well-kept house, its windows clean and shining. Connie wondered if that was where the projectionist Leonard Gregory lived. The front door of the big house sat back on the pavement with no front garden, unlike the house belonging to Etta Hines. That had a broken mangle and a child's swing with the seat cast to the ground. Dirty milk bottles lay among the tall grass, while sweet wrappers, blown by the wind, and a soggy newspaper were undisturbed on the doorstep.

'Is this the house?' Queenie's voice was small. All the way, as they'd walked along the streets, she had been chattering nineteen to the dozen. A sure sign, Connie thought, that Queenie was worried about her meeting with Etta Hines and trying to pretend everything was fine.

'This is illegal, Queenie,' said Connie, suddenly. The three had earlier discussed Etta Hines and her business but no one had mentioned this.

'I can't have the baby! How will I manage?' Queenie looked small and frightened. Her eyes were unusually bright, and Connie knew she was close to tears.

'What else is she going to do?' persisted Gertie.

There was a moment's silence before Gertie spoke again. 'She could have washed out her milk bottles since yesterday.' Connie saw she was staring at the pile of dirty bottles, some filled with greenish-white slime. Gertie turned to her. 'Go on, then, Connie, knock.'

Connie wasn't sure why it was her job to alert the woman to their presence. She looked for the door knocker, saw there wasn't one and discovered a hole where a letterbox had once been and which now had a piece of grubby cardboard behind it. She banged heavily on the door, its paint blistered.

'C'mon,' said Gertie, now standing at her side. 'Knock again. I'm sure we're being watched by neighbours.'

Connie said, 'Ssh! I can hear someone coming.'

The door opened, not fully but enough for a woman

to peer round it, look at Gertie, and say, 'Oh, it's you. Brought a bloody army with you with you by the look of it.' A heavy waft of something like boiled cabbage came out from inside the house. Connie shuddered. She didn't like the way the woman's eyes rested judgementally on her, almost as if she knew she was the interloper. She felt behind her for Queenie's hand and squeezed it tightly. Obviously, the woman had expected two visitors, not three.

Gertie opened her mouth to speak but before she could get any words out the woman opened the door wide. She wore a short-sleeved brown jumper and a dark skirt topped with a grubby apron. 'Come on in, then, don't hang about!'

Etta was thin. Her emaciated face made her nose look large. Her long greasy hair was plaited and wound in circlets about her ears. She stepped back against the hallway wall so Connie, Gertie and Queenie could enter. The door closed behind them. It was barely light inside the house. A wireless was playing.

'Go on through. Everything's ready,' the woman said.

Connie walked past two closed doors and a flight of stairs, then emerged into a scullery. Gertie and Queenie were close on her heels.

The woman, Etta, said, 'Have you got the money, Gertie Mullins?'

'Would I go to the fish shop if I didn't have the price of cod and chips?' Gertie snapped.

'It's always money first.' The reply was swift and tart.

Gertie stood in the doorway of the scullery, fumbled in her coat pocket and brought out a brown envelope. Connie saw she was about to put it on a low shelf alongside a dirty mug with a dog-end floating in tea when Etta grabbed it and, without looking inside to check it was all there, said, 'I trust you, Gertie. Now, which one of you two beauties has an unwanted bun in the oven?' She stuffed the money into her skirt pocket. Etta's small rat-like eyes flicked from Connie to Queenie and back again. Queenie said quietly, 'It's me.'

'You wait here,' Etta said to Connie. To Gertie she said, 'Take her upstairs to the back bedroom. There's no sense in hanging about.'

Connie watched as Gertie gently pulled Queenie back into the hallway and pushed her ahead to climb the uncarpeted stairs.

'How long will you be?' Connie asked.

'As long as it takes,' Etta said. She leaned forward and grabbed Gertie's arm. Gertie turned back to her. 'Just to remind you that you've not been in this house. You know what I mean?' Etta leaned forward and glared at her.

'Whatever happens when you leave,' a dirty finger poked Gertie in the chest, 'is nothing to do with me.'

Etta's eyes, now piercing Gertie's face, reminded Connie of steel knitting needles stuck in a ball of wool. She couldn't help asking, 'Do things go wrong?'

'Only to stupid women who don't do as I tell 'em,' Etta snapped. Her eyes followed Queenie's figure as she neared the top. 'That one's smart. Up to three months is a piece of cake. She'll be dancing at the Connaught Hall in a couple of days an' this'll be a memory.'

Connie heard a door open. But then Queenie, who had been remarkably quiet and calm while everything was going on around her, called down, 'I want Connie with me!'

Etta glared at Connie and snapped, 'Get up there, then, girl.' Her voice rose to a shout. 'You'll have to come down, Gertie Mullins. There's no space in that little boxroom, and my lodger won't appreciate anyone waiting about in his bedroom. Very particular he is.'

Connie said, 'Why don't you do your . . .' she searched for the right words to describe what Etta Hines did '. . . medical operations downstairs, then?'

Gertie was clumping down on the bare boards. Even her footsteps sounded angry at being turned away, thought Connie.

'Nosy, aren't you? That's my special room up there an' I keep it locked. I can leave stuff up there I'd have to hide away down here, can't I?'

Connie thought Etta's lodger must have a very strong stomach to sleep next to a small room where murder was regularly carried out. Etta must have read her mind, for she said, 'Don't go making no drama out of it. Like I said, that room is kept locked.'

Now Gertie was in front of them. 'If she wants you, you'd better go to her,' she said, addressing Connie. Her lips settled into a disgruntled thin line. Her hand fiddled in her coat pocket and she brought out her Woodbines. 'I'm not stopping in here where I'm not wanted.' Connie saw Gertie look towards the rear door. 'I'll be out the back,' she said. For a single second Connie envied her aunt getting out of the foetid air inside the house.

'I haven't got all bleedin' morning,' snapped Etta, pushing past Connie and going upstairs. 'You sort yourselves out.'

Connie didn't look at Gertie but followed Etta up and through a good-sized bedroom where a candlewick bed-spread was pulled across bed-linen that Connie felt must be as dingy as the uncovered pillowcase. A suit was hanging from the dado rail and a wooden hairbrush full of grey hairs sat next to a jar of Brylcreem on top of a dusty chest of drawers. A long mirror was propped against a wall devoid of pictures. An overflowing ashtray lay on the floor next to the bed. The same thick cabbage smell that pervaded the rest of the house hung in the room.

Connie's eyes sought Queenie's. In them she could see her fear. Connie didn't speak but deep in her heart she admired the bravery of her friend to bear all this filth and neglect to try to get her life back to normality.

Pushing the pair out of the way, Etta took a key from her pocket and opened the padlock on the door. She stepped inside, her hand finding Queenie's arm and dragging her in. 'Take your knickers off,' she barked. Her eyes then slid to Connie. 'I prefer not to do this in front of an audience so I'll thank you to keep your mouth shut during and after.'

From a shelf she took a bottle of murky liquid, poured a hefty measure into a cup with a broken handle and gave it to Queenie. 'Get that down you, fast. Don't taste it, just swallow.'

Amazingly, Queenie did as she was told. She screwed up her eyes with distaste and made a peculiar face after she'd swallowed, then handed the cup back to Etta without asking what it was. Connie saw the torn and dirty bottle label that said, 'Plymouth Gin'. She knew from working in the Sailor's Return that it was a strong drink the Royal Navy doled out to the sailors. This bottle looked like it had been on the shelf for years. In all her time of working in a pub she'd never seen Plymouth gin that colour.

'You can have a nip, if you like.' Etta had a glint in her eye as she saw Connie looking at the label. Connie shook her head. Who knew what that bottle really contained?

'Get up on the table, lie back and let your legs fall open,' demanded Etta. Queenie stood on a small stool to climb onto the newspaper-covered table. A smaller table stood to her right. The newspaper crackled when she moved.

'Is there somewhere I can sit?' Connie asked.

'Jesus, you ain't in the pictures now,' cackled Etta, fumbling in an open wooden container that looked like a handyman's toolbox. Connie could see long sharp metal implements. One was spoon-shaped. Connie wished she and Queenie hadn't worn their usherette uniforms.

Queenie whispered Connie's name, fear on her face. Connie forced a smile for her. 'It'll be over soon,' she said to her friend hopefully, for she was sure that was what Queenie wanted to hear. Queenie, who looked as if she was about to burst into tears, closed her eyes.

The small room was windowless. It might have been cold outside in the street but in there it was stifling A pile of washed but faded towels were stacked on the smaller table.

Lying on top was a thin hose with a rubber ball-like object at the end. Connie's attention was now on Etta who was muttering about some instrument that seemed to be missing.

'How d'you feel?' Etta asked Queenie suddenly.

Queenie didn't answer. She was obviously relaxed enough to be lying flat on her back, her eyes still closed and her mouth slightly open, as if she was sleeping. Her breathing was deep and regular. Her clothes were rucked up around her waist and her knees sagged outwards.

'Bloody good stuff that is,' Etta said, glancing up at the bottle on the shelf. 'Suits anyone not used to strong drink. Of course a little additive works wonders.'

Out of the box came a long, thin, curved metal instrument. Etta put her left hand on Queenie's stomach. With the right she began to insert the implement inside Queenie, who neither moved nor uttered a single word.

Connie felt revulsion and sickness. She was praying that Etta Hines hadn't lied when she'd promised it would be over in no time at all. But what she really wanted to do was shake Queenie out of her stupor and get her out of this awful house, far away from Etta Hines. Except that decision wasn't hers to make, was it?

The long thin object clattered onto the table and made the paper rustle.

'She needs opening up before it can come out,' said Etta. Now she had the scooped instrument in her hand. Connie knew if she looked at what was going on her stomach would void all the tea she'd drunk that morning and the night before.

'Pass me that tube, over there on the towel.'

Connie had no choice but to hand her the object.

She felt it being snatched from her hand. A sucking noise started up. Connie kept her eyes on the blue-and-white label saying 'Plymouth Gin' and its drawing of a galleon.

'All done,' rasped Etta Hines. Connie drew her eyes away from the gin. Queenie looked dead to the world. Connie wondered if she'd been dreaming.

Etta smacked Queenie's face. 'Come on, this isn't beddy-byes time now, dearie.' To Connie she said, 'Did she bring sanitary towels? Looks like she could be a bleeder.'

'In her coat pocket,' said Connie.

'You find 'em,' said Etta. She was fumbling with Queenie's skirt.

Somehow, beneath the reek of the room, Connie caught the fragrance of Californian Poppy, Queenie's perfume. She looked at her friend now, trying hard to climb off the table. It was as if she was drunk. Connie felt like crying but what good would that do now?

'Get her downstairs and out of this house,' said Etta. 'I got another lady coming this afternoon. I can't have anyone hanging about here.' She began wiping off her instruments with a discoloured towel. 'Remember, what's happened today hasn't happened here. I perform a service greatly valued in this area and no one wants it stopped.'

Getting Queenie downstairs was harder than Connie had imagined, but as she reached the last step she called to Gertie. 'I need help here!'

Queenie squeezed Connie's hand. 'Is it over?' Perspiration stood out on her forehead and her words were slurred.

'It's done,' said Connie.

Gertie appeared, smelling of fresh cigarette smoke, and walked down the passage to open the front door. 'Let's get the poor girl home,' she said.

Queenie whispered, 'I'll be all right in a minute.' She was telling herself she'd be all right because she wanted to believe it, Connie thought. Walking arm in arm on the pavement, she hoped they resembled any three women going to work.

Women were chatting on doorsteps wearing headscarves over curlers. A little further up the road the children Connie had noticed before were now playing five-stones on the pavement.

Gertie said, 'If we get to Stoke Road, we can catch a bus down to the Criterion.'

With that thought in mind, Connie and Gertie walked Queenie along in the cold sunshine. Alver Creek was a river of mud. Gulls lined rusted iron bedsteads sticking out of the mire. On the far shore an old lady was throwing bits from a bag and birds were hovering ready to snatch them.

Queenie spoke. 'I don't feel very . . . very well . . . I got cramping in my stomach . . .' She doubled over and slipped through their arms to the pavement.

'Pull her up. Lean her against the wall,' Connie said. Together they dragged her towards it, and Connie made sure Queenie was supported by the low brick structure dividing the creek from the pavement.

'My insides are falling out . . .' mumbled Queenie.

Connie looked at Gertie but didn't speak at first: where Queenie had fallen, bright blood smeared the paving stones. Queenie's face was grey, her eyes glazed.

'Stay with her. I'll get help,' Connie hissed. She turned and ran back the way they'd walked. When she reached Etta Hines's door she banged loudly. There was no answer but a corner of the dirty curtain at the window twitched. Connie went on banging. After a while a voice came through the open slit of the letterbox.

'Who is it?'

'My friend's very poorly. Can you come?'

There was silence for a moment. Then, 'It's nothing to do with me, get her home!'

'Please?'

'We talked about this. Get her home.'

'Can I at least phone for an ambulance?'

'Who d'you think I am? The Queen? No phone here, nearest box is on the main road.'

Connie bent down, peered through the open oblong and saw the back of Etta walking resolutely away up the passage.

She turned and began running again. If she could get to the main road she could find a red telephone box, and . . .

She saw the large house on the corner of Old Road. Without stopping to think she got to the front door and began hammering.

Chapter Twenty-two

'Is everything all right, Tommo love?'

He looked down at Angela Keating. He could feel no desire for the woman in his arms, despite the extreme kindness she'd shown him during the past weeks when his mother's death and subsequent burial had left him inconsolable.

The band in Ace's club was playing 'I'll Never Smile Again' and that was exactly how Tommo felt.

'Of course,' he murmured. He bent his head and kissed her hair, inhaling the scent of Joy. He was beginning to hate the smell.

Eleanora Simmonds was sitting at a table at the side of the room, trying to gain his attention. She was holding, high in the air between her podgy fingers, several tickets. He felt as if he was a piece of meat. Eleanora was a big ungainly woman, whose flesh seemed to spill in folds from her clothes.

At the back of the busy bar Ace was standing next to Jerome while the bar-man and pretty girl attendants served a flood of customers. He could tell Ace and Jerome were talking about him.

'I'll have to leave you,' he said to Angela. 'I don't want to but my boss is giving me the evil eye.' He laughed softly, trying to turn his words into teasing banter. He knew he'd not been pulling his weight just lately. Luring gullible rich women up to the gaming tables was low on his list of priorities. Ever since his mother's funeral he'd allowed himself the solace of Angela's sympathetic arms. He was digging a hole deeper and deeper in misery for himself and losing the will to climb out.

'I'll wait for you later?' The question came from her as the music ended and he led her back to her table to gather her handbag and wrap. He squeezed her arm gently. She would go upstairs to sit at the gambling tables. They were almost as big a drug to her as he was. He watched her weave her way through the customers and at the bottom of the stairs she turned and gave him a small wave, which he returned before he began edging his way towards Eleanora. His brain dredged up her history. Scrap iron. Her husband had amassed a tidy fortune before dropping dead in his office and leaving the lot to Eleanora.

'Tommo, come and have a drink. She'll wait.' Ace's voice reached him and he caught the boss's nod towards Eleanora.

'Whisky, Tommo?' Jerome asked, as Tommo neared the bar.

He shook his head. 'Something light would be good,' he said. 'Got to keep my mind on my job.' He grinned at Jerome.

He thought he was about to receive a lecture on his indifferent performances, but Ace said, 'Tommo, you're my number-one man. You know that, don't you?'

He noted the half-pint of beer set on the bar in front of him and smiled his thanks. He stared into Ace's eyes, wondering what he was up to and how he should answer him. Ace continued without waiting for Tommo to speak. 'I've got a proposition for you. A kind of thank-you, if you like, for all you've done before the bomb decimated this place and since. You might look on this offer as a pay-off, which it is, in a way . . .'

'You sacking me?' Tommo's words came out quicker than he'd meant them to.

'Why would I sack one of the best just because he's going through a bad patch?'

Tommo drank some beer and set the glass very carefully on a mat to give himself time to think. Was Ace asking for payback already for the money he'd advanced Tommo for his mum's funeral? Or was it something more? When Ace had told him to make sure his mother had a good send-off and not to skimp because he'd take care of it, he'd never dreamed he might want repaying so soon.

'What's the one thing you couldn't have while you were nursing your mother?'

The music had changed to a quicker tempo. The air in the club was stuffy with cigarettes and body odour, each vying for top place.

'A lot of things, boss,' Tommo answered. He took another swallow of the tepid beer.

The thing . . . or person . . . he wanted couldn't be his because Tommo was ashamed of the way he made a living. Connie's smile flashed before him. 'There was this girl,' he said. Was it his imagination or had Ace's forehead suddenly creased into a frown?

Ace reached for his whisky and downed it in one.

Jerome said quickly, 'I thought you wanted to join the services? The navy, wasn't it?'

'They wouldn't have me.' He stared at Jerome. 'You know how badly I took it.'

Jerome curved his lips into a smile that never reached his eyes.

'Would you like another chance?' Ace's words were sharp.

'Of course I would,' Tommo said, just as quickly. 'But what's the point?'

'The point is I can guarantee you'll get into the navy this time.'

'But how?'

'Ask no questions and you'll get told no lies,' said Jerome. He removed his spectacles and polished them on a large handkerchief, which he had taken from his pocket, then replaced them on his nose. He put the handkerchief back where it had come from.

All Jerome's movements were well thought-out and methodical, mused Tommo.

There was a moment of silence between the three of them. Tommo drank the rest of his beer but kept his fingers on the glass, turning it thoughtfully round and round in his hand. 'So, you'd go to a great deal of trouble to get rid of me, then?' He stared at Ace.

'If you want to look at it that way, please yourself. But you're no damn good to me the way you are, moping about the way you have for months . . .'

Tommo opened his mouth to excuse himself. Surely Ace couldn't be so insensitive. His mother was barely cold in her coffin . . .

Ace didn't let him speak. 'You're a mate, a good worker, the best. I don't want to lose you but you're useless at the moment. If there wasn't a war on, I'd give you the money for a holiday so you could have a few women your own age, not these worn-out tarts. That would have you up to scratch in no time . . .' He paused. 'I asked you what you wanted and I can make it happen.'

Before Tommo could reply, Ace put up his hand to one of the girls behind the bar. 'Refills, here, love.' Tommo watched as the pert blonde began filling the empty glasses. 'This is first of my Four Aces clubs. I need someone like you to fill my shoes when I open my second in Southsea. But I want you as you were, not the shell you've become . . .'

Tommo looked at Jerome. 'Don't look at me, mate. My days of running anything are over and done with. . .' His voice halted as the girl set the beers and a whisky on the bar top, grinned and flounced away. Jerome looked after her longingly. 'If only . . .' he said.

'You've had your share,' Ace said to him, with a smile.

Tommo's head was whirling. Was he hearing right? Ever since he'd begun working at the club, he'd modelled himself on Ace. He wore the sharpest suits he could afford, two-tone shoes. He'd never been able to run to silk shirts but his mother had made sure he'd had a clean cotton one, nightly.

Ace wanted him to run the club? Not be a ghost dancer? Not a gigolo? He'd be proud as Punch to tell anyone he managed a club. Wouldn't he just!

He thought about the navy. The war wasn't going to last for ever. If Ace could swing him a few months in the services the experience would give him the head start and confidence he needed to do justice as manager of a club like this.

Ace hadn't done time in the services: he'd wangled a way out of that. But he already had confidence in bucket loads. Look how he'd come up smiling when this club had been bombed. Money and confidence had given him the nerve to get back on his feet in no time. Sadly, with all the hard knocks Tommo had had in the past year, his confidence was nil. Why, he hadn't even had the guts to ask Connie out.

Connie. He remembered the electricity running between them when he'd touched her hand. He'd had nothing to offer her then, but maybe . . .

How he'd love to be able to say to her, 'I've served my country and now I run one of the Four Aces . . .'

'I didn't pass the medical when I last applied . . .'

'Let me worry about that,' Ace said. 'My own medical was fiddled so I could stay out. I can make sure your new one shows you're A1.' He gave a little laugh. 'Let's face it, Tommo, those doctors couldn't have known what they were doing when they downgraded you. You're the fittest bloke I know. You've got to be medically fit to dance the night away like you do. Am I right or am I right?' He bestowed a big smile on Tommo, then picked up one of the drinks and handed it to him.

'That makes sense,' admitted Tommo. He looked first at Jerome, then at Ace. 'Of course, there is another problem, quite a big one, in fact . . .'

'And what would that be?' Ace was smiling like the cat that had got the cream.

'We're at war. Are you sending me into it in the hope I'll get killed?'

'What a nasty mind you've got, my son.' Ace glanced at Jerome and shook his head, then smoothed back the lock of hair that had tumbled forward. He looked at Tommo and put a hand on his shoulder in a fatherly gesture. 'If I can arrange to have you accepted as medically fit for the navy, I can arrange for you to spend your days and nights somewhere you'll come to no harm and have all your home comforts.' He squeezed Tommo's shoulder. 'You're like a son to me. You should know that, Tommo.'

Ace was looking across the room, his mind as ever on money he might lose, thought Tommo, as he said, 'Don't forget Eleanora's waiting for you.'

Chapter Twenty-three

'Come on, open this door,' Connie was saying, willing someone to appear. If this was Leonard Gregory's house then surely it was much too early for him to have left for his job as projectionist at the Criterion picture house. Bang! Bang! Bang! Her knuckles were sore hammering against the wood. If she'd made a mistake and Len didn't live here then she'd – she'd – she'd . . . Connie thought quickly. She'd ask the person who answered the door if they had a telephone so she could ring for help. Yes, that's what she would do.

'All right! I'm here!' She heard a chain being lifted inside, the door opened a little and Len peered through the gap.

'You've got to come. Now!' Connie said quickly. 'Queenie's in trouble.'

The door opened wider and Leonard Gregory stood in the doorway, barefoot. He was dressed in trousers and shirt, both hastily thrown on, and with shaving cream covering the lower half of his face. When he saw who was creating the disturbance, he wiped the back of his hand across his mouth.

'Calm down and tell me what's the matter,' he said, standing back so she could squeeze past him and into the surprisingly bright hallway. Before closing the door, he looked out and along the street.

'Thank God I've found you,' Connie gabbled. 'Queenie's up the road near Alver Bridge. She's ill! She can't walk—'

'Slow down, Connie!' His voice was sharp. He pulled out a large handkerchief from his trouser pocket and swiped the white foam from his face. 'Now tell me,' he said, pushing the hanky back out of sight.

Connie knew that if she wanted help she must tell him the truth. Or at least her version of it to save Queenie's reputation. 'Queenie's took bad. We daren't move her. Oh, Len, please come!'

He looked into her face, then down at the linoleum floor where his shoes sat inside the door. He slipped his bare feet into them. 'Show me!' Without grabbing a coat for himself, he was pushing her back out onto the street, the door slamming behind them.

He turned left and ran down the road towards Alver Bridge. Connie tried to keep up with him but his long legs meant he reached Gertie first. She was bending over Queenie, trying to prop her up before she slid further down onto the cold pavement.

Queenie's face was ashen, her eyes were closed and her head was lying to one side. Connie thought she'd aged ten years in the time she'd been gone.

'The blood's made a mess of her uniform,' Gertie whispered to Connie.

'Let me get at her,' Len said, pushing Gertie out of the way and magically catching Queenie up in his arms before she fell. 'I've got you,' he said, sweeping her chest high, then turning and striding back the way he'd come. He was carrying Queenie as though she weighed no more than a doll.

Connie looked about her. Across the road in one of the cottages facing the creek she thought she saw a net curtain fall back.

Gertie seemed to read her mind. 'Not one person came out to see what was the matter with her. Nosy lot but they keeps themselves to themselves. That's what the neighbours are like round here.'

Connie was hastily kicking dirt over the mess that spattered the pavement.

She looked up to see Gertie chasing Len down the pavement.

'Key's in my pocket,' Len said, as they reached his door.

Gertie said, 'We wouldn't be so eager to put our hands in your pocket if you were Ol' Mangle!' It wasn't a good time to make a joke but Connie's spirits rose.

Perhaps, just perhaps, everything might be all right.

Inside the house, Len carried Queenie through to the scullery, deposited her on a chair near the sink and immediately began removing her coat.

Queenie was like a dead thing as Len knelt in front of her. He saw the red stains on her clothing and the brightness of fresh-flowing blood. 'Only one reason she's in such a state and you're down here in Old Road.' Len sat back on his heels and sighed.

'Are we to get an ambulance?' Gertie asked, already puffing on a cigarette.

He looked at her. 'You do know what Etta Hines has done is a criminal offence?'

Gertie narrowed her eyes.

'This could have serious repercussions on Queenie. If ever she gets over it. Gertie, I want you to go right to the bottom of Old Road, the last house near the gasometers, and tell Edith Stimson I need her to come here immediately.'

'Who—'

'Go!' It was practically a shout and Gertie scurried away.

To Connie he said, 'I'm going upstairs to make up a bed for her.' Connie opened her mouth to speak but he stopped her: 'I'll find a clean shirt so she can get out of that stupid uniform when Edith's examined her.' He took a deep breath. 'Of course, sorry, you have no idea what I'm on about. Edith's a midwife, or was when she was younger, but everyone calls her when they need a doctor. Not many can afford a doctor's charges around here and I . . .' he paused '. . . would rather rely on her.' He took in a deep breath, then let it out slowly. 'It wouldn't be the first time Edith's cleaned up after Etta.'

Before Connie had time to ask him anything he'd gone. She heard footsteps going upstairs. Left alone with Queenie, she saw her poor face was streaked with dirt. Tears filled Connie's eyes as, using Imperial Leather soap, a clean flannel and fresh towels she discovered in a cupboard, she carefully washed her insensible friend.

When Len returned, she said, 'I hope you don't mind, I've used a couple of clean towels I found.'

He shook his head, handed her the shirt, 'You keep hold of that,' he said, after entering the scullery.

'She is going to be all right, isn't she?'

'That'll be up to Edith,' he said.

She'd read somewhere you weren't supposed to move

injured people so she'd done the best she could without undressing Queenie. She guessed Edith would strip the messy clothes from Queenie's body before she did anything else.

When Connie had first met Len, she'd thought he was a kind man. Now she added 'good' to her mental list. It was obvious he cared about Queenie for when he noticed her hair was straggling down the sides of her face, he picked up his hairbrush and gently smoothed back the curls. As he brushed the blonde hair off her forehead, he said tenderly, 'It shouldn't have come to this, Queenie, love.'

Everything seemed to happen at once when Gertie swept back into the house, followed by a small, round woman with apple cheeks. She was wearing a white apron that was so bright it almost hurt Connie's eyes.

'Hello, Len, I came as quick as I could.' The woman bent towards Queenie but didn't touch her. Connie caught the smell of vanilla – she had probably been baking before she'd been called away. 'Can you carry her upstairs to a bed for me to look at her properly?' Len nodded. The woman turned to Connie. 'You stay down here, love. If I need anything, Gertie can help me.' Gertie put on her important look and used the sink to stub out a cigarette she'd lit the moment she'd got into the house. 'Gertie, for God's sake, put the kettle on,' Edith said, as she followed Len from the scullery with Queenie held in his arms.

When Len came back downstairs, he said, 'I hope one day that that blasted Etta Hines gets her comeuppance.'

'I'm sure she will,' came Connie's response. Again, she asked, 'Is Queenie going to be all right?'

'Edith will do the best she can for her. She's had me putting books beneath the bottom legs of the bed to lower the head.' Connie guessed that was to help staunch the flow of blood.

'Connie, we need to talk about work,' he said. All thoughts of her job had flown from her mind with what was happening to Queenie. 'You have to go to work today as though nothing out of the ordinary has happened. We don't want Mangle getting a sniff of anything. Queenie'll need this job, when she recovers enough to get back to work . . . or if,' he said.

'I can't leave her, she needs me.'

'She needs Edith,' he said firmly. 'Gertie can do the running around – she'll make a good job of that – and I can't possibly leave here until I know what's happening.'

'You're telling me to go to work at the picture house but the projectionist won't be there?'

'A projectionist will be there. Young Gary can do

everything I can and he'll make a good job of it. We can't let the patrons down and I don't want any of this becoming public knowledge. Do you understand?'

Connie could see that what he was saying made sense but she couldn't get her head round the fact that upstairs Queenie was possibly fighting for her life while down here Len was arranging for the Criterion picture house to open as usual.

'I suppose you're going to tell me the film's already set up.'

'Of course, Abbott and Costello's *Hold that Ghost.*'

'What do I say about Queenie's absence?'

'You'll think of something. And it wouldn't hurt you to take over the ice-cream sales. That'll put Ol' Mangle's mind at rest about the routine being upset because his best usherette is missing. Anyway, you know what a shirker he is – he might not even come in today.'

'That's quite possible,' Connie said. She'd calmed down a little and realized his words made sense. 'What about Gertie?'

'Oy! I am here you know!' Gertie, cigarette in her mouth, was warming the teapot.

'She's not due in until tomorrow morning and I see no reason why she shouldn't be back in Alma Street tonight, if Edith's allowed to do her job properly.'

'So, you're going to telephone Gary,' said Connie.

'I don't have a phone,' he answered, shaking his head.

'Oh!' Why had she automatically thought he had a telephone? Not everyone possessed one – Gertie certainly didn't.

'But I know Gary won't let me down and he'll be in early to do a check on the equipment. If necessary, he'll start things rolling without me. I trust the lad. You go up to the projection room later and explain.' He took a deep breath. 'If between us we can make sure the Criterion functions as usual, with a bit of luck all this will stay secret.'

'As long as . . .' Connie couldn't utter the words but she could tell by the look on his face that he knew exactly what she meant.

'Queenie's in good hands. Put some cups on a tray. Tea's needed upstairs.'

Chapter Twenty-four

Connie felt funny walking home alone. She missed Queenie's chatter. No matter what she had done that afternoon or evening, or how many people she'd spoken to in the course of her work as an usherette at the Criterion, her mind had been continually focused on Queenie. How she'd not left the picture house to be at Old Road with her friend, she didn't know. But she trusted Leonard Gregory. He was a good man. Still, it didn't feel right going home to Alma Street when she wanted to bang on Len's door at the other end of town to find out how her friend was. But she'd promised him she'd do her best to carry on as normal, and by now Gertie would be home and hopefully could put her mind at rest.

It wasn't as dark as usual because the moon was so much brighter tonight. Summer had gone, and the remaining leaves on the trees were brown and shrivelled, yet still the war rolled on.

Connie remembered two of the items on Pathé News earlier. Women were no longer required to wear hats in church and, due to rationing, cardboard wedding cakes were now popular! The whole damn world had gone mad, she thought. What kind of news was that to broadcast when the Germans sending bombers over almost nightly was enough to put the fear of God into everyone? Did people really order cardboard cakes?

Len had been right about young Gary Pink. After she'd climbed up to the projection room and told him that, due to unforeseen circumstances, he was to take over for the afternoon and evening and Len would explain everything tomorrow, he'd puffed out his chest and said, 'Leave it all to me. I won't let Len down.' Connie had had no doubt he'd do exactly as he had promised, and he had. She'd even noted that after the National Anthem had been played, before the Criterion closed for the night, Gary had operated the switch to open and close the screen curtains, a daily safety requirement.

Mangle had been alone in his office when she'd first arrived at the picture house. Determined not to allow him to intimidate her, when she'd heard him call, 'Come in, the door's not locked,' she'd simply banged again and again until he'd had to come and open the door. She'd wanted to speak to him without going inside his office. He stood in the doorway, glaring at her.

Connie had taken one look at him and announced, 'Sorry to be the bearer of bad news, Mr Mangle, but Queenie's been taken ill with a stomach upset. She's in bed but you aren't to worry. To save you the bother of finding someone to do her duties she's told me exactly what needs to be done. I promise you, Mr Mangle, I can cope adequately.' She was hoping he'd remember how he'd praised her for working on her own initiative when those lads had been causing bother in the stalls. She also knew how lazy he was and that he didn't like putting himself out to do extra work so would be more than willing to go along with her suggestion.

He'd stared at her. 'She'll be back tomorrow, I presume?' He didn't look at all happy.

'I should think so, Mr Mangle,' she'd simpered. 'But you won't want the rest of the staff catching it so she might not.'

'And can you cash up when we close? I have to go out later.'

Connie knew exactly what to do. She'd checked the sales money in the till enough times when the Sailor's Return had closed at night and she'd left the correct float ready in the drawer for the next day. Cashing up was easy. Besides, many times she'd watched Queenie tallying the money against the number of tickets sold. Afterwards, Tom Doyle could check the place over and lock up for the night.

'Oh, yes, Mr Mangle,' she'd answered, breathing a sigh of relief that he'd believed her and she'd managed to escape his clutches.

As she walked away, he'd come to the door and shouted, 'I'll not be here after seven this evening. There's a council meeting my wife and I need to attend. I'm sure you'll manage, though.'

Connie didn't like to lie to anyone about why Queenie wasn't at work, but she didn't consider being economical with the truth a bad thing. The usherettes crowded around her asking questions and she'd replied, 'Hopefully she'll be back at work soon.' Which, again, was the truth, wasn't it? Connie was well aware that not only were Queenie's health and possibly her life at stake but so was her reputation.

During the afternoon she'd watched the patrons, hoping to catch a glimpse of Tommo Smith, but it wasn't to be. She hadn't seen him for some time now and consoled herself with the thought that perhaps the smart young man had changed his working hours and it wasn't possible now for him to spend time at the pictures. She knew she'd never forget the magic tingle that had coursed through her when their fingers had touched.

Taking over Queenie's job made her understand just how much the manager depended on her friend. Queenie, with Tom Doyle's help and Len Gregory's knowledge of film, practically ran the Criterion, not Mr Mangle.

There was one job, however, that Connie had never attempted.

'Has any of you ever stood in for Queenie selling ices?'

For a moment there was silence. Connie's heart began beating wildly.

'I'll do it!' Sara Cantrell's voice piped up from the back of the small gathering. Connie knew the woman had worked diligently after her run-in with Gertie. She'd made the jump from cleaner to usherette. That job paid better and had allowed her to start settling some of the debts that had accumulated.

Connie was glad Gertie wasn't there. She was sure her aunt would have a lot to say about why the spotlight shouldn't shine on her old enemy. If Sara felt confident enough to stand in for Queenie during the intervals when the ice-creams had to be sold then Connie could only thank Sara from the bottom of her heart.

'It's usually me what fills the tray for her, anyway,' Sara added.

'Thank you, Sara,' Connie said. What she didn't add was that she could no more stand beneath that bright spotlight being stared at by a picture house full of people than she could think of flying a Spitfire.

She would also think about telling Gertie that Sara was taking over that job later, perhaps much later, when she was less tired and better equipped to deal with any argument Gertie might start.

Connie shivered. When she got home, she wanted nothing more than a good strip-wash in the scullery, after she'd had a cup of tea, of course. Later she could fall into bed and blissful sleep. Though she doubted she'd rest properly unless she could be assured Queenie was comfortable. It had been a tiring day, much worse for Queenie than anyone else, of course.

She thanked God she didn't have to go into work until six in the afternoon tomorrow. The staff were aware of their duties for the following day and all Queenie's were covered. Today had also shown her how hard Queenie worked to keep the Criterion picture house running. It had also proved to her what a useless lump of a man Arthur Mangle was. He was a worm, a rotter. No doubt his wages were far higher than an usherette's, yet he made sure his workload was much lighter.

As Connie rounded the corner into Alma Street, she saw Ace's car parked outside the house. She wondered how Gertie was, what news there was of Queenie, and whether it would be possible to sneak in without seeing or talking to Ace. She was so tired she knew she wouldn't be able to think of any quick come-backs if he started teasing her. Today's events and all the heartache they had engendered had also made her think a great deal about her mother and how much she missed her. One minute Connie had been a child and the next she had been thrown into adulthood when she wasn't ready for it. The war had done that, she thought. And no doubt many, many people were experiencing the same tragedy.

She walked up the street, mindful of the cracked paving stones, and was about to slip her hand into the letterbox to pull out the key when the door opened and the clean, lemony scent of cologne assailed her.

'I heard your footsteps,' Ace said. 'I've been waiting for you. I'm so glad you're home.'

Chapter Twenty-five

Ace was downstairs alone.

'Where's Gertie?' Connie said. The smell of stale cigarette smoke hung in the kitchen and a saucer full of dog-ends lay on the table. There was also an oily smell that reminded Connie she'd had little to eat all day and it made her feel hungrier. She kicked off her shoes and breathed deeply, glad to be rid of her high heels, which had made blisters form on her feet.

'She went to bed some time ago, said she was worn out with all the drama of today. Probably asleep by now.' Ace raked his fingers through his hair and she waited, knowing the heavy waves would immediately fall back onto his forehead.

Connie took off her coat and threw it over the back of a kitchen chair, then collapsed into the old armchair near the window. 'I so needed to talk to her,' she said, and was dismayed to see him disappearing into the scullery. Naturally she wanted to see Gertie. She had been worrying all day about Queenie and now Gertie was sleeping! She listened to Ace making noises outside with cups and kettles. It dawned on her that if Queenie had taken a turn for the worse, Gertie wouldn't be asleep, would she?

Ace's voice came to her. 'She's really upset with that Etta Hines. She said she wishes she was dead so she could dance on her grave. Gertie also said if you go down to the lavatory don't walk into the wet washing.'

She pondered his words. Sometimes, she thought, wriggling her toes to get some feeling back into them, I swear Gertie Mullins is quite mad! So much for keeping everything a secret! 'Gertie can't keep her mouth shut,' she called to him.

His voice came back to her from the scullery. 'She was worried about you taking things bad so soon after your mum, an' all. She needed to talk and I'm here.' Then he added, 'She said you were really upset about that woman in Old Road butchering others and getting away with it. I told her if there was anything I could do for you, I would. And, of course, I don't gossip.'

Ace bustled into the kitchen with a tray of tea. He had his shirtsleeves rolled up, showing the soft down of red-gold hairs on his arms. Somehow, thought Connie, it made him look endearing.

'I'm to tell you that Queenie's going to be all right eventually.' He put the tray on the table. 'Well, she's going to live,' he added. 'That stupid Hines woman has made a bit of a mess of her insides but there's some good news. She's still carrying the baby.'

Connie let his words wash over her as his strong hands poured the tea into cups. Her mind went back to that horrible woman, Etta Hines, her filthy house and that stinking upstairs room.

'Oh, my God!' How is that possible? she wondered. All that blood . . . 'So, it was all for nothing,' said Connie, eventually, quietly. She felt the tears rise. She couldn't do anything to stop them spilling over. She took a deep breath. She used her hand to wipe them away. 'I'm really surprised Gertie told you,' she said. 'It was supposed to be kept quiet, for Queenie's sake.' Her tears kept falling, faster now.

'When I got home, she was in a hell of a state. Told me it was all her fault because she'd arranged for Queenie to go to that woman . . . And she was worrying about you having to do so much, taking on responsibilities you weren't used to when you hadn't been working long in the job – and she knew you'd had nothing to eat today.'

'Stupid woman!' Connie let out another deep breath as though she'd been storing the air inside her. Again, she used the back of her hand to wipe her wet cheeks. She rose from the chair to walk to her coat to get the handkerchief from her pocket. Ace stood in front of her, in her way, and she couldn't pass him. Connie didn't know whether to be irritated or comforted by him being there.

Then his arms were around her crushing her to his chest. All the emotion she'd kept pent up burst from her and more tears fell, unheeded. Big noisy sobs that had been held back all morning, afternoon and evening.

Suddenly she was weeping not just for Queenie but for herself because she missed her mother and it was hard trying to keep everything together. And Ace's chest felt hard, secure, and in his arms she was safe.

After a while, she gave a few hiccups and said, 'I'm sorry.'

He looked down at her and said, 'This is something sticking film stars' pictures in scrapbooks can't mend, isn't it?'

Connie tried to smile, unsuccessfully. As she pulled away from him, a long string of dribble broke from the corner of her mouth and settled on Ace's silk shirt. 'I'm so sorry.' She tried to wipe it away but instead made it into a wet, grubby mess. Looking at it only made her feel worse.

He laughed. 'Buggered that up, haven't you?' He smiled down at her, then sat her on one of the kitchen chairs. She felt like a wet paper bag that needed to be thrown away. He turned to the table and finished pouring her a cup of tea that he set in front of her. 'Drink that and you'll feel better.'

Connie picked up the cup and held it in both hands in an effort to stop herself shaking tea all over the place. Ace pulled up a kitchen chair and sat watching her.

When she'd drained the tea, she set it back on the tray.

'Better now?' he asked. Connie gave a small nod. 'Right,' he said. 'Take your time and tell me your version of what happened today.' Connie opened her mouth to speak but he placed his hand on her arm and said, 'Afterwards, I expect you could do with a tidy-up. There's plenty of hot water on the stove outside, and I've taken the liberty of fetching your nightie and dressing-gown from your bedroom for you. As Gertie kept moaning about your empty stomach, I visited the fish shop and there's cod and chips in paper warming in the oven.'

Connie was suddenly overwhelmed by his kindness. But she stopped more tears from leaking out and began telling him about Etta Hines, Len Gregory, Arthur Mangle, and how the usherettes at the Criterion had all rallied round to take on extra responsibilities because they liked Queenie.

And all the time Ace sat at the table watching and listening to her.

Eventually when she had finished, she added, 'Queenie's a good friend. Gertie and me, we didn't want her to lose her job, be talked about and have everyone shun her and make her life a misery because she'd fallen in love with some American who got what he wanted from her, then left her high and dry. She deserves better.'

Connie could feel herself getting angrier and angrier. Ace picked up her hand. His touch was gentle. 'Look,' he said. 'It's no good upsetting yourself, you're no use to your friend like this.'

He let her hand drop and began pouring more tea for them. Connie was staring at him. She wondered now how she could ever have thought this man too cocky to have feelings.

'Gertie said to tell you . . .' he frowned and she realized he was searching his brain for a name '. . . Edith, the midwife, is staying with your friend tonight at Len Gregory's house. Gertie's going into work as usual in the morning and she won't say anything.'

Connie grimaced. Could she believe that Gertie really wouldn't talk?

As if reading her mind, he said, 'She won't say a thing. She promised me. Things will get easier.'

He sounded so positive, Connie thought. The extra work today hadn't been exactly hard but she wasn't used to the responsibilities that Queenie took in her stride. But then, she thought, if Queenie could manage so could she.

'I really like working there,' Connie said. 'You know how much I love films.'

He was looking at her intently. She yawned, managing to put her hand over her mouth. He laughed. 'Go and get washed,' he said, as he stood up, 'but first let me bring in that washing. It won't get any drier by being out all night. I'll leave it on the line in the scullery. You finish your tea.'

He left the kitchen and a waft of lemony cologne followed him.

Connie was a bit apprehensive about taking off her clothes and washing in the scullery while Ace was sitting in the kitchen. He came back in, saying, 'I've locked the back door and hung Queenie's uniform over the string line. The scullery is all yours. There's food in the oven in the range,' he reminded her, pointing towards the fireplace. 'It's already late and I know you probably won't sleep much but you should try. I promised Gertie I'd get you to Len Gregory's house in the morning.'

'Queenie? I can go and see her?' There was nothing she'd like more than that.

'Of course. But it's a fair trek to the other end of town to Len's house . . .'

Connie stared at him.

'So, young lady,' he added, and then he winked at her, 'at last I get to give you a lift in my car.'

She couldn't help it. A smile creased Connie's mouth.

Chapter Twenty-six

'Did you sleep all right last night?' Ace had opened her door unannounced.

Connie sat up in bed while clutching her nightdress, which had lost its top button. The alarm clock said it was half past seven. She groaned. It was too early for her to wake up, especially as she didn't have to go in to work until six o'clock today.

He was washed, shaved, and dressed in dark blue trousers and a clean pale blue shirt. Again, he had his sleeves rolled up and it gave Connie a particular thrill to see the golden-red hairs on his arms. He brought in with him that gorgeous citrus smell she loved and a cup of tea, which he set down on the chair next to her bed.

'I did,' she said. 'And I ate the fish and chips.' She paused. 'Nearly all of them but they'd got a bit dried up.'

'So would you, if you'd been warming in that oven as long as they had.' He stared at her for a moment. 'In case you're wondering why I'm giving you an early call, it's because last night I promised to take you round to check up on Queenie. If we can leave reasonably soon, I can drop you at Len Gregory's house, so you can help out there if it's needed. I'll pick you up again after I've been down to the club. I've got someone coming in to see me this morning but I shouldn't be any longer than a couple of hours.'

He took a deep breath. 'I know you don't need to be at the Criterion until later today so I thought you might like a drive and a meal somewhere . . .' His voice tailed off. He reminded her of a naughty boy who was asking for a biscuit. What he was suggesting sounded wonderful, especially now she'd got to know him and had decided he really was a nice man.

'I'd like that,' she said, picking up her teacup. 'But if Queenie's taken a turn for the worse, I'll have to stay with her. You do understand that, don't you?'

A look of relief swept over his face. 'Of course,' he said. Then, 'Gertie and I had a little talk this morning before she left. She knows you'll be in later so she's staying at the picture house longer than she normally does. She said you'd be more likely to accept my offer if you knew that.'

'Oh,' said Connie, with a smile. 'She likes to keep her finger on the pulse of things, doesn't she?'

He nodded and his auburn hair fell across his forehead.

'I haven't been out for a meal for ages,' Connie said. Already she could feel excitement rising within her.

'And you've no need to worry. I'll get you back here this afternoon in plenty of time to change for work.'

Her eyes went to the back of the door where her uniform hung. She was glad she'd taken the time to brush it last night and clean the marks from it, so it would be fresh and ready for today.

He was waiting for her to hand him her empty cup, so she gave it to him.

'Can you be ready in about an hour?

She knew it would take her at least half an hour to find something nice to wear from her meagre selection of clothes, but Connie smiled at him. 'Of course,' she said.

In the cellar of the Four Aces Jerome had already checked a shipment of cigarettes, tobacco, drink, tea, butter, sugar and tinned goods that had been delivered. Ace smiled at the brown carrier bag full of food that the old man had left out especially for him to take to Gertie later. He'd also written Ace a note: 'Tell Gertie this fish needs using up.' He looked inside the newspaper parcel and saw at least a couple of pounds of cod that smelt sea-fresh.

Ace decided if he got through his business quickly at the club, he could deliver the bag to Alma Street before he drove to Old Road to pick up Connie. He dropped another packet of Woodbines into it and left the cellar.

Ace handed the young man an envelope. His visitor had been waiting a while in the Four Aces but Jerome had been looking after him. The man promptly pulled out the wad of notes and counted them. 'Thanks. Happy to be of service. Glad you got the notification through the post that a Tom Smith of this address has passed the medical, with flying colours, for naval training.'

Jerome standing behind the bar, said, 'And why wouldn't we get the letter? You cost us enough. Fancy a drink?'

The young man shook his head. Ace watched him look keenly around the club. 'Nice place you've got here,' he said.

'I think so,' Ace replied. 'Obviously you didn't come up against any problems while taking the medical?'

'Never did before, didn't this time,' he said.

Ace was aware the man was used to taking the place of real candidates and having the doctors unknowingly examine him. It worked for insurance purposes as well.

He didn't like the man's condescending manner but they

were hardly likely to come into contact again in the near future so Ace smiled with his mouth but not his eyes.

The medical for the healthy bloke had been a walk-over. Tommo Smith was now in the navy.

'Just as a matter of interest,' said the man, nodding towards the official letter in Ace's hand, 'are you going to tell me where Tom Smith is going to do his training? We got more naval training bases here on the south coast in Portsmouth, Gosport and Fareham than anywhere else in the country, haven't we?'

Ace smiled again, a real smile this time. 'Tom Smith is to report to Faslane, Gare Loch. It's five miles from Helensburgh and they've enclosed a West Highland Line train ticket to Scotland.'

The young man slipped the money into his inside pocket, 'Couldn't be much further away, could it?' He nodded at Ace and left.

Jerome said, 'Now to tell our real Tommo Smith he's got his wish to join the navy.' He began polishing his spectacles.

Connie waved to Ace as his car slowly moved down Old Road. She'd never been in a sports car before and at first thought the cold November air would freeze her to death. Ace had asked her if she wanted to have the hood of the

MG VA Tourer up or down and she'd been so excited she'd opted to have it down. She'd been surprised at how low and comfortable the black car was and how it wasn't at all cold, despite the light wind ruffling her hair. In fact, sitting next to Ace as he deftly manoeuvred the controls made her feel quite special.

She'd already thumped on Len's front door and was touched to see Ace going very slowly until he was sure Len had opened it. The scent of antiseptic met her, along with Len's broad smile. His dark hair, slightly damp at the front, no doubt after his morning wash, curled on his forehead. His corduroy trousers were old but clean, and from his collarless shirt, open at the neck, she spied curly dark chest hair. He smelt of Imperial Leather soap.

'Queenie will be so happy to see you,' he said. 'She must be getting fed up with only us two to talk to. Give us your coat – it's warm upstairs.' Connie took it off and handed it to him. 'That's a pretty dress,' he said. 'But, then, I'm used to seeing you in your usherette's uniform.'

'This old thing! Thank you, anyway,' Connie said.

She didn't tell him that she had tried on all the clothes she had to find something that would look half decent for a meal out later with Ace. He wore smart suits, and his cashmere overcoat always matched the colour of his trilby hat.

The green woollen knee-length dress, tightly belted at the waist and with padded shoulders, was one of Marlene's cast-offs but she didn't tell him that.

From the kitchen she could hear the wireless playing jaunty band music, and from the ambience inside the house and Len's cheery manner she knew she should stop worrying so much about Queenie. She was obviously being well looked after. As she climbed the stairs Connie pondered Len's words.

'Us two,' he'd said. Of course, she thought. The midwife, Edith Stimson, had no doubt stayed the night sitting up with Queenie. No matter how bad Queenie had been it wouldn't have been right for her and Len to spend the night alone in his house, would it? Len would never compromise Queenie's reputation.

When she reached the hall at the top of the stairs there were two doors, one closed. Connie knocked on the one that was ajar.

'Don't be daft, I know it's you!'

Connie pushed open the door and entered with a smile that grew wider when she saw Queenie half lying, half sitting up in a iron-framed double bed with a patchwork quilt covering her. The base of the bed was higher than the head, propped up on stacks of books.

Connie couldn't believe her eyes. She'd expected to see a ghostly wraith lying there, but although Queenie's face was devoid of make-up and pale, she looked like a blonde angel reclining in the bed. Connie's mouth fell open.

'I know. I look better than I should, don't I? But don't be fooled. Edith has dosed me up with aspirins and I'm as weak as a kitten. The smile on my face is especially for you. Actually, I feel bloody awful.'

All Connie could do was nod. Yesterday she'd thought her friend was going to die. Today, thankfully, she could believe she might live. She was certainly chirpy enough, unless she was putting on an act to stop Connie worrying. And that might be exactly what Queenie was doing.

'I'm lucky to be alive. I could have bled to death. That stupid butcher of a woman has messed up my insides but I've been told with luck, hopefully she's not harmed the baby. Edith, the midwife, sat by my bedside, looking after me all night. And Len, poor lamb, has been running up- and downstairs at her beck and call. If it hadn't been for your quick thinking and their kindness I wouldn't be here.' She shook her head. 'I'm so sorry, Connie, for bringing all this unhappiness to your door.'

'You didn't know that visiting Etta Hines was going to end up like this, did you.'

Queenie shook her head. 'I blame myself,' she said. 'I thought everything would be so easy.' Suddenly her face screwed up in pain. Connie watched her hold her breath, then let it out slowly. Eventually the pain must have eased for Queenie carried on talking. 'When I fainted down by the bridge, I was glad to be out of it. Out of the shame I was bringing to everyone – and most for believing I'd killed my baby. A poor little scrap that I'd taken life from even before it had begun. I thought I was dying, Connie, and I knew I deserved it.'

Connie sat on the side of the bed and picked up one of Queenie's hands. She noticed Queenie was wearing a high-necked flannelette nightie, probably one of Edith's, she thought. 'You're not to blame. That awful woman is,' she said.

Queenie gripped Connie's fingers. 'No. It's my fault for believing a pack of lies from a man who said he loved me.'

Connie saw the brightness of tears in Queenie's eyes. Her voice was very small as she added, 'Edith says I haven't lost the baby. I'm so relieved about that. I've been given a second chance to love the little mite I'm carrying and I'm going to make sure I give it as much love as I've got.'

The bedroom door opened and Len came in, carrying two mugs. 'Thought you could both do with a cuppa,' he said. Connie saw his smile couldn't hide his tiredness. She also saw something else: the tenderness in his eyes as he set Queenie's mug on the bedside table, then looked at her. 'It's hot and I dare say too heavy for you at present. I'll help you with it later,' he said to her.

Connie took a sip of her tea and said, simply because she didn't know what else to say, 'Your lad Gary made a really good job of showing the films yesterday.'

'I knew he would,' Len said. 'He'll make fine projectionist. I'm going to the Criterion myself today.'

Connie couldn't help asking, 'Will there be someone with Queenie?' as if Queenie wasn't in the same room.

'Edith will be here,' he said. 'Tell me now, how did Mangle get over Queenie not turning up for work?'

'If you want the honest truth, I don't think he even noticed, because everyone rallied round.' Connie looked at Queenie. 'You're so well liked that no one minded doing a bit extra.'

Queenie at last had some colour in her face. She was actually blushing at Connie's words. 'They don't know do they?' she said, agitated.

'They believe you've got a bad stomach upset.'

'Thank God for that. With a bit of luck, I should be back—'

'You'll go back when you're fit enough. You'd be daft to do otherwise,' snapped Len. He looked quite fierce.

'Did the midwife say how long it'll be—' Connie was only going to ask when Edith thought Queenie might be well enough to get out of bed, but again Len jumped in.

'If she tries to do too much too soon it might have disastrous results.'

'Of course,' said Connie, chastened.

'Len told Gertie I could stay here indefinitely,' said Queenie, giving him a smile.

'Oh, yes,' said Connie. 'And what did she say to that?'

'She said he'd better get hold of my ration book.'

Len blushed, the colour rising from his neck. 'You going to try to drink this tea now?' Queenie nodded, and he held the mug to her lips. It was then Connie realized that the mug was too heavy for her to hold unaided. For all her forced high spirits Queenie was not well at all.

Connie heard the sound of the front door opening and a voice cried, 'Yoo-hoo! It's only me! I hope you like a nice rice pudding because that's what I've cooked for you.'

Connie looked at Len. 'Edith,' he said, replacing Queenie's mug on the table.

'I gathered that,' said Connie. As the front door closed downstairs a car's horn sounded. Connie rose from the bed, bent towards Queenie and kissed her cheek. 'That's Ace. I'd know the sound of that horn anywhere. He's picking me up so I'd better go. I can see you're being well looked after.' She turned to Len. 'Can I come and visit again tomorrow?'

'You come whenever you like,' he said, and she could tell by his tone that he meant it. 'I'll get your coat.'

Going downstairs, Connie could hear the rattling of pots in the scullery so she popped her head around the door to say hello. Edith was measuring out powder from screws of brown paper. On the table there were rolls of cotton wool and sanitary pads.

'Is that for Queenie?' Connie asked, then felt ridiculous: of course it was for Queenie. She saw the rice pudding, covered with a plate and keeping warm on the flat top of the range.

'Oh, hello, love.' Edith turned to face Connie. 'What did you think of Queenie?'

The question took Connie by surprise. 'She's a credit to you,' she said. 'She's well, considering.'

'"Considering" is a funny word,' the midwife said. 'I hope you weren't taken in by all the flannel she might have been giving you about feeling fine.'

Connie stared at her.

'You might well look at me like that,' Edith said. 'I

thought we were going to lose her last night. That woman up there,' she nodded towards the ceiling, 'should have a medal for pretending.'

Connie began, 'I didn't realize—' but Edith hadn't finished.

'Etta Hines wants hounding out of Gosport. One day she's going to kill some poor girl.' She paused. 'It was your auntie Gertie put her in touch with the woman, wasn't it?'

Connie knew where Edith's words were taking her. 'If Gertie had known more about Etta Hines, she wouldn't have allowed Queenie anywhere near that butcher,' she said.

'Come on, ladies,' broke in Len. 'This isn't the time for recriminations.'

'You saved Queenie's life, Edith. I can never thank you enough for that,' Connie said. 'She's the best friend I've ever had.'

She glanced at Len for reassurance, but it was Edith who said, 'I'm sorry, love. I didn't mean to let my feelings get the better of me but that woman and her botched abortions cause so much unhappiness.' She sighed. 'I shouldn't have ranted at you.' She stepped forward and enclosed Connie in a warm hug. 'Just you make sure you don't allow it to happen to you, my love.' She pushed Connie away and held her at arm's length. 'Promise me?'

'I promise,' said Connie. The words were hardly out

of her mouth when the MG's horn pierced the air again. Connie didn't want to keep Ace waiting any longer than was necessary.

Doing up her coat while walking along the passage to the front door she said to Len, 'Make sure she doesn't worry about her job. She's got good friends covering for her.'

Len opened the door, saw Ace sitting in the car and gave him a manly nod. He put his hand on Connie's shoulder. 'And you mustn't worry about her, either. I'm looking after her.'

Chapter Twenty-seven

Gertie sat with one foot in a bowl of hot salt water and breathed a sigh of relief as she lowered in the other. Next to her was the kitchen table, with a cup of tea, the brown teapot, and a packet of Woodbines she'd taken from the bag of groceries Ace had brought round. A clean towel was draped over the back of her chair.

'He's a good boy,' she said out loud. She reached for the cigarettes and matches, and before she lit up she lifted out her left foot and looked at the bunion near her big toe. 'You devil, you,' she addressed the bunion. 'You're making yourself known to me now, aren't you?' She examined her toenails and decided she would cut them later. For a moment she listened to the wireless. That nice girl with the long hair and clear voice was singing 'We'll Meet Again'. Very pretty, she is, thought Gertie, Vera somebody.

With both feet back in the water she took a long drag on the cigarette she'd just lit and sat back comfortably on the chair.

She knew exactly what she was going to make for a meal later on. A nice fish pie with the cod, and a syrup sponge with the tin of syrup she'd found in the bottom of the carrier bag. The fish was lovely and fresh now but it needed to be used up before it went off.

Gertie swivelled round, laid her cigarette in the saucer and picked up her cup. She took a long swallow. 'That's nectar, that is,' she informed the room. She thought about her morning's cleaning job at the Criterion. Not much had been said by the staff about Queenie's absence. There had been commiserations, of course. Queenie's duties would be covered. People mucked in, didn't they? But everyone knew it was foolhardy to come back to work before stomach upsets were properly better. Diarrhoea and sickness could lay people low like ninepins, couldn't they?

Mr Mangle had been absent. He'd left a message saying he'd be away tonight as well. Gertie clicked her false teeth. That man, she thought, didn't care about the picture house one little bit. She drank the rest of her tea and picked a stray tea leaf from her lip.

Her cigarette on the saucer had gone out. She relit it, taking a long drag to settle her nerves. Well, she thought, when your fag goes out for no proper reason, of course it makes you nervy.

She thought about the peculiar thing that Doris Castle, a new cleaner, had said this morning after Gertie had finished collecting her dog-ends from the ashtrays for Mr Mason.

Doris had said that Fanny Taylor, who lived next door to Etta Hines in Old Road, had found Etta in a right mood as she was going to the lavatory at the bottom of her garden. Apparently, last night someone had pushed a letter through the hole in Etta's front door.

Etta had shown Fanny the letter that was in her apron pocket. It was on posh cream paper and the envelope matched. Fanny said it must have come from someone with a bit of money – who would waste an unmarked envelope like that on something hand-delivered?

The single page said, 'You may want to rethink the help you give pregnant women.'

Fanny said there was no stamp on the envelope, no names on the letter. It was definitely meant for Etta, because everyone knew what she got up to in her upstairs back room.

The letter was typewritten and Etta Hines had probably never seen a typewriter, let alone knew anyone who owned one or could type. Etta had been up all night, worrying about what it really meant, Fanny said.

'I told Doris what it meant, didn't I?' said Gertie, to the empty room. 'Those posh words mean she's to stop messing about with women's insides.' Gertie thought for a moment. 'If I'd known what was going to happen to poor Queenie, I'd never have let her go anywhere near Old Road.' Gertie felt the sadness close down over her. 'I wish I'd never heard of Etta Hines.'

Gertie gave a big sigh. The water in the bowl had gone cold. She reached for the packet of Woodbines and lit up gratefully. The tea in the pot was probably still warm.

The music had stopped on the wireless and the news was now on. Alvar Liddell was talking. She liked his voice. Gertie stared at the blackout curtains and listened in amazement. A health service for after the war? The Beveridge Report? Means testing to be abolished? The government to bring in a comprehensive compulsory insurance scheme? Free medical and hospital treatment? Retirement pensions, possibly two pounds a week for a husband and wife?

Gertie took a long lungful of nicotine. She hadn't heard all of it but it sounded too good to be true.

Well, that information certainly hadn't been shown on the Pathé News at the Criterion picture house, had it? And all this was going to come from a deduction of four shillings and threepence from men's weekly wages? And even less from women's pay? Employers would contribute half a crown a week. Well, they'd have to chip in something, wouldn't they? Stands to reason, doesn't it? she thought.

Gertie tried to listen carefully so she could tell Ace. He'd want to know about this. Just imagine all that really happening. Wouldn't it be wonderful not to have to find money, when there was no money to be found, for a doctor?

Thinking of telling Ace about the new welfare state reminded her she had planned to make a fish pie with the cod. And a syrup sponge for afters.

She began to hum along to the wireless after she'd stubbed out her fag. The news was finished now. Artie Shaw's band was playing 'Frenesi', one of her favourites. He'd been going around with Betty Grable, hadn't he? The Hollywood star! But he'd dumped her! Imagine a bloke dumping the girl with the Million Dollar Legs! There must be some lovely places to go to in Hollywood.

That made her think of Connie going out for a meal with Ace. It was about time that girl got out and about. Ace would be kind to her – he was a lovely man. But eating in the middle of the day meant they'd both be starving tonight after they'd finished work.

Gertie felt the teapot under the cosy. It was barely warm. She screwed up her face. She'd make fresh tea in a minute.

The ration of two ounces a week didn't go anywhere, did it? But she had plenty of tea: Ace saw to that.

Gertie pulled the towel from the back of her chair, dried one foot thoroughly, put on a slipper with a pom-pom on the top, then dried the other and pushed it into the slipper with a hole cut into it to accommodate her bunion. Picking up the bowl of water, she put it on the kitchen table so she wouldn't fall over it while she was cooking. Her feet definitely felt better than they had when she'd first come home from work.

She opened the cupboard door near the window where she kept most of her food and took out the block of salt. She'd need that, and pepper. Flour and bicarbonate of soda, for the syrup sponge.

Leaving those on the table, she scrabbled in the sideboard drawer for the potato knife, spoons and a fork and put them ready on the table. The fish was in the scullery, and she'd already taken the tin of syrup out of the carrier bag. Gertie found her oven dish, her cake tin, enough potatoes to peel, a couple of onions, and saw she had nearly a pint of milk standing on the draining-board, which she carried separately. After piling the ingredients into the oven dish she managed to carry it all into the kitchen. With her back to the warmth of the range, she could prepare the fish pie and the syrup sponge. Neither would take more than half an hour to cook.

But first, Gertie thought, a cup of tea and a fag would go down very well.

Chapter Twenty-eight

'Are you sure you're not cold?' Ace took his eyes from the road for a moment to stare at Connie.

'Not at all,' she said. She had snuggled down in the seat next to him and felt the warmth of his body close to her in the MG VA Tourer. The sun had decided to make an appearance and a breeze swept her hair away from her face. He'd turned back to watch the road and she studied her side view of him. She liked what she saw: his brandy-coloured hair doing exactly what it wanted to do, even with the light sheen of Brylcreem, his nose, aquiline, his lips pressed together as he studied the light traffic ahead on the road out of Gosport and his chin, determined. Watching him made her feel happy inside. He was a good-looking man, but not chocolate-box pretty, more rugged, and again she thought of Clark Gable. Every so often she caught a hint of his lemony cologne.

He must have felt her staring for he turned again, 'What?' he asked, with a little laugh, as though he knew exactly what she was thinking. 'How well do you know that Len Gregory bloke?'

'Not well,' she answered immediately. 'We work together – well, not exactly together. He's the projectionist.'

'He put his hand on you.' Ace gave her a quick enquiring look.

Smartly she retorted, 'He should have given me kiss and a cuddle for the way I nearly killed myself running down to his house to get help for his Queenie.'

Ace laughed. 'Like that, is it?'

'It's early days but I've seen the way he looks at her.'

'So, you can tell by the way a man looks at a woman if he likes her?'

'I can tell by the way you keep looking at me instead of the road that you like me.' She smiled at him.

'Damn! I was hoping to keep it a secret,' he said.

They were out of Gosport now, with the bombed buildings and their rubble piled back from the main road, but the stink of cordite and burning still swept over her. Like Gertie's Woodbines, she thought, and smiled to herself. She stared at the passing scenery. On her left Portchester Harbour looked inviting in the brief sunshine. Shipbuilding premises lined the shore, and Connie saw they were heading towards Portsmouth. For a moment panic gripped her. She hadn't been back to Portsmouth since her mother had died. She certainly had no wish to be reminded further of that terrible period in her life. She was trying to forget, wasn't she?

He must have been reading her mind again for Ace put his hand on her knee. 'Don't worry, we're going nowhere near where you used to live.'

He drove through a maze of small streets, many of them with gaps between the houses where enemy bombs had blown them to smithereens.

And then there was the sea! Glittering in the sunshine, with tiny white waves breaking up its blue-grey surface. The stony beach was covered with barbed wire to help keep away marauding Germans.

'Is the beach mined as well?' she asked.

'Probably, but if it is, it'll be where we're not allowed to wander.'

Across the water she could see the Isle of Wight, lying like a green jewel in the Solent.

Now they were driving past the large hotels set back on Southsea's sea-front. She wondered if they were going to one of the sumptuous white-painted buildings but he carried on past the ornamental gardens and the common, heading towards the pier.

Despite the wind off the sea bringing the pungent smell of salt and ozone, she could also smell chestnuts, their shells burning on an open fire, and onions frying, greasy and sweet, the combination making her feel suddenly hungry. And then she heard the music, Jimmie Davis singing 'You Are My Sunshine'. Her spirits lifted even more, if that were possible, and she started to sing along with the American's cheery voice, which seemed to be growing louder.

Ace started laughing. 'It doesn't take a great deal to make you happy, does it?'

And then she saw where he had brought her.

He parked the car on a nearby road and, without waiting for him to open the door for her, she scrambled out and stood looking at the fairground on the sea-front.

'I thought things like this were all closed down,' Connie said. The music, the smells, the voices calling for people to spend money, the laughter of kids on the roundabouts instantly transformed her into a child again.

'It'll close as soon as it becomes dusk,' he said. 'The blackout takes care of that. But the government decided we need entertainment so this time round the funfairs go on trading. During the Great War the fairs closed and many showmen went out of business – it was a bad time all round. Now, despite the men joining the services, their families, the women mostly, keep up the country's morale.' He paused. 'I thought I'd bring you here before we go and have a meal—'

Connie interrupted him: 'Does that mean I don't get to eat any hot chestnuts?' She'd listened to him talking, telling her about things she knew nothing about, and decided there was a lot she didn't know about Ace Gallagher but would like to learn.

'You can have what you like,' he said, gripping her elbow with one hand and picking up his hat from behind the driver's seat with the other, setting it at a jaunty angle on his head. Connie gazed at him, a thought running through her mind: I could really, really get to like this man.

He grabbed her hand and dragged her across the road towards the fair's entrance.

'Where first?' he asked. He probably saw it before she did: the rotund man standing beside the burning brazier with a grill across its top steaming chestnuts, their shells brown, the smell achingly wonderful cutting through the air towards them. 'Aha!' shouted Ace. 'Your wish is my command!' And in a very short while she was passing the brown paper bag of hot chestnuts from hand to hand as it burned her fingers.

'They taste as good as they look,' she said, passing the bag to him and laughing as his face contorted with mock pain at the heat. He bit into one after shelling it, then clutched his throat as though the chestnut had poisoned him.

'You fool!' she said. 'The horses. We must go on the horses.'

Again, pulling her by the arm, he hurried past people, dragging her to the majestic roundabout, which had just stopped. He stepped up onto it and put his hand on the head of a noble horse. 'This must be yours, Her name's Emma.'

Connie breathless, just managed to ask, 'And which one's yours?'

Ace helped her climb onto its back, then straddled the one next to Emma and said, 'This one, of course. His name's Bert.'

She offered him the last chestnut in the bag.

'You eat it,' he said. 'I don't want to spoil my lunch.'

When it was gone, Connie looked for somewhere to put the screw of paper now it contained only bits of shell. Ace held out his hand and she ceremoniously dropped the paper into it.

Within a very short while, all the steeds had people sitting on them and the hurdy-gurdy music started up again. A young lad, wearing a flat cap and with a red kerchief tied jauntily around his neck, took the fares from Ace and the other passengers, and the ride started. The horses rose and fell as they travelled round and round. Every so often as their horses passed each other, Ace smiled widely at her.

Connie could see high above the people walking around the fairground. The excitement she felt at being out on such a wonderful day with a man like Ace made her feel twice as tall as the ride.

Eventually the music stopped and the customers climbed down.

'Look, there's the rifle range. C'mon, I'll win you a teddy bear!'

A woman stood behind the stall. She was extraordinarily pretty, Connie thought, with curly dark hair hanging down her back, a long skirt, and a shawl covering a white blouse. Gold hoops swung from her ears. Toy animals hung all around her, but the biggest and best were the huge golden bears with brown glass eyes.

'Have a go, sir? This rifle's spare,' said the woman, giving Ace change. 'Gonna win your girl a prize?' She handed him the rifle and he stood next to a young man who wasn't having any luck hitting the line of ducks as they bobbed along at the back of the stall. Connie felt proud to be mistaken for Ace's girl, and grinned at the young woman.

'Try again, sir,' said the woman, to the disgruntled young fellow edging away. 'Maybe your luck's changed.'

Connie noticed he didn't turn his head to reply.

Ace raised the gun to his shoulder and looked along the sights. He fired. Connie gasped. A little yellow duck keeled over. He aimed, fired again, and a second duck slid sideways. He looked at Connie, winked, and fired a third time, causing his third duck to fall.

The woman cried, 'See, you lot? Everyone's a winner at my rifle range!' Two men from the crowd, urged on by her enthusiasm, waited for rifles. To Ace the woman whispered, 'You don't get another go, mate.' Loudly she cried, 'Well done, sir, pick your prize. Anything on the stall except me!' She laughed.

'What's your choice, Connie?' Ace asked.

'A bear! A bear!' Connie was overjoyed. As they walked away, Connie cuddling the teddy, which smelt of toffee apples and cigarettes, she said, 'I didn't know you were a crack shot.'

Ace put his arm around her. 'There's a lot you don't know about me, Connie.'

Connie lowered her eyes, then looked up shyly. 'Perhaps it's time I found out.'

His arm tightened around her while he stood looking at

her. It was as if some magic wand had been waved over them, she thought, and she and Ace were the only people present, although the fairground was filled with people, noise and music. How long they stood gazing at each other Connie couldn't tell, but it was Ace who broke the spell by looking at his watch. 'We have work to get to later and I promised you lunch. We can go on one more ride. Which would you like it to be?'

Connie was about to tell him he should choose when she spotted the Dodgem cars.

His eyes followed hers and he said, 'Good choice.' She liked it that he could practically read her thoughts. 'Give us that,' he said, taking the bear from her and propelling her through the crowds. While they waited for the customers to climb out of the brightly coloured bumper cars and the next session to begin, he said, 'I'm thinking you'd like a car to yourself!'

Connie's mouth opened involuntarily. The idea of sitting alone next to the huge stuffed toy while trying to escape being crashed into filled her with alarm. He started laughing.

'I guess not!' The cars slowed to a halt. 'Quick!' he said. 'The green one!' From all round the edges of the covered area where the squat cars were electrically operated people surged forward to get into them almost before the current drivers had left. And then Connie, the bear and Ace were tightly fitted into the little green car and the roustabout, with his leather purse, was leaning in for payment.

'Three, is it?' the greasy-haired youth asked, staring at the bear.

Connie was still laughing as Ace paid their fares. She could hardly move in the small space and suddenly, illogically, wished she was sitting next to Ace, which was where the bear was propped.

With the music blaring, the car being shunted this way and that, and every so often either Ace or herself pulling the bear back onto the seat from the floor, Connie was screaming and laughing like the rest of the bumper-car occupants. 'Oh!' she said, as the music stopped. She felt quite sad as Ace stepped out of the little car and put out a hand to help her. With the bear under his arm and his hand gripping Connie's, they moved away from the Dodgems. 'I'm having such a lovely day,' Connie said. 'I can't remember when I ever laughed so much.'

They were heading towards the exit.

'It's not over yet.' Ace hoisted up the bear – it had slipped down – stopped on the pavement and stared at her. 'What's this bear's name? We can't go on calling it, him, Bear?'

Connie thought quickly as she looked up into Ace's

smiling face. 'Bert,' she said. 'I know it was your horse's name on the roundabout but it can be a bear's name as well, can't it?'

Ace held the big soft toy out in front of him. 'Welcome to our world, Bertie Bear!'

Connie began laughing again. 'Oh, you are daft!' But she knew she loved him for his daftness. And as they ran hand in hand, Ace grasping the bear, towards the MG waiting for them at the side of the road, it suddenly struck her which word she'd just used in her mind about Ace. Love him?

What did she know about love? All the love she'd ever experienced between men and women had occurred while she was sitting in a picture house! Love to her was the hero-worship she felt when cutting out handsome male stars from magazines and pasting them into scrapbooks. In films she'd seen what happiness love could bring and the unhappiness it wreaked when it all went wrong.

Ace was making her happy. A man had never done that before. Was that love, though? It was exciting being with him and surely she didn't want anything more than that, did she?

Chapter Twenty-nine

Connie gazed around the hotel restaurant in wonder. Potted palms, tall and feathery, stood around the edges of the huge room as though guarding all the guests sitting and eating at the tables, which bore startlingly white cloths.

On a dais a small orchestra, the musicians dressed in evening suits, played popular music, encouraging a few well-dressed couples to move rhythmically on the highly polished floor. Connie took a deep breath of the air, which smelt of perfume and cigars.

'This way, Mr Gallagher.' The head waiter, obviously knowing Ace, led them to a table for two where the large ceiling-to-floor window gave an uninterrupted view of the sea yet was fairly secluded from the other diners.

Ace nodded at the man, who presented each of them with a leather-bound menu and disappeared. Connie, now sitting down, looked from the menu to the other patrons, some eating, some dancing. Her stomach was full of butterflies.

Earlier today she'd been happy with how she looked in Marlene's cast-off green dress. Now, her coat left with the cloakroom attendant, she felt out of place. Some of the women were dressed up to the nines in glittery clothing, but she also spotted servicewomen in their uniforms sitting at tables and at the bar, which helped her confidence to return.

'What do you fancy to eat?' Ace looked across the small table at her.

Connie had been staring at two men in smart suits who were tucking into chops, the biggest she had ever seen, with golden chips and green peas. Her mouth watered.

'Those look nice,' she said, inclining her head towards the table and the piled plates.

'You do realize Gertie will leave out something for us for later?' Ace was smiling at her.

'Of course, but I'll have done a shift at the Criterion by then and I'll be starving again.' She thought for a moment, then glanced at Ace with his unruly brandy-coloured hair falling across his forehead and his eyes scanning his menu. 'Would a big chop like that be very expensive?' She didn't want to appear greedy or expect him to have to pay for something that cost a lot of money.

From the amusement on his face she realized once more that he had read her mind. 'Connie, my love, you can have anything on the menu your heart desires!'

'I want the chop, then.'

'Good girl,' he said. 'I'll have the same. What d'you want to drink?'

'A cup of tea.'

Again, his lips pressed together, then rose in a smile. A waiter was now hovering. Ace said, 'A large whisky for me, a pot of tea for the lady and pork chops for the two of us.'

The waiter wrote down the order, then asked, 'Something to start?' Ace shook his head. The waiter thanked him and was gone.

Connie hadn't thought before that Ace was well off. To her, he was Ace, Gertie's lodger. And a lodger often lives with a family because he or she has nowhere else to stay. But, of course, that wasn't true of Ace Gallagher. He owned a prosperous club. She had never set foot in it, but Gertie had, and apparently above the club there was a huge apartment that was very well furnished. Gertie had also told her that a man named Jerome, who was like a father to Ace, also had a flat above the club. Connie had never met Jerome either. That was not surprising as she worked late at the picture house and seldom went out. Since coming to Gosport from Portsmouth she had considered herself very lucky to be doing a job she adored, especially as she'd become firm friends with Queenie. Connie had also decided she was fortunate to live with her aunt, who really cared about her. She wondered if Ace, now that the club had been rebuilt, was still lodging with her aunt because he, too, liked Gertie mothering him. She treated him like a son, didn't she? Connie wondered if, deep down, Ace was lonely. Not that he was short of women, so Gertie said. He simply hadn't found the right one, yet.

'When you offered to buy me a meal, I never expected it to be in a place like this,' she said.

'Don't you like it?'

'Yes!'

'I thought we could dance.' His silvery eyes were staring at her as he waited for a reply.

'Oh dear.'

'What's the matter?'

'I can't dance,' she said.

He was quiet for a moment. 'That never occurred to me.' She could see he was very deep in thought now. Then he asked, 'Have you never met anyone who could teach you?'

Connie shook her head. 'Queenie said, "You just let yourself move to the rhythm." We were planning on going dancing together but then all this horrible stuff happened.'

'Who's "we"?' A frown line had appeared across his forehead.

'Why, me and Queenie,' she said.

It seemed to Connie that Ace had been looking at her in a most peculiar way before he gave a sort of relieved sigh. Just then the waiter arrived with their order and she forgot about their conversation.

Obviously Ace hadn't, for when the waiter had finished setting out side plates and adjusting serviettes, which he called napkins and Connie thought were almost as big as babies' nappies, Ace asked, 'So, you've not been dancing with anyone while you've been living with Gertie?'

Connie shook her head. He was becoming quite persistent about this dancing lark, she thought, but dismissed it because their waiter was serving their lunch.

'Just look at the size of this chop!' It lay across her plate from side to side, its outer edge crispy and succulent. She took a deep breath. 'Oh, I am glad you brought me here,' she said. 'I can't remember the last time I saw so much meat. This war has spoiled everything!' Then she grimaced. 'I'm sorry, Ace,' she said. 'I don't mean that the extras you give Gertie aren't very welcome, very welcome indeed,' she repeated. 'But, come on now, have you seen a chop as big as this lately?'

She didn't wait for his answer but began cutting into the juicy flesh. She looked up from her plate and Ace was still watching her. He said, 'I need an answer from you as to why you'll eat black-market food I bring to the house but you wouldn't accept the lipstick.'

'That's a good question,' she said. 'We both know Gertie works hard to provide the best she can for both you and me. Food is impersonal – all three of us eat what you sometimes provide. To me that lipstick was a personal item. At that time, I didn't want to feel beholden to a man I knew nothing about and who might expect more than I wanted to give in return for a present.' She smiled. 'Your reputation, you know—'

'But now you're willing to come out with me?'

She nodded. 'Time's passed and I don't believe you'd do anything to compromise me. I feel sure you have only my best interests at heart.' She was looking into his eyes, and was surprised when he narrowed his gaze, picked up his glass and finished his drink without speaking.

Something hitting the window almost but not quite took her rapturous attention away from the chop and Ace. 'It's raining!' she said, and grinned at him, lightening the atmosphere. 'It was a good idea of yours to put up the hood on the car. Bertie Bear won't get wet now, will he?' She swallowed another mouthful of meat, sat back in her chair and raised her eyes heavenwards. 'Oh, lovely,' she murmured.

'What are you going to do with that thing?'

'If by "thing" you mean Bertie,' she speared a chip with her fork and thought for a moment, 'I might put one of my nighties on him and sit him on a chair in my room. When Gertie puts the light on, she'll have a fit, won't she?' He was staring at her again and, for a moment, she thought he was cross with her for suggesting such a thing, but then he laughed and she knew it was going to be all right. She could say what she wanted to this man without fear of him thinking she meant to harm anyone.

Connie relaxed and went on with the business of eating. She couldn't manage it all but when she looked at Ace's plate, she saw that, although he'd drunk his whisky, he'd hardly touched his food.

'Didn't you like it?' she asked, placing her knife and fork together on her plate to signify she'd finished.

'I prefer to watch you eat. Anyway, I can't dance on a full stomach,' he said.

'I told you, I don't know how to dance.' She poured herself tea from the small metal teapot.

'Name a favourite song of yours.'

She looked at him as though he'd suddenly gone mad but instantly she replied, '"Green Eyes".'

Ace pushed back his chair and rose. She saw him signal to a waiter, probably to announce they'd eaten and the table could be cleared, then watched as he walked through the dancers on the floor to the musicians on the dais. The conductor, still waving his baton, turned to listen to him and nodded. Within moments Ace was back at the table, his hand held out to her.

'"Green Eyes" is a waltz. Queenie has told you the truth. The steps are simple, so just let your body move to the rhythm.'

Her heart was thumping against her ribcage so loudly Connie thought it would eclipse the music. She wanted to refuse, to sit on the chair and not move from it. But if she did that the other diners and dancers would see and she'd feel so embarrassed she'd want to die.

Connie took his hand and stood up. Her napkin, which had been lying across her lap, fell under the table. Ignore it or pick it up? Ace's hand felt warm, inviting. Disregarding the napkin, she allowed it to stay where it had fallen and followed her heart and Ace onto the floor.

He stood in front of her. 'First, don't worry about what anyone else is doing. They're too busy worrying about themselves to look at you.' He put out his hand and invited her to hold it. His other encircled her back and she automatically allowed her arm to lie along his. 'That's good,' he said. 'Now for the easy part. Count one, two, three, and again, one, two, three. It's called a box step. Just follow me and repeat.'

The music, 'Green Eyes', filled her heart and within moments she found she could move along with him without concentrating on the steps. Connie, wearing heels, still found she had to look up to Ace. She liked being in his arms.

'I'm dancing,' she said, her amazement in her voice.

'And you're doing it very well.' He smiled down at her.

She discovered she liked being held by him: he was light on his feet and the fresh citrus smell of his cologne made her want to press herself closer to him. Eventually the waltz finished but almost immediately the orchestra began playing again, this time with a faster tempo.

She frowned. 'My feet don't fit with this music,' she said, falling against him. He pulled her close to stop her stumbling and held her perhaps just a little too long. 'Whoops!' she said. He didn't move but looked down at her, still cocooned in his arms. She was quite content to stay there, but as their eyes met, she thought she saw a wave of regret in his.

'That's because it's a different dance,' he said kindly. Then, 'Connie, my love, I hate to say it but I think we're finished with our lesson for today.' He glanced at his watch, then at her. 'And, sadly, we're both due back in Gosport.'

Chapter Thirty

Connie heard light footsteps approaching the door as she waited outside Leonard Gregory's house. 'What are you doing out of bed?' she couldn't help saying, as Queenie, wrapped in an over-large dressing-gown, opened the door.

'I'm feeling stronger each day now.' Queenie pulled Connie into the hallway. 'I was hoping you'd visit,' she said. 'I can get out of bed and potter about, so Edith said, as long as I don't lift anything heavy.'

Connie hugged her. 'Well, that's good, isn't it?'

Queenie nodded. 'I can't wait to get back to work.' She put her hands across her stomach. 'That awful sickness has gone and I need to earn some money.' Then she added, 'That butcher woman, Etta Hines, has had another funny letter posted through her door.'

'Another?' Connie knew about the first.

'Edith told me.'

'What did it say?'

'That's the peculiar thing. Apparently, it said exactly the same as the other one. "You may want to rethink the help you give pregnant women."'

Connie looked at her. 'And has she?'

Queenie shrugged her shoulders. 'Edith didn't say anything about that but it's got Etta all scared.'

'No one's hurt her or anything?'

'No,' said Queenie. 'But that's the frightening part, isn't it? Her wondering if, or when, something awful might happen.'

Connie knew she was right. Whoever the mystery letter writer was, if they frightened that awful woman into stopping her horrible craft, it could only be to the good, couldn't it? Queenie led her into the kitchen. As she followed, Connie was aware of the scent of Californian Poppy. 'Sit down and I'll make tea.'

'On your own?' Connie couldn't hear anyone else in the house. The wireless was playing softly, Frank Sinatra singing 'How Deep Is The Ocean'. Queenie had gone into the scullery.

'You've just missed Edith,' called Queenie. 'She's gone home to her own house and she'll be back later. Len's at work.'

'Early for him, isn't it?' Connie asked. She took off her coat and put it over the back of a kitchen chair.

'He wanted to get in before Mangle, if our beloved manager turns up, that is. Len trusts young Gary but was worried Mangle was sniffing about. He could quite easily sack Gary for not informing on Len taking time off without good reason. Besides, today's the day the van comes to exchange the films.'

'I would have thought you're a good enough reason,' said Connie.

'But Mangle doesn't know about me, does he? Hopefully he still thinks I've got a stomach upset. Len's trying to help me keep my job.'

'That man's useless at running the Criterion. You'd make a better job of it than he does.' Connie was thoughtful. 'When you're there, you do his work for him.' Queenie loved her job and worked extra hours without pay making sure the patrons were satisfied.

'I heard he'd even got you doing the accounts.'

'I don't mind that. The man's not good with figures.'

Connie heard Queenie giggling to herself. 'What's so funny?' Connie went to the scullery door. Queenie was still giggling.

'I said Mangle's not good with figures – but he thinks he

is, doesn't he? The way he gets so close so he can run his hands over girls' bodies!'

Connie shivered. 'Shut up! He gives me the creeps!'

She watched Queenie placing cups and saucers on a tray, then filling the teapot with boiling water.

'What's showing next?' Connie wanted to know the titles of the next films to appear on screen.

'*You'll Never Get Rich*, with Fred Astaire and Rita Hayworth.'

'That'll be good. What's the second feature?'

'Some British film with Arthur Askey.'

Connie wrinkled her nose as Queenie picked up the tray. 'Thought you weren't supposed to carry heavy things.' She was cross with Queenie and took the tray from her hands.

'Stop fussing and tell me how your afternoon out with Ace went.' Queenie allowed Connie to carry the tray into the kitchen, sinking down on a chair opposite the one Connie had vacated. 'Did he kiss you?'

Connie frowned at her. 'No.'

Queenie tutted. 'Why not?'

'Because he didn't! But he won me a huge teddy bear on the rifle range.'

Queenie was waiting for her to go on.

Connie giggled. 'I mean a really big soft teddy. When we got back to Alma Street, Gertie was in the kitchen pressing your usherette uniform that she'd washed. I managed to get the bear upstairs to her bedroom without her seeing it and tucked it in her bed. Ace gave me a flat cap, and from the doorway the bear looked just like a real man asleep in Gertie's bed!' Connie was laughing. 'I know it was a really unkind thing to do.'

'What happened?' Queenie asked.

'When Gertie went up to her room, she started screaming! I know we shouldn't but we laughed ourselves silly, me and Ace. Gertie was ever so put out! We had to make it up to her by lighting her fags and making her tea for the rest of the time we were with her.'

Queenie was laughing now. 'That's not nice,' she said. 'I still don't understand why he didn't kiss you.'

Connie had asked herself the same question. 'There were times when we were so close and I thought he might, but he was a perfect gentleman.'

Queenie stared at her. 'If my American had been a perfect gentleman, I wouldn't be in this mess, would I?'

Connie thought it better she didn't answer that. Instead she said, 'I always think things are meant to be. What goes around, comes around When I first met Ace, I believed he thought he was God's gift to women. I wouldn't even let him give me a lift in that posh car of his, remember? But now I know there's more to him than meets the eye.'

Queenie began pouring the tea. 'What do you mean?'

'I think he's lonely.' She got no further for Queenie gave a big guffaw.

'Lonely, be buggered! Hasn't he got a flourishing club, money, his pick of all them girls he employs? How can he be lonely?' She was leaning forward across the table waiting for Connie to answer.

'Right, Miss Know-It-All.' Connie was ready with her answer. 'How come, even though he has a perfectly good, fully furnished place to live at the club, he prefers to stay with our Gertie?'

Queenie stared at her, her eyes unflinching. 'I would have thought that was obvious. He wants you!'

There was silence. A log spat in the range. Connie let her eyes travel around the homely kitchen with its serviceable furniture. The room was devoid of a woman's touch, she noticed. But didn't Len live here alone? At least he had, until he'd taken Queenie in out of the goodness of his heart.

Quietly, pulling her cup of tea towards her, she asked, 'Do you really think that?'

Queenie nodded. 'Don't you?' she asked.

'But why? I'm nothing special.'

'There you go again, always putting yourself down. Connie, you're a beautiful human being and you're totally unspoiled. I doubt you've ever made love with a man, have you?'

Connie knew she was colouring. 'If you mean, had "it" with a feller then the answer is no.' She picked up her cup. The conversation had made her nervous and her hand was shaking. 'I don't want to talk about it any more,' she said. 'I came round here to see you – ask if you needed anything from your own home.'

Queenie laughed. 'Gertie went and picked up some bits and pieces. She forgot quite a lot, too.' She ran a hand across the dressing-gown. 'But Len looks after me.'

'Do you think you and he . . .'

Queenie took a deep breath. 'Don't you dare go reading anything into me being looked after by Leonard Gregory as anything more than a friendly gesture. He's a kind man, that's all.'

Connie smiled at her. 'Just a thought,' she said.

Chapter Thirty-one

Tommo slid out of his bunk and went to his locker. The wooden floor was freezing to his feet and made him shiver, even though he wore thick socks. The air inside the Nissen hut smelt of fags, farts and ashes because the pot-bellied stove had gone out while he and his mates slept. It was so cold his breath frosted over.

He didn't light a lamp because he didn't want to wake any of them. He fumbled around in the metal compartment and lifted out the extra blanket he'd begged from the stores. He'd never experienced cold like this, he thought, never. And when it wasn't cold it was raining and the wind blew you off your feet. And anything outside the hut that wasn't nailed down in the open air got blown away and you never saw it again. Snow, too, had been a problem when they'd had to dig themselves out to get to the canteen.

'This is Scotland, Tommo, old mate. Sometimes we get four different lots of weather in one day. Can't you lily-livered soft southerner of an Englishman take real weather?'

'Hamish, I can take anything you or the weather or His Majesty's Naval Boatyard can dish out,' he'd said, and put his back into shovelling away the ice.

Of course, it was fine in the hut when the stove was alight but when it had burned itself out, like now, it was like Hell iced over. But Tommo smiled to himself, ruefully. He'd got what he'd wanted and he was in the navy now.

He folded the blanket in two and laid it on his bunk. Once inside his covers he thought back to the evening Ace had sent Jerome to the club's bar to accompany Tommo to his office.

'He won't be long. Hang about outside until he calls you in.' Jerome had smiled at him. He'd had that cat in his arms he was so fond of and it was purring away like a bleedin' alarm clock. 'He's just finishing typing up some correspondence. You know what it's like when you get disturbed doing anything. The train of thought goes, don't it?'

Tommo had nodded, letting Jerome know he understood, and the elderly man had pushed his spectacles onto the bridge of his nose and ambled off. Tommo had waited, wondering what was going on but knowing it couldn't be work-related: lately he'd charmed more old dears up to the gambling tables than ever before.

It wasn't long before Ace opened the door saying, 'Come on in, Tommo. You've had a letter delivered here.' He held an official envelope. 'It looks important,' he said, going over to his desk and sitting down on his leather armchair.

Tommo's stomach had turned somersaults. 'You said I could use this address to apply to go in the services.'

'Course I did,' said Ace. 'And didn't I arrange for someone else to take your medical? Someone who also provided forged papers?'

He handed Tommo the letter and he turned it over and over in his hands, not daring to open it.

'Go on, mate, open it.'

So Tommo had, and after reading it, his heart was full of pride and excitement. 'You've done it!' he cried. 'You promised to get me into the navy even though I'm sup-posed to have a heart murmur and you've bloody gone and done it!'

Tommo could remember his excitement. He'd wanted to crush Ace in his arms, like he was his father, but didn't feel that was quite appropriate. 'You're the best mate anyone could have. You've made my dream come true,' Tommo had said.

'So, where are they sending you?' Ace had been really interested, happy for him.

Tommo had reread the letter. 'Scotland,' he'd said. Ace had taken it from him and read it himself.

'Leaving so soon?' Ace had said. 'And they've issued a travel warrant. How do you feel about it all?'

'Bloody marvellous,' Tommo had said. And he had, then.

It was a little different when he'd arrived for basic training at Faslane.

Gare Loch was home to submarines and ships, and boasted easy access to the north Atlantic and the Norwegian Sea. It was also an emergency port and marshalling yard, handling supplies, weapons and storage. Isolated, surrounded by moorland and heather, and incredibly windswept. Built in 1941 and five miles from Helensburgh, it had taken Tommo quite a while to become used to a different way of life from the one he had left in Gosport.

The work was hard. He was lifting weights he'd never thought possible, working long hours and using muscles he never knew he had. Tools that were so heavy that at first he hadn't been able to lift them were lightweight now and used to repair engines and parts of machines that were becoming increasingly familiar to him. It was certainly more strenuous than dancing, though that could be tiring enough.

How he'd survived the strenuous training was a miracle to him. Running, marching with packs on his back that weighed a ton. Being shouted at by a higher- ranking bloke he had to obey when all he wanted to do was kill him. And cleaning! Every little thing had to be bloody polished so he could see his face in it. Yet somehow he had emerged from it all with a smile on his face and a dark blue uniform to be proud of.

The food was plentiful and of excellent quality, and most nights he slept as soon as his head hit the pillow.

Tommo had always considered himself a bit of a loner. But perhaps the seclusion of the port made him integrate more with his fellow men. Hamish McKay, a beefy Glasgow bloke who read thrillers, had decided early on in Tommo's basic training that he should become an avid reader as well by throwing a Raymond Chandler novel onto his bunk and telling him to give it a go. And so he became one of the lads.

His one regret was that he'd not been able to see Connie before he'd left Gosport. The date on the travel warrant had given him precious little time to sort out his affairs.

He often thought about the charge of electricity that had passed through their fingertips that day in the Criterion. She'd felt it, too, he knew she had. What is to be will be, he thought. And when he'd finished his term of employment in the navy he'd go back to Gosport a new man, a different man, with everything to offer a girl like her, and he'd find her. If Connie was meant to be his woman, she would be.

Of course there was nothing to stop him writing a letter to her, care of the picture house. But that would be cheating. Trying to manoeuvre Fate into doing what he wanted before he was ready. No, he had to prove himself first.

If his plans went awry – well, he'd still be a better man than he was when he left Gosport, wouldn't he?

His mum would have liked that, too.

Chapter Thirty-two

'You were right, old man!' Ace said, pouring himself a whisky. He didn't ask Jerome if he wanted one because he knew his friend would rather have a cup of tea.

The bar staff were gathering glasses to be washed before the club closed and Ace was smiling because the takings were up and he felt good. He had his coat and hat on and was ready to leave for Alma Street.

'I'm glad to hear it,' said Jerome. 'You gonna tell me what I'm right about?'

'Connie and Tommo didn't get together, as I'd mistakenly thought. The romance never got off the ground.' Ace took a gulp and swirled the whisky around in his mouth.

'And now it never will because there's hundreds of miles between them,' said Jerome. 'I hope you think sending him away is worth losing the money he brought to this place.'

'Peace of mind is worth any price,' said Ace. 'There are plenty of pretty young ghost dancers ready to fleece rich old ladies.' He sipped his drink, the wireless playing softly in the background. 'Will you listen to those three girls' singing "You'll Never Know"?'

'That's the Bluebirds. They're a local group. You ought to book them in for a session here. They'd bring in the customers,' said Jerome.

'Again, you're right,' said Ace. He took a deep breath and said clearly, 'I'm going to ask her to marry me.'

He saw Jerome narrow his eyes. 'I don't suppose you mean one of the Bluebirds?'

'Very funny, old man. You know damn well I mean Connie.' Ace waited for a further reply but none came. 'Not got a right answer to that, Jerome?'

After a while, Jerome took off his spectacles, wiped them on a handkerchief from his pocket, then settled them back on his nose. Carefully he looked at Ace. 'What about Belle and your boy, Leon?'

'What about them? I'll go on supporting them both. Nothing will change.' Ace picked up a beer mat and began tapping it on the bar.

'You going to tell young Connie everything?'

'What do you mean, "everything"?' Ace stared at him.

'She don't know you run with the black-market.'

'Actually, old man, she's not as naïve as she looks.' He was remembering his and Connie's conversation about the lipstick and the extra food he sent round to Gertie's.

'What about when she knows you sent Tommo away?'

'I don't see why she should find out. She's never set foot in here so she's not likely to know he worked for me, is she? To tell the truth, I don't believe they ever had much more than a very brief conversation.' Ace swallowed the rest of his drink.

Jerome shrugged. 'It's not good to start married life with secrets between you. You going to invite Billy Hill and some of the other London mob to tea when you're set up together in your little love nest? When are you going to tell her you're behind the letters to Etta Hines?' Jerome went on, 'I'm not a bleedin' mushroom to be kept in the dark. Those letters were typed, and you just happen to have an Underwood machine that you use for all your club correspondence. That girl was really upset by that woman and her abortion business. You going to tell her you're the person responsible for those thought-provoking letters Etta Hines keeps getting in the hope she stops messing with women's insides?'

Ace opened his mouth to protest, thought better of it and closed it again. He was surprised Jerome had found out. Especially after all the trouble he'd gone to, delivering the letters on his way back to Alma Street after the club had closed, and when there was no one on the streets to see him. 'Does anyone else know I write them?'

Jerome shook his head. 'You know I'd never betray you. You and I both know you wouldn't physically harm that old bag but you thought if she gets enough letters it'd frighten her off and she'd pack it in . . . You can't do things like that just because Connie gets upset by life.'

Ace tried to excuse himself: 'But she's already had so much sadness in her past . . .'

'And marrying you and taking on all your dirty baggage will make her future easier, will it?'

When Ace didn't reply, Jerome said, 'She's a nice girl. And you're going to contaminate her and break her heart when she finds out all the bad stuff you're trying to keep hidden from her. You've got to tell her everything. You can't keep secrets from her. Not if you love her.'

'Damn you!' Ace tore the beer-mat in two, threw it onto the bar, and walked out of his club, the door slamming behind him.

Ace stepped into the hallway, hung his overcoat and hat on the peg near the front door and headed towards the kitchen, where he found Connie sitting at the table with her scrapbook and a cup of flour and water paste in front of her. Her head was bent over a picture of Robert Mitchum and she was trying to smooth out the lumps the paste contained. He saw the glossy picture-house stills that Len had given her, next to a pair of scissors.

'You haven't been attending to that for a while,' he said, still trying to keep the anger from his voice after his run-in with Jerome. Driving back to Alma Street in the pitch-black streets had helped him realize that every word Jerome had spoken was true.

Jerome, and now Connie, were the only people he really cared about. Even his own son was simply a cheque he signed every month that was sent to Belle. His mind worked on the assumption that what you never had you never missed. She didn't send him photographs and he never asked for any.

He was well aware he used people to make money. Money had been his god all his life because, from a very early age, he'd found that it brought him what he wanted: food, respect and, later, women.

He put his hand on the back of her chair and leaned over her shoulder. He could smell her hair was freshly washed in Amami shampoo and it excited him more than the expensive perfumes some of his clientele habitually wore.

'I find it helps to soothe my nerves,' she said.

'A good-looking man like Robert Mitchum could probably soothe any woman's nerves,' he said.

'Oh, you.' She tutted. 'Gertie's left some corned-beef hash in the oven.'

He stepped away from her. With her dressing-gown over a flannelette night-dress and her scrubbed face, she looked vulnerable. She gazed up at him. 'Can I ask you a question?'

He shrugged. 'If you must.'

'Why does Gertie go to all the bother of cooking a meal for you to eat late at night, when you own a club where your customers eat better food?'

He stared at her for a long time before he answered. 'She likes to look after me and I like being looked after. It's not the quality of the food, it's the care that goes into it.'

Her eyes were searching his face. He had an almost overwhelming desire to bend down to her again, gather her up and kiss her. Instead, he said, 'Well?'

'Well, what?'

'Why do your nerves need soothing?'

She smiled at him. Her small teeth were very white. 'Queenie's planning on returning to work soon. I worry about her. Do you think it will harm the baby?'

He thought for a while. 'The exercise will probably do her

good as long as she doesn't overtire herself. She'll feel more contented knowing she's earning again and not relying on Len's generosity. Women do work when they're pregnant.' He pressed his lips together, then gave a big sigh. 'I'm no expert on working women with babies, though.'

She was staring at him and he thought her green eyes were like wondrous pools he could disappear into and all his own problems would evaporate. 'I'm not thinking about that,' she said. 'I'm worried that Etta Hines may have harmed Queenie's baby.'

He let out a breath. 'What did that midwife person, that . . .'

'Edith Stimson?' Connie supplied the woman's name that was on the tip of his tongue.

'Yes, what did she say?'

'She said the baby floats in its own sac of water. Possibly it's fine. It's Queenie who was harmed.'

He stared at her, at her eyes brimming with tears. 'Once a midwife, always a midwife,' he consoled. 'Edith's a marvel but Queenie also needs to be examined by a doctor.'

'But then she'll have to tell him what happened . . . And there's the cost . . .'

He thought for a moment. 'I happen to know of a doctor who won't ask questions and he owes me a favour.'

Connie jumped up from her seat, scattering the papers she'd been cutting, and threw her arms around his neck. 'Could you ask him to do a check-up on Queenie and her baby?'

Her body was squashed tightly to his, her head against his chest. He looked down at her, then gently lifted her head and kissed her lightly on the lips. She tasted sweet, like strawberries. He felt her respond. He didn't want to but he pulled away. Now wasn't the time or the place. 'For you, anything,' Ace whispered.

Chapter Thirty-three

'You're going to tell me in a minute that I'm to sit here, and when a patron walks in, I must ignore them. You'll be the usherette to show them to their seats!'

Connie could feel herself getting cross with Queenie. 'Anything to stop you jumping up and down like a demented jack-in-the-box. It can't be good for you,' she whispered. For a change both of them were working upstairs in the circle.

'We won't get many patrons in now the big picture's started. Why d'you think I'm working this evening shift from six until eleven? I'm easing myself back into the job carefully. The stronger I get, the more hours I'll take on.' Queenie looked around. 'Anyway, it's pretty quiet tonight. And Sara Cantrell's quite happy selling the ice-creams. That tray weighs a ton.'

Connie sighed. There were only about twenty seats taken

up with patrons. She wasn't surprised Queenie had decided to come back to the Criterion. She'd got fed up with being alone in Len's house. Edith still popped in for a chat every so often but Queenie, used to being with people, had decided to move back to her own house and to come to work. She believed she'd feel better when she was looking after herself again. She'd also told her Len hadn't wanted her to leave and they'd had a few words about it.

Connie wondered if she was being overprotective of her friend.

The Lady Eve was the big picture. Connie said, 'Do you like Barbara Stanwyck?' She could smell Queenie's Californian Poppy. She thought how nice it was to have her friend back with her and that tonight, after watching this extremely funny film, they'd walk home together just like they used to.

Queenie wrinkled her nose. 'I'm not keen on her. She's a good actress but for me she doesn't have the star quality that Joan Crawford or Bette Davis has. And she hasn't got big boobies like Betty Grable or Jane Russell.'

Connie stared at her. 'What's that got to do with it?'

'Everything. Men like women with big boobies!'

Connie looked down at herself. 'That's probably why I haven't had as many blokes as you.'

Queenie giggled. 'My boobies seem to be getting

enormous.' The smile left her face and she grew serious. 'I don't, er, show yet, do I?'

Connie shook her head. She knew her friend was referring to her pregnancy. 'So far, you've hardly put on any weight at all. Anyway, a lot of it will be swallowed up by the seams Gertie unpicked and let out when she washed your uniform. She was worried the material would shrink in the wash.'

'I don't know what I'd do if I didn't have you and Gertie.'

'Ssh!' Connie was embarrassed. 'Everyone was so pleased to see you back again tonight.'

'They'd soon talk if they knew the truth,' said Queenie. 'I even felt awful trying to convince Ol' Mangle I was feeling better.'

'Oh, so his lordship's deigned to come to work, has he?' The manager had had quite a bit of time off lately. Staff had thought it unfair as they were working to cover Queenie's shifts and could have done with a bit of help and compassion from him.

'Didn't you know he's interviewing two young girls as usherettes?' Queenie said. 'We get really busy in the few weeks' run-up to Christmas. That's when we show Disney and other cartoon films so the mums can pack the kids off to the pictures. Len says we're lucky – we've got some smashing kids' films to show. *Dumbo*, *The Reluctant Dragon*,

The Night Before Christmas, Mr Bug Goes to Town and, wait for it, *Captain Marvel.* They're all lined up for showing.' Queenie's eyes were sparkling, even in the dull light of the auditorium. 'Anyway, just because Mangle's interviewing it doesn't mean the young girls will get the jobs and stay on. They can earn more money in Priddy's armaments yard, can't they?'

'I suppose so,' said Connie, thoughtfully. 'If this place needs more money why doesn't he put on a Saturday matinee for the kids, like the Forum does? That picture house in Stoke Road has been operating a children's show on Saturday mornings for ages.'

Queenie shrugged. 'Mangle's really not interested in this place,' she said. 'It would mean more work for him and he'd have to pay out extra wages.' She giggled again. 'There might not be many people up here but both the lovers' seats are taken.'

'The what seats?' Connie was mystified.

'The lovers' seats. Didn't no one ever tell you about them? Haven't you noticed them?'

'I wish I knew what you're on about.'

Queenie whispered in her ear, 'Down there, see that couple having a really intimate kiss and cuddle . . .'

Connie stared. 'It looks like they're in the same seat,' she said.

'In a way, they are. There's no middle armrest between those seats so a couple can get really close . . .'

'Well,' said Connie. 'Fancy that!'

'There's two sets of seats here upstairs like that.'

Connie's eyes moved along the few patrons sitting in front of them. She was looking for snuggled-up couples who were even more tightly entwined. 'I don't think I'd like to be sitting next to them if they . . .' she paused '. . . they, you know, got carried away,' she finished.

Queenie laughed. 'Couples come to the pictures to be really close to each other, don't they?' For a moment she was thoughtful. 'I think you might be surprised at some of the things the cleaners find when they clear up after people.'

'Gertie sells the dog-ends.'

'And good luck to her, I say,' Queenie said. 'But I'm talking about French letters.'

Connie gasped. 'Really?'

'Yes, and they're not always by the lovers' seats! Money gets found on the floor, scarves and gloves. Sometimes jewellery, but we always keep lost stuff so it can be reclaimed. But mostly it's umbrellas get left behind . . . Knickers are found a lot, as well,' she added, 'especially up here by the lovers' seats!'

Connie was blushing. 'Why are the seats like that? Surely they weren't made that way.'

'Probably not,' said Queenie. 'I expect they got broken, and you know what Mangle's like – he can't be bothered to pay to get things mended.'

Connie had to tear her eyes away from the couple in the lovers' seat.

Queenie said, 'Guess what?'

'I shudder to think,' said Connie.

'No, this is good news. Etta Hines reckons she's going to pack in doing abortions.'

Connie said, 'How do you know?'

'Edith told me yesterday that Etta's had more letters. It's really frightened her. She knows they must be from someone important as they always say the same thing and they're always on that posh paper. It's really upset her. She knows it's not a joke.'

'You're telling me that Etta Hines, an abortionist in a part of town where burglars live and women are constantly beaten up by their men, is frightened of letters?'

Queenie stared at her. 'That's just it! Everyone under-stands those things – they can see violence – but posh letters with the same message written over and over again? Apparently, Etta really is scared.'

'I'd say the person writing those letters is very clever. Doesn't anyone know who it is?'

'No one. But she's frightened to go out now or to let anyone through the front door, except her lodger, that is. She's so scared she's making him do the shopping.'

'That's good news, isn't it?' asked Connie.

'Not for Etta, it isn't. The first time she gave him money for shopping, he spent it all in the Robin Hood pub and came home drunk.'

'Oh, you do make me laugh,' said Connie, chuckling. 'That reminds me, Gertie told me to ask you about Christmas Day. Do you want to come round to our house for your dinner? Ace usually brings home something nice.'

'Whoa, hold your horses,' said Queenie. 'I'd have come like a shot – no one likes being on their own on Christmas Day – but Len's already asked me to his house and I've said yes. I can't very well break a promise, can I?'

Chapter Thirty-four

Naïve millionaire adventurer Henry Fonda, complete with snake, on board an ocean liner, was trying hard to escape the clutches of Barbara Stanwyck when Moaning Minnie screamed into action.

The groans from the picturegoers filled the Criterion as the familiar message appeared on the screen: 'All those patrons wishing to take advantage of the local shelters may do so through the exits provided and at their own risk. For those wishing to stay, the film will continue.'

The lights had come on. People were moving from their seats. The dust and cigarette smoke caught in the powerful beam directed by Len from the projection room above danced and swirled.

Queenie was already on her feet, 'Let's make sure the

patrons don't hurt themselves stampeding out to the air-raid shelters,' she said.

Connie was suddenly cross. Even in the pictures, that palace of dreams, real life had intruded and fantasy had been shattered. She moved to an exit door and began marshalling the few people downstairs.

'No need to rush,' she said, in as calm a voice as she could muster.

The young man and his girlfriend who had been sitting in one of the lovers' seats shuffled past, the girl hastily adjusting her clothing.

'Good night, keep safe, hope to see you again,' called Queenie to the couple.

Connie glared at her because she knew she was being sarcastic. 'Mind the stairs. No need to rush,' she advised again.

Suddenly a scream rang out.

'Someone downstairs in the stalls must have tripped over.' Queenie looked worried. 'I'll go and see. The upstairs patrons have all gone now. Luckily there's not many in tonight.'

Connie let her eyes sweep the circle's empty seats.

'Why don't you watch the end of the picture?' Queenie said. 'It's nearly finished and so far it's been a good laugh. There's enough usherettes to sort out whatever's going on downstairs and Tom Doyle's there as well.'

'Are you sure?'

'Course,' said Queenie, immediately leaving her. Connie went back to her seat and sat down again. Then she rose, went to the balcony and looked down to the stalls. There were hardly any picturegoers sitting there. She sat and waited for the darkness, for the light to be turned off and for the film to begin again, so the magic could continue. Within a little while, it did.

A deafening noise disturbed her enjoyment. Somewhere close a bomb had exploded. The picture house seemed to shudder. Automatically Connie ducked. She hoped the patrons who had left had already found shelter. And she prayed that Gertie was safe in the Anderson. She knew some people had developed a relaxed attitude towards the bombing, especially as some of the warnings were groundless. She looked around her at the vacated seats and suddenly felt very much alone.

Connie knew she was being irrational as, downstairs in the foyer, the usherettes, including Queenie, would be ignoring the noise of the planes and taking advantage of the lack of patrons to embark on the nightly tidy-up before leaving the premises. Probably, though, Queenie was cashing-up. For sure there would be no more people paying to come in tonight now that *The Lady Eve* was practically at an end.

It was silly of her to feel as alone as she did. Wasn't Len up in the projection room, no doubt ably assisted by young Gary?

Connie heard another whine of hurtling bombs but this time the Criterion didn't move. The bombs must have landed close by, for the loud noise, followed by the clatter of shrapnel, like hailstones, rained down on the roof of the picture house.

Connie could feel panic invading her body. She didn't think for one moment the enemy were purposely hoping to obliterate Gosport. Of course not. It was Portsmouth Dockyard, the maintenance yards and naval bases that the German aircraft wanted to destroy. Unfortunately for the town, Gosport was in the way.

She made herself concentrate on the picture and by the time the credits rolled she realized the outside clatter was no more. She got up, stretched, flipping up the seat and was satisfied to hear the all-clear. She stood perfectly still while the National Anthem played and was relieved when the lights came on again. She could hear the sounds of ambulances now, and recovery vehicles. On her way to the exit, along the row, she flipped up the seats, suddenly surprised that Queenie hadn't returned. As the two of them were the circle's usherettes they'd be expected to do that chore together, ready for tomorrow's cleaners.

The further down the stairs she went, the louder the raised voices became. The foyer was fully lit, the blackout curtains tightly pulled across the glass doors.

Two policemen were chatting to Tom Doyle, and Sara Cantrell was interrupting. The air seemed to be charged with expectancy. Connie stood on the bottom step and watched the usherettes milling about, talking nineteen to the dozen.

'You've missed all the excitement,' said Queenie, appearing in front of her.

Connie knew she looked mystified.

'Ol' Mangle's handcuffed in a police car outside. The girl's been taken off.'

'What?' That was as far as she got, because Queenie said, 'That was the scream we heard.'

'Are you going to tell me what's happened?' Connie asked curtly.

'Mangle. Interviewing the two young girls, one at a time. When the first one came out, apparently she said, "I wouldn't work here for twice the wages." She flounced out, that's according to Sara Cantrell, who'd just come back with the ice-creams.' Queenie took a breath. 'Mangle called the second girl into his office – that's what I heard from Sara – and after that all hell was let loose. Tom Doyle heard a scream. He put two and two together – the pretty girl and the possible locked office door – and warned Mangle to unlock it immediately. Tom said he could hear the girl crying inside.

'Mangle shouted that the girl was frightened by the bombing. Tom wasn't having any of that. He took a chance and put his shoulder to the door.'

'And Sara was watching all this?' Connie asked.

Queenie nodded.

The policemen were now leaving the picture house. Tom Doyle was bidding them goodnight and thanking them. As soon as he'd closed the main door the usherettes were crowding around him, all chattering at once.

Tom said a few words to them, then looked around as though he was searching for someone. When his eyes fell on Queenie, he came across to her. 'I've promised to go down to South Street and talk to them at the police station in the morning, Queenie. I know it's your first night back and you must be worn out, but can you be here to oversee everything? They need a statement from me, you see.'

He smiled at Connie, then looked again at Queenie, who nodded. 'Of course.'

Connie thought how tired he looked. Tom hadn't finished: 'They said we can open up as usual tomorrow. I said you and I can take over until we hear from the big bosses. It was all right to say that, wasn't it?'

'Of course,' said Queenie again.

His shoulder epaulette was hanging by a thread on one side. He saw Connie looking at it. 'My missus'll need to fix that for me. That damned door was harder than I thought.'

'I think you were very brave. Is your shoulder all right? What happened when you got into his office?' Connie asked.

He gave a weak smile. 'One question at a time. My shoulder's a bit painful but nothing some wintergreen rub won't cure. In the office that little girl was crying and trying to cover herself up where the bastard had torn her blouse.' Tom must have seen Connie's curious look for he added, 'He'd told her to take off her coat and be comfortable, so she said to me. Then I suppose he made a move on her.'

'She should have thumped him one,' Queenie put in.

'Yes, well, she probably would have,' confirmed Tom, 'had she realized what sort of bloke he was. But that poor kid wanted the job so much that when she wrote in about it she told him she was eighteen.'

'Wasn't she?'

Tom looked downcast. 'She's fifteen years old, that kid.'

Queenie made a whistling sound. 'Jesus! That'll scar her for life,' she said.

Connie saw tears in her eyes. She put her arm around her friend and asked Tom, 'Is that when the police were called?'

'Sara saw what had gone on. She saw me hit Mangle.'

Connie couldn't help shouting in amazement, 'You hit him?'

'He disgusted me, the bloody pervert! We've all closed our eyes to the way he treats women like pieces of meat, and everyone so scared of losing their jobs.'

Tom took in a deep breath, then exhaled. 'That bastard was trying to get out so he could run away! Sara had just come back from selling ices. I thumped Mangle and swore at him. Yelled at Sara to get the coppers. Sara wouldn't come in the office to use the phone. She dropped the tray of ices and ran to the phone-box on the corner.' He looked at Queenie. 'Thank God you came downstairs when you did, assessed the situation and carted the usherettes who were hanging around into the auditorium to flip up the seats.' He sighed. 'Everything happened so quickly. The ice-creams are ruined, melted. Sorry, Queenie. I know that's your department.'

Queenie put her hand on his arm. 'Well, it's not like Mangle's going to have a few words with me about it, is it?'

'Where was Mangle while Sara was gone?' Connie asked.

'I didn't want to leave the bugger in case he tried to run off again, and I didn't think that little girl would appreciate another big man hovering over her. Mangle was sitting there,' he pointed to the bottom step in the foyer, 'holding his chin and snivelling, and I stood over him. When Sara came back, she went in to the girl. The police were here almost immediately, which surprised me because by that time the bloody Germans were putting their five eggs in as well.'

'So, what's going to happen now, Tom?' asked Queenie.

'Well, Queenie girl. You know what goes on in the Criterion as well as I do. I'm sure we can cope until the powers that be either send us a new manager or . . .' he paused '. . . close us down.'

Chapter Thirty-five

Tommo looked around the interior of the Kilted Pig and sighed. Hamish was standing at the bar waiting to be served. The place wasn't busy but the barman was nowhere to be seen. Even Hamish's shoulders were hunched, making him seem sad. There was no music in the place and the only movement came from the gnarled fingers of the two old men sitting at a table in the corner playing dominoes.

It had been Tommo's idea to leave base and borrow transport to spend precious time off in Helensburgh. He wished now that he hadn't bothered. This place is all brown, he thought. Dirty brown varnished floor, brown fag-smoked ceiling. The few tables were brown, the chairs brown wood, the bar was brown and the curtains over the blackout shutters were a tweedy brown material. There were even two brown logs on the fire that weren't giving out any heat.

He thought back to that afternoon when they'd arrived at the Victorian resort.

The object of the outing, five miles from base, was to cheer up Hamish who, when he wasn't on duty, was moping about the hut. Some bastard had sent Hamish an anonymous letter telling him all about the American soldiers who were regularly beating a path to his girlfriend's tenement in Glasgow's Cowcaddens Road.

Hamish was now making his way back to the table carefully carrying two pints of ale.

'Took his time serving you, didn't he?' Tommo grabbed his glass before Hamish spilled any more. The table-top already resembled a loch.

'Aye,' Hamish said. 'He was outside in the lavatory. I heard the flush when he came out.'

Tommo thought that didn't warrant an answer so he asked, 'What do you think of Helensburgh?'

'This place is pish. The streets were fine with their trees lining the roads and the park could have done with some flowers.'

'It's only days to Christmas – there's no flowers. Even in England there's no plants flowering at Christmas.'

'We don't really pay much attention to Christmas.' Hamish took a good pull at his beer.

Tommo looked around the brown bar, which was devoid of paper chains. 'I can see that,' he said, taking a gulp.

'Christmas is for kids. Hogmanay is for grown-ups,' Hamish said. 'First footing with a piece of coal for good luck and plenty of wee drams.'

Tommo let him talk for at least the conversation wasn't about Adaira, his girlfriend. Tommo felt sorry for the big bluff Scot. Last night he'd heard him sobbing softly into the pillow in his bunk. He didn't say anything, knowing how ashamed the man would feel to think his grief had been overheard. Tommo had really thought a change of scene would help. But this afternoon all Hamish had talked about was Adaira. And now he'd started again.

'She works in McCormack's music shop in Cowcaddens. You must have heard of McCormacks? Opened in 1940, everybody knows McCormack's.'

Tommo shook his head and drank more beer.

'I expect that's where she meets the bloody Americans.'

'Hamish, you've got to snap out of this.'

'Saving up to get married we're supposed to be,' Hamish supplied.

'So you said.'

'Adaira means "beauty" in the Gaelic.' Tommo saw him fishing in his top pocket.

'I've seen the photo and she is beautiful.' Tommo looked again at the girl in the black-and-white picture. She had blonde hair and a nice smile.

It made him think of Connie and he wondered what kind of Christmas she was going to have. Hamish was fumbling with his top pocket, trying to fit the photo back in. When he'd succeeded, he said, 'Your turn to get the drinks in.'

Tommo finished his pint, picked up the glasses and stood up.

'At least the barman's not in the lavatory this time,' said Hamish, with a bleary-eyed grin.

When Tommo got back to the table with two mugs of beer he'd managed to hold in one hand and two tots of whisky he'd carried with the other, he saw Hamish had been crying. The tears on his cheeks gave it away.

Tommo's heart went out to him. He'd never cared about anyone until he'd met Connie, except for his mum, of course, but he could imagine the grief Hamish was going through. His mate had told him yesterday he couldn't read his book any more because the words were running into each other and didn't make any sense. That told Tommo that his friend couldn't get the hurt out of his mind. He couldn't escape into his beloved novels.

'Of course that letter could have come from someone

Adaira turned down. Some people need to cause trouble because it makes them feel better about themselves. I've known of jealous buggers who've written anonymous letters before.'

Hamish caught his eyes and held them. 'Really? Have you really?' He sounded hopeful.

Jesus, you're a mess, my friend, thought Tommo. Of course he didn't say that to Hamish, just put the whisky into Hamish's hand and mouthed the Gaelic for 'water of life', meaning the whisky, '*Uisge beatha.*' Hamish smiled at him and repeated it.

When the glasses were empty, Hamish asked, 'So, do you really think someone's having me on?'

'Does the picture house close for Christmas?'

Ace put the lump of bread pudding back on the plate, licked his lips, because it was so delicious, and looked at Connie.

She hastily swallowed a mouthful of mixed fruit, sugar, bread and fat. 'I've got Christmas Eve, Christmas Day and Boxing Day off. Why?'

He didn't answer her but looked at Gertie, who was sitting by the range, a cigarette in her mouth with a long grey ash on it, and a cup of tea near her elbow on a small table. Her eyes were closed. 'Have you got the same break, Gertie?'

'What? Eh? I wasn't asleep, just resting my eyes. Oh!'

She'd obviously forgotten she had a cigarette in her

mouth when she dozed off for when she answered the stub had dropped to her lap.

Ace laughed. 'What hours are you working over the holiday?'

'Why?'

'Because I'm asking.'

'I'm cleaning Christmas Eve morning but then off until the morning after Boxing Day.' She was looking at him expectantly. Every lock of her grey hair was fastened by a metal curler.

'I'm closing the club on Christmas Day. Obviously, I don't want to offend anyone, it being a special day. Christmas Eve is profitable but Jerome can manage and Boxing Day is either very good financially or extremely bad. Again, Jerome said he can cope. I wondered if you'd both like to come away on a little holiday.'

Gertie had opened her mouth but nothing came out, so Ace went on, 'Just for a couple of days. We'll be back in time for you,' he nodded at Gertie, 'to go in early to work. What do you both think?'

'Why?' Gertie was suspicious.

'For God's sake, woman! You're always doing things for me so I thought I'd repay your kindness – a sort of Christmas present, if you like.' Gertie wasn't used to kindness. He looked at the photograph of her daughter on the mantelpiece. 'Are you hesitating because Marlene's paying a Christmas visit?' He knew they seldom wrote to each other.

She looked at him in amazement. 'I've probably seen the last of her, though she might come back if and when she's ready.' He noted her bitterness. 'Anyway, you don't have to . . .' she began.

'Gertie, there's precious little to buy in the shops as gifts to give each other. Come on, say yes!' He turned to Connie. 'What d'you think?'

'Anything to get away from the planes coming over . . .'

Since it had taken him a great deal of patience to persuade Connie to go to the fair with him, then on to a meal afterwards, he knew she would agree if Gertie did.

'Where?' Gertie had picked up her cold tea, taken a mouthful, made a face and spat it back into the cup.

'I'll put the kettle on, shall I, while you make up your mind?' He got up from his chair with a sigh, after giving her a black look. 'I forgot you were such a great traveller that a couple of days in the bloody country wouldn't be good enough for you, Gertie Mullins!'

In the scullery, as he struck a match beneath the kettle on the gas stove, he was smiling. He counted in his head, one, two, three . . . and then, 'That'd be brilliant! Not 'alf! When will we be leaving?' shouted Gertie.

Chapter Thirty-six

'Doesn't this stuff sting your head?' Len was carefully dab-bing the pasty-white mixture of peroxide and ammonia, which stank to high Heaven and was causing his eyes to water, on the partings he had made in Queenie's hair.

'Of course it does,' she said. 'But pride is painful and I can't go around with blonde hair and dark roots, can I?' She pulled the towel closer to her neck in case he spilled any on her skin. 'No one's ever offered to bleach my hair for me before,' she said. 'I'm surprised you, being a man, would offer to do it.'

'Can't think why you're surprised. I looked after you when you were poorly, upstairs in my bed, didn't I?'

'That was different,' she said. 'Edith was here most of the time then.'

'Do you wish she was here now?'

'Don't be daft!' Queenie said quickly. 'She'd say something like "You'll rot your head putting that rubbish on it!"'

He began to laugh. 'I always thought your hair was natural,' he said.

'That's where us women fool you men!' she retorted.

He put down the paintbrush he was using and said, 'Finished. All the mixture's used up and I'm pretty sure I've not missed any bits.' He stretched his back. 'What happens now?'

'We wait for my hair to fall out, then go and buy me a hat!'

He smiled at her. 'That's why I care about you,' he said. 'You make me laugh.'

And she did, he thought. That was also why the house seemed so empty now she wasn't clattering about and singing along to the wireless. She'd returned to her own place to live. He didn't like it. Not one little bit. 'I'll make us some tea,' he said. He turned the wireless up a bit. Bing Crosby was singing 'White Christmas'.

He left her sitting by the range in the kitchen while he washed his hands at the stone sink in the scullery. 'I'm glad you're coming to me for Christmas Day,' he called. 'I've got a chicken promised me.'

He heard her gasp. 'Proper chicken?'

'Yes, I thought we could have a traditional roast.'

'I forgot you can cook,' she called back.

He remembered making her dainty meals with Bovril to raise her strength when she was lying in bed and he'd feared for her life. He wanted to tell her how much he cared for her but the moment didn't seem right. He watched the flames beneath the kettle changing from blue, to red, to orange, then shouted, 'Have you heard anything about a new manager?'

'Nothing,' she yelled back at him. 'Most young blokes are away fighting, so if we get anyone it'll be someone with one foot in the grave, I expect.'

She knew why the services didn't want Len. He'd told her about the accident to his fingers when he was a kid. Funny, he thought, he didn't normally like talking about it, though Connie knew, and he found it easy to talk to Queenie about anything and everything. 'We're managing, aren't we?' he asked.

Queenie had now taken over the book-keeping.

'Managing? We're making more money than we did before. I think Mangle was creaming some off the top for his own personal use.'

That wouldn't surprise me at all, Len thought. Nobody at the picture house had asked about Mangle, or his wife, for that matter. And he didn't care what happened to the weasel, except that he got what he deserved for attacking that young girl. Tom Doyle had had a lovely letter from the girl's parents, praising him for his quick thinking. The rest of the staff thought that was well deserved.

He stirred the teapot and set it on the tray ready to take into the kitchen.

He sighed.

He walked over to the sink, put his hands on the wooden draining-board and stared out of the window. It was cold outside. Last night there'd been a frost.

It was no good, he thought, he was going to have to say something to her. Not knowing was eating him up inside.

He picked up the tray, carried it into the kitchen and put it on the table.

He looked at Queenie. In the warmth of the kitchen some of the bleach had dried on her hair, which was sticking out from her head at angles that reminded him of a hedgehog that used to visit his garden. He'd leave saucers of bread and milk for it. He shook his head, smiling at her looking so comical.

'If I keep coming round your house like this people are going to start talking about us,' she said.

'If we got married it wouldn't matter,' Len said quickly.

Her mouth had fallen open. There was a silence. Her

mouth closed, then opened enough to ask, 'Did I just hear you ask me to marry you?'

He nodded.

'But I'm pregnant with someone else's baby?'

'I'd love it as if it was my own,' he said.

Now she wasn't saying anything and it unnerved him. 'It makes a lot of sense,' he said. 'You tried to get rid of the kiddie because you knew what it would be like. Having to give up your job, no money. People talking behind your back. The kiddie being called a bastard. I can change all that, Queenie . . .'

'But . . .'

'But nothing! I've cared about you for ages. Every time I shone that bloody spotlight down on you, I wished you belonged to me. I couldn't say anything, though. You didn't even know I existed up there in the projection room.'

His voice failed him. He had nothing left to say to her.

'Are you asking me because you feel sorry for me?'

'Sorry? You think I'd want to spend the rest of my life with a woman I felt sorry for? I don't feel sorry for you, you silly thing, I love you. I've always loved you. I loved you the moment I saw that tray of ice-creams around your neck . . .'

He stopped ranting and stared at her when she said, 'I love you too, you know.'

'You do?'

'Of course I do. Why wouldn't I love the kindest, gentlest, cleverest man ever?'

He couldn't believe his ears. Queenie had said she loved him! 'And you'll marry me?'

'Yes.'

He started to laugh. 'I suppose we ought to kiss then, seal the deal and all that?'

She folded her arms, sat back in the chair and said, 'I'm doing nothing until I've had a cuppa and you've helped me wash this bleach off my hair.'

'We'll make up for it then, shall we?'

'We certainly will,' Queenie said. 'Oh, I do love you.'

'And I love you.'

Chapter Thirty-seven

'Aren't we having the top down?' Gertie looked disgruntled.

'Not unless you want to freeze to death before we get there,' Ace said. He'd not thought getting Gertie Mullins into his car would be so difficult. First, she'd wanted to sit in the front seat. He wasn't happy about that because he'd have preferred Connie next to him. But when she'd realized that sitting behind Ace meant she could talk in his ear, she'd moved happily, and he'd breathed a sigh of short-lived relief.

'Did I take the key from the front door? I don't want any looters in my house.' He put his hand into his pocket, took out the front-door key on its tangle of string and passed it back to her.

'I picked it up from the doorstep,' he said. Connie put her hand over her mouth and tried not to giggle. 'Don't you start or you can walk,' he said, with a grin.

'Now, have you both got everything?' He was driving up Fareham Road and didn't intend to go back but thought he'd better ask.

The silence told him the two big bags of God knew what, jammed into the boot, held everything they needed for a couple of nights away. His small overnight case on the back seat next to Gertie even contained a spare suit, carefully folded, of course, which he'd take out and hang up the moment they arrived at the hotel he'd booked. He took a hand from the wheel and patted his inside pocket, which contained a small present for Connie.

He wouldn't admit it but he was just as excited as they were. Neither Gertie nor Connie had ever spent Christmas Day anywhere but in their own homes and he wanted to make things special for them.

In the car there was enough contraband petrol to get them to Devon, and in his wallet, he had plenty of illicit petrol coupons that could easily pass inspection.

Last night at the club, Jerome had helped him raid his well-stocked kitchen, so he could prepare a picnic for them to eat when they stopped for a break on the way. 'It makes sense as the food you've got here is probably better than any you'll get from a café. Besides, them two women will like it that you've been so thoughtful.'

Despite the cold, a weak sun was shining, making everything outside the car look bright and cheerful. He was trying not to notice the damage wreaked by German planes. Gaps in the rows of houses where families had once loved and lived.

Once-profitable shops now just piles of rubble. He shuddered.

'Are you all right?' Connie asked.

He gave her a grin. 'I'm fine,' he said. He thought how pretty she looked today. She could do with a new coat – the one she wore was a tired and grubby green gaberdine. He'd have bought her another – she could have anything she wanted from him, he thought – but she'd only just accepted that lipstick. It had sat on the sideboard in Gertie's kitchen for ages, until the day after he'd taken her to Southsea for a meal. Then it had disappeared. The next time he'd seen her she had blushed almost as deeply red as the colour on her lips. He knew she'd not appreciate him drawing attention to it so he hadn't. But he felt a milestone had been reached between them.

Gertie had fallen asleep, her head on his case. She'd filled the car with the smell of her Woodbines. She'd probably have something to say about the crick in her back when she woke, but as he looked in his rear-view mirror, he appreciated the silence so decided not to wake her.

Connie sat beside him, calm and quiet. Every so often he'd steal a glance at her to find her looking back at him and they'd exchange smiles. Ace was happier than he'd been in a long while.

The silence was broken near Lyndhurst in the New Forest: 'I need a wee! And I'm gasping for a cup of tea.'

He looked at Connie and said, 'Guess who's awake?'

'Can we stop for a while?' Connie asked. 'I'd like to stretch my legs.'

He turned off the main road and down a gravel lane, pulling up where several ponies were grazing on the heather.

'I'm not getting out here!' Gertie was horrified. 'Not with them about.'

'They're ponies and they'll be more frightened of you than you should be of them,' said Connie.

Ace was already out of the car and adjusting the hood, pulling it down to let in some fresh air. The grass was short, wiry and, amazingly, dry. Everything felt new and clean, he thought. There were no houses, no traffic on the road and barely any noise. He could hear insects chirruping in the hedges. 'There's a nice clump of trees over there.' He waved an arm in the opposite direction to the ponies, which were munching grass quite contentedly and hadn't moved. He smiled to himself as Gertie and Connie walked off in the direction of cover. He brought out the wicker picnic basket and set it down on a blanket Jerome had persuaded him to bring.

Connie and Gertie had spotted the basket in the boot of the car and wheedled it out of him that it contained food and a flask of tea. By the time they came back he had set out his offerings on the blanket.

'Ham? I haven't tasted ham as good as this for ages.' Gertie was looking inside her sandwich. She ate it quickly then began inspecting some of the others. 'Not a bit of corned beef in sight,' she said, with a grin. He refilled her tin mug with tea. She gave him a lovely smile and he saw that for his benefit and the holiday she had put in her false teeth.

Jerome had boiled six eggs and even included a salt cellar. Ace watched Connie peel off the shell from one. 'I like boiled eggs,' she said. 'Dried egg isn't the same. Won't it be lovely when the war's over and we can buy as many fresh eggs as we want?'

Ace made a mental note to include more eggs in the bags of offerings he left for Gertie. He picked up a piece of cheese that Jerome had thoughtfully cut into squares and popped it into his mouth.

Gertie was putting the remains of the picnic carefully back into the basket. 'That was a real treat,' she said. 'Something

I never expected.' She stood up, picked up the blanket and shook the crumbs from it.

Ace lay back on the grass enjoying the last rays of the sun. Connie was lying next to him. 'Hear that?' she said.

He shrugged.

'Birds singing their hearts out.'

He could hear a skylark. 'We don't take much notice of them in the town,' he said.

'That's because we're used to sparrows, pigeons and sea-gulls,' she said. 'So used to them we don't hear or see them any more.'

Ace thought he could lie all day talking to Connie, but just then Gertie gave a squeal of terror.

'What the—' Ace and Connie shot up to a sitting position. Gertie was pointing to the ponies that were ambling towards them, no doubt interested in picnic leftovers.

'I think it's time we made a move,' said Ace.

It was dark when they reached the Anchor Hotel in Beer and he signed the register. Ace was pleased he'd reserved accommodation in the friendly hostelry, but wished they could have left Gosport earlier. He knew the Devon countryside was spellbinding but he'd not been able to show his passengers its beauty. Gertie had had to work in the morning and there was nothing he could do about that, but he resolved that during the time they stayed at the Anchor he would take the women out to see the sights.

He'd asked for two rooms, one for himself and he'd decided Gertie and Connie would prefer to share. He didn't want Connie to be unsure of herself in different surroundings and knew Gertie would look after her. Of course he'd have preferred a room for himself and Connie, but that was too soon to contemplate.

Beer was a place Ace remembered. Jerome had taken him there when he was younger and he hoped he could recreate with Connie and Gertie some of the magic he had felt then, in the picture-postcard quaint fishing village.

Perhaps he could suggest a boat trip on Boxing Day. He doubted either of them had ever been on a boat smaller than the Gosport ferry. And the walks along the high cliffs were awe-inspiring . . .

He said, after they'd unpacked, that he wanted to treat Connie and Gertie to a slap-up meal in the restaurant, but Gertie asked only for a pot of tea, saying the car trip had tired her and her bed was calling.

'I don't think I want to eat,' Connie said, gazing wide-eyed at the beamed ceilings and unique furnishings in the foyer of the old building. 'But I wouldn't mind a walk in the fresh air. I feel as though I've smoked as many fags as Gertie has today.'

'We'll go down to the beach,' he said. 'It's only at the end of the road. But I could do with a whisky first.'

'That sounds a good idea,' she said. They agreed to meet later after they'd freshened up.

'Isn't it pretty?' Connie exclaimed.

Paper chains and gaudy bell-shaped decorations hung in the Anchor's bar. Holly with berries was tucked behind fox-hunting and fishing prints on the walls and ivy lingered along the big fireplace's mantel. In the corner a little Christmas tree was ablaze with tiny lit candles.

'It's just like a real Christmas!' Connie was as excited as a child.

'Well, it is Christmas Eve,' he said. That was another thing he liked about Connie: she didn't hold back on her feelings. He patted his breast pocket, wondering if he should present her with the gift tonight or tomorrow. He looked around for mistletoe. The centuries-old tradition meant he could steal a kiss from her beneath its boughs. Holly and ivy in abundance but no mistletoe. Oh, well, when the time was right, he'd enfold her in his arms and show her how much he cared. But the timing had to be exactly right: he didn't want to scare her away.

'It smells so lovely in here,' she said. Frank Sinatra was singing on the wireless.

He took a deep breath and detected spices, orange and alcohol. Apple logs were burning on the open fire. He immediately realized what the spicy smell was. A few moments later he returned from the bar carrying a large whisky and a thick glass of liquid that steamed and bubbled and smelt of cinnamon, cloves and oranges. He set it on the table in front of Connie.

She looked at it dubiously. She sniffed the glass. 'It smells heavenly but what is it?'

'Spiced wine, or some call it mulled wine. The Victorians loved it and it's a pity it's usually made only at Christmas. Taste it.'

Connie touched the glass, decided it was not too hot to hold and picked it up. After a couple of sips, he saw her smile widen. The glass was half empty when she set it back on the table. 'That's the loveliest drink I've ever tasted,' she said. 'I've never heard of it before. Spiced wine?'

'Sometimes called mulled wine,' he reminded her.

'How come I worked in a pub next to Portsmouth Dockyard and I've never heard of it?'

'Pubs sell what their customers want to buy. I bet you never sold many cocktails, either.' He was teasing her but he could tell by Connie's blank look that he'd possibly taken it too far. Cocktails were sold in the better hotels in Southsea but beer and spirits were king in the city's pubs.

Connie picked up the glass and finished the drink. 'Can I have another, please?'

She looked so happy, how could he possibly refuse her? He went up to the bar and ordered.

'Your ladyfriend knows a good thing when she tastes it,' said the barman. 'I know I should mind my own business but it contains a red wine that's very potent . . .'

'I'm not offended. Thanks for telling me,' said Ace. He carried the glass back to her at the table. No matter how much Connie liked the drink, this was the last he would buy her tonight. He didn't think Gertie would appreciate being woken by Connie being sick.

There were only a few other customers in the bar but sitting, watching the fire, drinking whisky and listening to Connie chatting to him, he was surprised when the barman rang a ship's bell and called time. Connie yawned. He stared at her and saw she was obviously too tired to walk anywhere now and her rose-red cheeks and frequent giggles told him she was ready for her bed.

He called goodnight to the barman and helped Connie upstairs. At the room she shared with Gertie, she stopped, turned and threw her arms around his neck. 'Thank you for a lovely day and night,' she slurred. He thought she was about to kiss him, when the door opened and Gertie stood there in a flannelette nightdress, her hair bristling with metal curlers and the eternal cigarette hanging on her lip.

'About time, too,' she said, hauling Connie inside. 'Goodnight, Ace.'

And the door closed on him.

Chapter Thirty-eight

The moment he woke, Tommo knew something was wrong. The door to the Nissen hut was slightly ajar and the air coming in was maliciously cold. Tiny white flakes of snow were blowing through the gap but melting almost immediately. He cursed the last person in, who had probably forgotten to shut it securely. Still swearing beneath his breath, he slid out of his blankets, went over and quietly closed the door, then padded back to his bunk. That should have been the end of it but still something bothered him.

He glanced around the hut. Humped figures moaned and snored as they slept. The hut was cold but still stank of men and sweat. He picked up the clock on his locker and stared at it. Three in the morning.

Hamish had been sobbing again last night. One of the other men had obviously heard him, had possibly been awakened by his friend's grief. 'Shut up!' had been yelled into the darkness, briefly waking Tommo, but he'd soon slid back into sleep. Tommo's unease gathered momentum. He stared at Hamish's bunk, rubbed his eyes in the gloom and stared again. It was empty.

Illogically Tommo's first thought was that there was nowhere he could hide in the hut. But it didn't stop him creeping soundlessly along the gangway between the bunks. But the door was open, he told himself. Hamish had to be outside.

On Hamish's locker his folded clothes lay ready for the morning. His polished boots were on the floor, confirming he wasn't wearing much more than his pyjamas.

Tommo pulled open the door and lunged out into the darkness, shouting behind him, 'Wake up, you bastards. Hamish is missing!'

The thick socks on his feet became wet and frozen in no time at all.

The snow fell wetly in his hair and on his skin, and the cold gnawed at him.

When his eyes were accustomed to the darkness they scanned between Nissen huts and buildings. He ran to the ablutions block, shouting, 'Hamish!' and clattered open every lavatory door in his quest.

'Whassamatter?' came a sleepy, disgruntled, disembodied voice from the darkness.

'It's Hamish! He's out in this lot! Tell the guards!' Tommo shouted, as he searched dark corners, peered beneath and inside parked vehicles.

His pyjamas were wet, clinging icily to his skin, but he mustn't think about that. His mind wouldn't shake away the heartrending sobs of his friend in his bunk, while others slept.

Hamish hadn't been able to get that bloody letter out of his mind. Tommo had told him to ask for leave, but with Christmas upon them, the port was already running on skeleton crew. The end of January was the only time on offer.

For want of somewhere else to search, Tommo frenzied, attacked the rubbish containers, throwing lids to the snowy concrete when he found the huge bins empty.

When his wrath was extinguished, he stood on the jetty by the steps leading down to the loch and tried hard to analyse what his friend might do.

Standing there, looking at the freezing water with the snow melting as soon as it touched the surface, he saw what at first he took to be an old coat floating and swaying about. Common sense took over and he yelled to voices he could hear, to a bobbing light he could make out, 'Down here!'

And then he dived in.

The cold took his breath away. He forced himself to strike out towards the bundle of clothing. The fiendish cold numbed his body but his mechanical strokes kept him moving. As soon as he reached his goal, he saw it was his friend.

He managed to hook an arm beneath Hamish's body, grabbing at his clothing, grasping his pyjama jacket, fist clenched. It took him several attempts, the numbness hampering his grip, but when he was sure he had a handhold, he struck out, swimming as best he could towards the jetty. Almost blinded by snow and loch water, he used the sound of voices to guide him and Hamish to refuge.

And then hands were pulling them both from the water, onto the jetty. He managed to haul himself to a sitting position.

A blanket landed across his shoulders.

'Hamish?' His mouth could barely form the word. His teeth were chattering with the extreme cold. He turned his head and saw Hamish's body flat on the wooden planking, face up. Men were kneeling and bending over him. One man was practically astride Hamish using his hands to pump air into his chest.

'You all right, mate?'

Tommo wanted to speak but vomit inexplicably poured from his mouth.

'Get it all up, my son,' said the voice. Someone was kneeling at his side. Tommo felt suddenly lightheaded. Pain tightened across his chest so he could hardly breathe and he began to sweat. But the pain . . . the pain . . . Oh, it hurt . . .

'Heart attack, here!' Tommo heard the words, then blacked out.

Chapter Thirty-nine

'Get up . . . Get up . . . Ace . . . Come and see!'

The banging and Gertie's throaty voice wouldn't stop so he groaned, slipped from the bed, grabbing his dressing-gown and slipped it over his shoulders, before making his way to the door and opening it.

'Quick! Come and see what there is for breakfast! Oh, and happy Christmas.'

He looked at her, at her head of curly hair, at the red lipstick already running into the creases around her smiling mouth, at her bright yellow hand-knitted jumper with the short sleeves, and at the hand that hadn't been banging on his door, clutching a packet of Woodbines. He groaned again, turned, marched resolutely back to bed and climbed in again.

'No, you must get up before it all gets eaten! There's food not seen since before the war.'

She was bending over him and he caught the smell of stale cigarettes that made his stomach want to rebel at the whisky he'd drunk in his room last night.

'There's kippers, eggs, bacon, toast, kidneys, little rolls, beans, something called kedgeree, porridge, cereal, and the waitress said the chef will make pancakes, and omelettes . . .'

'Shut up! You're making my head spin.' In truth he thought it was more the whisky than her voice, which had now dropped an octave.

'But you'll miss it all and the other guests will eat . . .' He looked at her shining eyes, her eager face.

He pushed back the blankets. 'Go and sit at a table and I'll be down in two ticks,' he said. He looked at the bedside clock. 'It's seven o'clock!' He glared at her.

'Well, I'm always up at this time,' she said.

He drew a long breath and let it out slowly. He sat on the edge of the bed and watched as she sashayed – as well as her bunion would let her – to the door. Before she opened it, she turned back and said, 'Five minutes? You promise? Me and Connie won't start without you.'

She turned the handle and he called to her, 'Gertie.'

She looked back at him, brow furrowed.

'Merry Christmas,' he said, and smiled.

*

By the time Ace climbed into bed on Christmas night his face hurt from constantly laughing. He'd had a marvellous day. The hotel had certainly fulfilled its promise of a day to remember. If he had any grievances, it was that he'd not set foot out of the building and had not been alone with Connie.

From breakfast, when the rain started and the heavens had opened, it was agreed that they would enter into the spirit of Christmas with the other guests and enjoy all the hotel could offer. A waitress served free drinks. Father Christmas appeared, looking uncannily, thought Ace, like the barman, who presented cigars to the men and little posies of holly, mistletoe and ivy tied with seasonal red ribbon to the women. Ace was still disgruntled that there was no mistletoe hanging overhead anywhere.

Colouring books, crayons and jigsaw puzzles were handed out to the children staying at the Anchor. He'd marvelled at that as, along with wrapping paper, toys were difficult to find in the shops. The hotel was indeed fulfilling its promise of a break to remember.

After a sumptuous Christmas lunch of pork (the barman told him more than three chickens were impossible to get hold of but a farmer had promised the pig), complete with all the vegetable trimmings, and plum pudding – Gertie swore she could taste carrots in it – no one wanted to do much more than laze around until some local schoolchildren came to sing carols. Gertie, who had had a few port and lemons, kept saying loudly, 'Bless 'em,' until Connie took her upstairs for a lie-down.

Ace had had a little sleep in a comfortable armchair near the fire while the rain clattered outside against the windows. He'd woken when Connie had come down again and coerced him into playing charades with everyone else. Board games followed. Strangely, no one seemed interested in playing the usual pub games of darts, shove-halfpenny or dominoes.

'This isn't like a proper hotel, is it?' Connie whispered. 'It's more like a proper family Christmas.'

'Are you enjoying yourself?' he asked.

Her smile gave him the answer.

Boxing Day dawned bright and clear. After breakfast Ace excused himself to check over his car. They were leaving after lunch because Gertie was due in work at the Criterion the following morning.

'I'll come with you,' said Connie.

'You sure?'

'I really enjoyed yesterday but I need some fresh air,' she said. 'I spend enough time inside at the picture house as it is.'

'How about you, Gertie? Want a little drive? I have to get petrol.'

Gertie had just lit a cigarette and she took a long draw on it. 'No, thanks. I'll be sitting down enough later on the way home.' He guessed she intended a gossip with a couple of women she'd played cards with yesterday afternoon. Edgar, the barman, Ace knew his name now, had told him of a small garage that would be open for petrol, so while Connie ran upstairs to get her coat, he went out and put the hood down on his car.

Ace drove away from the garage after giving up his coupons and paying for the petrol.

'I don't want to go back to the hotel,' Connie said.

'Then we won't. We've time for a cliff walk, if you like?'

He looked at her and she nodded. 'Yes, I would.'

He drove down country lanes keeping within sight of the sea. 'When I came here with Jerome it was all different,' he said, when for the third time he had to turn the car and go back the way they'd come. It was impossible to drive close to the beach because barbed wire and notices warned off motorists and pedestrians.

'I should have realized this is the way the Nazi Germans would try to come from across the sea,' he said. 'We can't walk on the pebbles at Lee-on-the-Solent or Stokes Bay, and this place is very close to France. I wasn't listening properly but Edgar was talking about the prisoner-of-war camp up here and how a great deal of the land has been taken over by the army.'

She looked sad. 'I've never walked across a cliff top before,' she said.

He turned his car again. 'I promised you a walk and a walk you shall have.'

Ace found a dry field where he could park just inside the gate and began the business of pulling up the hood. When he'd finished, he grabbed her hand and said, 'C'mon, we're going exploring.'

Other people must have had a similar idea because there was a path of sorts, albeit overgrown, that ran along the top of the cliffs. The grass was long but surprisingly dry after yesterday's downpour.

The sea was far below them, the waves breaking on the sand and stones with a whooshing noise. Barbed wire lined the edge of the cliffs, running far into the distance.

'Oh, it's so beautiful,' she said, pausing to stare. 'The defences can't disguise that.'

He saw Connie's coat was undone. Beneath the green gaberdine was the faded green dress he thought brought out the colour of her eyes. Moving close to her, he said,

'You'll get cold,' and began to fasten her buttons. He could feel the warmth coming from her body.

'Thank you for a wonderful Christmas,' she said softly.

'I've enjoyed being with you ... both,' he added, as an afterthought. 'You and Gertie,' he clarified. She moved to his side so that they were both staring out to sea. He put his arm across her shoulders.

'You can see for miles, can't you?'

'When the war's over we can come back and walk along the beach. There's some beautiful coves along here.'

She put a hand into her pocket and brought out the little winter bouquet she'd been given at the hotel. He stared at it and smiled. 'I'd like to kiss you,' she said. 'If I hold the mistletoe above our heads, will you kiss me back?'

Ace had never been at a loss for words with any woman, ever. But she, Connie, was taking the initiative and all he could do was think how wonderful she was and how much he loved her.

Then guilt attacked him: he hadn't told her the truth about himself, who he was or how he really made his money. He knew he could never tell her how his jealousy had made him send a young man far away from Gosport simply because she'd shown an interest in him. It certainly wasn't the right time to tell her about Belle and his son Leon, was it? He pushed those thoughts away, consoling himself with believing everything he'd done so far was to keep her safe and to stop her worrying about circumstances over which she had no control. Like the letters to Etta Hines that would frighten the woman into giving up her profession. He'd done that because Connie had feared losing her friend. He thought about Jerome's warning that love can't be built on lies. Connie was too innocent to understand that sometimes lies are necessary. He felt the wisest thing now was to keep his secrets to himself.

She was standing on tiptoe holding the ridiculous bouquet above his head.

'I know what I want,' he said. He gave her a smile. 'I want very much to kiss you. But sometimes a kiss leads to other things.' He knew if he kissed her it wouldn't stop there.

'Would that be so bad?'

'There's only one way to find out, isn't there?' He pulled her down onto the grass, only slightly damp after yesterday's rain. He felt the warmth of her breath as he leaned across and kissed her gently, softly. Her lips responded. They were warm, full and supple. She reached to the back of his neck and pulled his head closer still. Her tongue played inside his mouth until that one innocent kiss was as hot as flames. She pulled away, her eyes searching his.

'I've never been with anyone.' Her voice was very small.

'You are the most incredibly beautiful person I have ever known,' he said. 'You've nothing to fear from me, trust me.'

He could smell the freshness of the grass, the salt from the sea and the musk from her body as he began undoing the buttons on her coat that a few moments ago he had done up . . .

Looking into her green eyes, his fingers began exploring the silkiness of her blonde hair and then he allowed his hand to feel the curve of her breast, her waist, and lower to raise the skirt of her green dress until his hand rested between her thighs. He moved her beneath him. Their mouths were meeting with no hesitation and as familiar as if they had been kissing each other for years.

And then he was inside her. He came to her gently and discovered she was moving with him.

'I want you to stay inside me for ever,' she said.

He cried out her name.

Afterwards, he'd asked her to marry him. On the way back to the hotel she said yes. He stopped the car, kissed her again, put a hand into his pocket and took out a small square jeweller's box. Inside was a gold chain bracelet. He clipped it on her wrist and said, 'I've wanted to give you this since yesterday so it's a belated Christmas present. Before this year is out, I shall buy you a ring.'

'I've nothing for you,' she answered, 'except this,' and from the pocket of her green gaberdine coat she took the posy, kissed it, and tucked it into his top pocket.

On the way back to Gosport, Gertie slept. Connie and Ace kept stealing meaningful glances at each other. He loved having a secret with her. The secret bigger than all secrets. He loved her and she returned his love. With Gertie snoring in the rear of the car, they decided not to stop but to get her home as soon as possible.

Gertie woke when they reached Fareham.

Unable to keep it to himself any longer, Ace said, 'I asked Connie to marry me and she said yes.'

He heard a match struck and a cloud of smoke was blown into the front of the car. 'About bloody time,' she said. 'I been expecting it. But there'll be no hanky-panky in my house until she's walked up that aisle.'

Chapter Forty

'So, Queenie, the new manager will arrive next month?'

'That's what the letter says, Connie.'

'Wonder what he'll be like.'

'As long as he's nothing like Mangle, he'll be fine,' said Gertie.

Queenie was acting very strangely, Connie thought. Waving her hands about like some demented film star. Connie was making small-talk while having a cup of tea in the Criterion's staffroom. She was waiting for just the right moment to tell Queenie all about the trip and that she had accepted Ace's proposal of marriage.

She hadn't blurted it out as soon as she'd met Queenie because she thought her friend's quiet Christmas with Len Gregory deserved all of her and Gertie's attention first.

'Shall I get rid of those dog-ends for you, Gertie?' Queenie's hand hovered over the saucer.

'Don't be bloody daft. It's only half full,' said Gertie, enveloped in a cloud of Woodbine smoke.

Connie could hardly contain herself. What a lot she had to tell Queenie. About the hotel, the food … Of course country people probably had access to better-quality provisions than townies, but there was still a war on and rationing was rationing, wasn't it? But the Anchor Hotel had excelled itself. She didn't dare think how much Christmas had cost Ace.

And then, of course, there was that other thing …

She definitely wasn't going to confide in Queenie while Gertie was around.

Gertie acted as though Connie was a child. Her child. If she was like that with Marlene then no wonder Marlene had left home! Though remembering Marlene, her bossiness, her deviousness, Connie thought there must have been quite a few arguments between them. Maybe Gertie had been eager to see the back of her daughter.

'Would anyone like more tea?'

There she goes again, thought Connie, her hand high above the teapot, like she's royalty waving to her subjects. Gertie and Connie shook their heads.

'Anyway, Gertie, why are you still here?' Queenie was frowning at her. 'You should have finished cleaning this place ages ago.'

'Now Mangle's not around, it's nice to chat to everyone,' Gertie said.

'But your hours are over for the day and you should go home,' Queenie stressed. Gertie didn't look at all happy.

Connie was amazed when Queenie, who was getting quite a little tummy on her now, got up from the chair walked round to Gertie, pushed her left hand into Gertie's chest and began jabbing at her.

Gertie looked down in horror, watching Queenie's fingers poking at her wrap-around pinny. Ash fell onto the table.

She looked up into Queenie's eyes and said, after removing her cigarette from her mouth, 'Bugger me, Queenie's got a ring!'

Later, when Queenie had proudly told them about Len asking her to marry him and how she'd accepted his proposal, she said, 'We haven't got a lot of money and this engagement ring belonged to Len's mum so it's all the more special to me.'

This time the small sapphire was oohed and aahed over with the excitement it deserved.

'I wanted you two to be the first to know,' Queenie said.

'And when's the happy day? Soon, I hope.' Gertie, never one to mince her words, was looking at Queenie's stomach.

Queenie smoothed the front of her usherette's uniform.

'As soon as possible. It won't be a posh affair. Len's getting a special licence and there'll be a few drinks in a pub afterwards. We can't afford a big wedding and, anyway, people will look at me and know I'm in the family way. So, we thought a register office and a couple of special friends.' She paused, then went on, 'Len's eager for people to think it's his kiddie. I know he'll make a lovely dad . . .'

Gertie was staring at Connie while Queenie was rattling on and on. Connie knew exactly what that piercing glare meant. She turned away. She tucked her gold bracelet high up her sleeve so it couldn't be seen. Later she'd remove it. Anyway, it was too nice to wear for work. Supposing she lost it? She couldn't imagine it finding its way to the lost property box. Besides, it was quite obvious it was many times more expensive than Queenie's engagement ring. She couldn't draw attention to it, not without taking the limelight away from Queenie and her exciting news.

'You'll both come, won't you?'

Connie and Gertie spoke in unison, 'Of course, Queenie.'

Connie got up, went to Queenie and threw her arms around her. 'I'm so very happy for you, Len and the baby.' She felt Queenie breathe a sigh of contentment.

And Connie knew then she'd have to keep her own news locked inside her heart. There was no way she could destroy her best friend's happiness by saying anything about her own engagement.

'It's right on the sea-front at Southsea. You could buy the land for peanuts.'

'Why, old man, would I want to buy a bomb site?' Ace poured milk into a saucer and set it on the floor of the club's kitchen. It was late. The chef, waiters and bar staff had long gone to their homes. The black-and-white cat jumped from Jerome's arms to the floor and began lapping noisily.

'I always knew you liked him,' said Jerome, looking fondly first at Ace, then at the cat. 'At least go and look at the piece of land – make a good site for your second club.'

Ace took a deep breath. The old man was talking sense. It wasn't the price of the land that worried him, it was the expense of the building work. Councillors in Gosport had owed him favours. The Four Aces had been rebuilt in record time at minimal cost to him. No one in Portsmouth of any standing knew him or owed him.

'It costs money,' Ace said.

'You're not short of a bob or two, are you?'

'Not really,' Ace answered. Of course he had money. But he'd planned on a fancy wedding, a decent honeymoon, and in these days of austerity all that was going to cost plenty. He'd decided on a diamond engagement ring and that wouldn't be cheap. Well, it would be if he bought a stolen one from a spiv, but that wasn't what he wanted for Connie. He wanted everything new, bright, shiny, like her, and he wanted a house in Alverstoke, where the nobs lived. He wasn't bringing her back to a flat over a club, no matter how luxurious his flat was.

'Offers like this don't come along every day. If you don't jump in quick someone else will. Then you'll be kicking yourself.'

Ace walked over to his desk and opened a drawer. He looked at the jeweller's box containing the gold necklace to match the chain bracelet he'd given Connie on Boxing Day. It had cost him an arm and a leg but he could imagine it around her lovely neck. He'd buy her the world if he could.

'How did you find out about this bit of property, Jerome?'

'It's not on the open market yet,' he said.

Ace could feel the cogs in his mind ticking over. Jerome knew it was his dearest wish to have a chain of four clubs. One for each of the four aces in a pack of cards and each club bearing his name.

'Not got money earmarked for anything else, have you?'

Ace shook his head and his brandy-coloured hair fell across his forehead. He swept it back with his fingers, feeling the slight oiliness of Brylcreem.

He hadn't told Jerome he'd asked Connie to marry him, not because he wasn't his own man, he could please himself what he did, but because he remembered the argument he'd had with him. Everything that Jerome had thrown at him – about lies being no good as the bedrock of a happy relationship – was absolutely true. His plan was to organize the wedding first, then tell Jerome. Jerome would be put out but he'd soon come around after Ace had married Connie.

Connie deserved the best, and Ace would give her the best of everything. After they were married and he'd shown her he was a first-class husband, provider, lover, indeed whatever she wanted him to be, he would tell her why he wasn't so perfect. Little by little he would explain, and he was confident because they loved each other that all would be well.

'A. G. Knight, the Portsmouth builder whose business relies on his wife's inheritance, has been a naughty boy playing away from home. He's got the girl pregnant. If – I say if – his wife finds out, there'll be ructions. He'll lose the lot.

'Big house on Portsdown Hill, lovely car, his kids, his social standing . . .'

Ace shook his head again. 'How you find out these things I've no idea.'

'Be thankful that I do. Because if you lean on Knight and his wife doesn't hear a dickie-bird about what he's been up to, you'll have club number two up and running in no time. It'll still cost you money but . . .' Jerome's voice tailed off. He went over to the cupboard and took out a tin of sardines. He began winding the little key provided to open the tin. 'I know you want another club. You got to speculate to accumulate, son.'

'You feed that cat well at my expense,' said Ace. Nevertheless, he picked up the empty saucer, rinsed it under the tap and forked out the sardines.

'So tomorrow you and I will take a ferry-boat trip to see this bomb site?'

'If you like, Ace, if you like.'

As Ace put down the saucer and the greedy cat began eating, he thought about Connie. They hadn't set a date yet for the wedding. They loved each other, so they weren't in any hurry, were they? He'd give her the gold necklace. She'd like that.

He'd buy her the best engagement ring ever when his second club was up and running. Diamonds, yes, diamonds big enough to poke people's eyes out.

Chapter Forty-one

'It's been a lovely day for a wedding, hasn't it? I hope we don't get a raid, tonight.'

Gertie was sitting in the saloon bar of the pub with her shoes off. Connie didn't know what had possessed her to wear high heels – they were two-inch court shoes and her feet were as swollen as lumpy pastry. She pushed her aunt's port and lemon across the table towards her. 'It has, and she looks so happy, doesn't she?' The past few nights had been raid-free and she hoped tonight would be the same.

Queenie was on the little square of dance floor, her arms tight around Len, like she didn't want ever to let him go.

'When I first saw her outside the register office at Fareham I took one look at her short dress made of parachute silk with its ruched top, shoulder pads and long sleeves and I thought, that girl knows how to dress,' Gertie said. 'Then

I caught an eyeful of those red high heels, those red paper flowers and that bright red lipstick showing off her blonde hair and I thought, that's our Queenie. She's got to be different!'

Connie was staring at the couple. Len had his back to her. He looked so handsome in his navy suit, the trousers with turn-ups and his dark curls gleaming. Queenie had her hand on his shoulder and they were snuggled up. When Queenie saw Connie watching them, she wiggled her hand to show off her wedding ring, a plain gold band. Connie laughed at her, remembering that morning in the staffroom at the picture house when she'd waved her hands all over the place trying to get them to look at her engagement ring.

First thing this morning Gertie had looked a treat, as well. Her grey costume and matching grey hat that looked like a pancake on her grey hair had given her a mother-of-the-bride look. Of course she wasn't, but all morning she'd acted like one, ordering everyone about, telling them where to stand outside when young Gary Pink took the photographs with his dad's new camera. Connie had spent coupons and money on a new dress: knee-length, blue with padded shoulders and a sweetheart neckline. She'd gone to bed the night before with her hair in rags so it would be curly. Before she and Gertie had arrived at Fareham on the bus the curls had fallen out but it had left her with a wave across one eye, just like Veronica Lake, so it wasn't all bad.

Connie had wanted to ask Ace to come to the White Swan to celebrate Queenie and Len's wedding. The pub was on Forton Road and a very popular place. At present the saloon bar was packed, and people were dancing to the small group of men playing instruments on a dais.

Gertie had shaken her head. 'Oh, no. Neither Queenie nor Len know him properly. Len's only met him once, hasn't he? It might make them feel strange. And it's not your place to invite who you want to their do.'

She was quite right, thought Connie. Anyway, she'd seen little of Ace over the past weeks. He was heavily involved in the building of a club on some land he'd bought very near the funfair he'd taken her to ages ago. He'd told her it would make a lot of money when eventually the place was opened. Some nights he didn't come back to Alma Street at all but stayed at a bed-and-breakfast in Southsea, so he could be on hand to supervise the builder, A. G. Knight. Apparently, he liked to skive off jobs, Gertie said. Ace had told her so.

He'd given Connie a beautiful gold chain necklace. It matched the bracelet she'd put away in her bedroom drawer. She hadn't worn the necklace. She'd have preferred an engagement ring but when Ace had said, 'I don't want to buy you something I'd be ashamed for you to show people,' Gertie had translated that as 'I'm a bit strapped for cash at present but when the club's up and running . . .'

Connie didn't mind: she knew how much Ace loved her.

They were a bit like ships that passed in the night when Ace did spend time at Gertie's. Sometimes he was asleep when she came home from the Criterion. Sometimes it was the other way around and she was asleep first. When she woke in the mornings, mostly he had already left. But that didn't matter, she told herself. He was working hard to get the new place up and running so they'd have a better life together.

That's what love was all about, wasn't it? she thought. Trust and love. Anyway, not seeing so much of Ace gave her time to stick film stars' pictures in her scrapbook.

'Do you like the new manager?' Gertie asked, lighting up a Woodbine.

'He doesn't look old enough to be one, does he?' Connie said.

'He's twenty-four.'

'How d'you know?'

'I asked him,' Gertie answered. She turned her head and blew out smoke. 'He got injured by a horse when he was doing his army training so they got rid of him.'

'That's not nice,' Connie said.

Gertie started laughing.

'What's so funny?'

'I bet he hates cowboy films!' she said.

Queenie and Len came back to the table. Len held a tray with fresh drinks on it. 'Here you are,' he said. 'Port and lemon for Gertie and I got you a half of shandy, Connie, because I know you're not a big drinker.' Connie saw he had a pint for himself and another port and lemon for Queenie.

'Thanks,' said Gertie. She gave a cackle, eyeing his pint. 'Don't you have too many of them. It might put you off your stroke tonight, and that mustn't happen, it being your wedding night.'

Connie noticed how red Len's face had turned. 'Don't take any notice. I think our Gertie's had too many of those already.' She leaned across and touched Gertie's glass. Connie could smell Queenie's Californian Poppy and took a deep breath of it. It helped to disguise the smell of Gertie's dog-end she was stubbing out in the ashtray.

Queenie bent over and whispered in Connie's ear, 'You'll never guess who I saw in the public bar when I went through to the outside lavatory.'

Connie said, 'I can't possibly but you're going to tell me anyway, aren't you?'

'He recognized me, before I saw him. Called me over. I told him you were in here.' Queenie looked pleased with herself.

'Go on, tell me. It's Clark Gable, isn't it?'

'Don't be daft! You remember that young bloke who used to come into the Criterion in the afternoons I swear just to see you?'

Connie's heart skipped a beat.

'Always dressed so smartly?' Queenie added.

Connie nodded. 'I remember,' she said.

'I didn't recognize him at first, he looks so pale. He said he'd been ill.'

'I remember,' said Connie, again. She remembered the feeling, like a sort of tingling shock that had occurred when their fingers touched. 'Are you sure it's him? He hasn't been in the pictures for ages.'

Gertie suddenly piped up: 'Where's the lad, that Gary? Where's he got to?'

Len said, 'He's met some girl and he's talking to her outside.'

'He'll get frozen solid. It's like Antarctica out there, now.'

Connie said, 'Love doesn't notice the cold.'

'Is that so?' asked a voice behind her.

Connie turned. It was the man she'd first met in the Criterion. The man with the blond hair.

'Would you like to dance?' he asked.

Connie was about to say she was sorry but she didn't know how when the music changed to 'I'll Be Your Sweetheart' and she recognized it as a waltz. One, two, three, one, two, three.

She got up and said to him, 'I'd love to.'

Acknowledgements

Thank you, Juliet Burton, Jane Wood, Florence Hare, Hazel Orme, Ella Patel and all at Quercus who work so tirelessly for me.